Once Upon a Secret

Once Upon a Secret

Catherine Andorka

Five Star • Waterville, Maine

Copyright © 1999 Catherine Andorka

All rights reserved.

This book is a work of fiction. Any mention of real people, either living or dead, was for the purpose of entertainment only. All other characters are products of the author's imagination.

Five Star Romance Series.

Published in 2002 in conjunction with Catherine Andorka.

The text of this edition is unabridged.

Set in 11 pt. Plantin by Elena Picard.

Printed in the United States on permanent paper.

Library of Congress Cataloging-in-Publication Data

Andorka, Catherine.
   Once upon a secret / Catherine Andorka.
     p. cm.
   ISBN 0-7862-4601-4 (hc : alk. paper)
    1. Women physicians—Fiction. 2. Rock musicians—Fiction. I. Title.
PS3601.N549 O53 2002
   813'.6—dc21   2002026776

Acknowledgments

A very special thank you to Alan Cooper, D.C., caretaker and friend, for your infinite patience and attention to detail concerning all of my questions and dilemmas. (Any mistakes are mine.)

Enormous gratitude to my Publisher, Rhea Griffiths, for taking a chance on a story that is close to my heart.

I am also deeply indebted to the following people:

Laurie Brown, for providing perspective (especially late at night).

Sherry Henderson, for your constant words of support and encouragement. And yeah, for your badgering too.

Carmen Mallory, for sharing with me your knowledge of the music industry—and for all of your love and support.

Rosemary Paulas, for your loyal friendship, your on-target critiques, and certainly, for always being in my corner.

Patricia Pinianski, for your professional expertise in an area in which I had no clue.

To Greg,
with much gratitude and love
for your patience and support . . .
and for never imposing barriers
or limits on my dream quests.

Chapter One

"Dammit!" a male voice bellowed from the distance, outside the backstage room where Tori Glenn sat. She jumped at the sound, then glanced at Kevin, her fifteen-year-old brother. He was immersed in conversation with Mike Sweeney, the keyboard player of the famous Brad Daniels rock band, and the two of them seemed oblivious to the distraction.

Winning the statewide contest for young journalists had been a real coup for Kevin, and this interview with the band members was one of the payoffs. The resulting story would be appearing in all the area high school newspapers, and Tori was anxious for him to succeed.

She cocked an ear toward the closed hallway door to listen more intently, though the shouting appeared to be over. She'd been uneasy about coming here to begin with, but when Kevin had gotten the last-minute call from the man who'd arranged the interview, she'd had no choice but to drive her brother. The small town of Wheatfield, where she and Kevin lived, was an hour west of Chicago, and Kevin was too young for a license.

Rock music wasn't exactly high on her list of priorities. Still, Brad Daniels was featured on enough radio stations that even she was familiar with some of his songs. When she and Kevin had arrived at the Pavilion, Mike Sweeney had politely insisted she come in to meet everyone. So, while she'd been introduced to some members of one of the hottest bands in the industry, she'd yet to get a glance at the famed lead singer/guitar player.

Tori picked up a nearby news tabloid. There on the front cover was a picture of Brad Daniels himself. She had to admit; he certainly was good looking. The headlines were in bold print: *Rock's Sexiest Bad Boy Does It Again!* Does what again? she wondered, searching impatiently for the story. Why didn't the tabloids ever have a table of contents?

"You're going to get hurt!" the same voice thundered once more, followed by the sounds of hysterical female screams. Tori cast the cheap magazine aside. This time the disturbance could hardly be ignored. The back of her neck prickled as she, Kevin and Mike Sweeney rushed out into the hallway.

Three bodies lay sprawled on the floor. From the picture she'd just seen, Tori immediately recognized Brad Daniels. The other two were young girls, and she stepped out of the way as security people hurried by in an effort to remove both of them from the area.

"Get your hands off me!" one teenager demanded.

"Make sure they're okay before they leave here," Brad said.

He was surrounded by people offering assistance, but he waved them off, insisting that he was fine. "Jeez," he muttered, helping himself to an upright position. "I don't mind signing autographs, but it would be nice to live through the process. Both of them climbed on top of me at once. One of them even tried to grab my . . ."

"You know what they say, buddy," Mike Sweeney

quickly and loudly interrupted. "All's fair in love and . . ."

"War!" Brad finished, swiping at his T-shirt and jeans to rid them of the dust. "I feel like I'm in a freakin' war zone sometimes. I don't know how those two managed to sneak in here, but they were out for blood."

As the crowd thinned Tori gave Brad a more scrutinizing look. "You are bleeding," she emphasized, moving toward him.

His cobalt blue eyes were piercing, and they narrowed as he took a step backward. "Who the hell are you?" he asked, his voice heavy with suspicion.

Tori winced at his rudeness, wishing all the more that she could have just stayed home.

"Take it easy, man," Mike interjected, before Tori could answer. "She's with Kevin here, the kid who's doing the interview for his high school paper."

"Oh." He turned to Kevin, who was beaming at the introduction, though her brother stood silent as if he were temporarily paralyzed at seeing his hero in the flesh.

Brad visibly relaxed and extended his hand to the boy. "Sorry I kept you waiting for so long, but there's a lot to check on before a concert."

That seemed to put Kevin more at ease, and his smile widened. "No problem, Mr. Daniels. I'm just glad for the chance to do the story at all."

Brad's face twisted into an expression of disapproval. "When people call me Mister, it makes me feel like I should be wearing a suit or something. Brad will do just fine."

"Okay, Brad," Kevin responded, with an eager voice.

"Look kid," Mike said, throwing his arm over Kevin's shoulder and leading him back toward the small room. "Time's getting tight. Why don't you and I go finish while Brad gets cleaned up?"

"Don't worry," Brad called after them. "I can talk to you backstage after tonight's show. I'll see to it that you and your—uh—friend here get passes."

"Passes! Thanks, thanks a lot!" Kevin shouted as he disappeared down the hallway. Tori couldn't remember the last time she'd seen her brother get this excited about anything.

Suddenly she found herself alone with Brad Daniels. His earlier abruptness had put her off, and now she wasn't quite sure what to say.

"I suppose I owe you an apology too, Green Eyes. I'm not usually so short with my fans, but after those two kids attacked me, it really put me on my guard."

His arrogance made her bristle. "Let's get something straight right now, Mr. Daniels . . . Brad," she corrected herself at his instant cringe. "First off, I am not one of your fans, and secondly, my name is not *Green Eyes*."

He flashed her an amused grin that made the dimple on the right side of his face deepen. The man was disturbingly handsome. She had to give him that. Unlike the stereotypical long-haired rock star, his ebony hair was short and wavy, though thick strands of it lay over his forehead as if it had been washed but not combed.

"I stand corrected," he said, folding his arms over the wide expanse of his chest.

That smile of his was mesmerizing—not to mention his eyes. And the fact that her insides were reacting to him like some star-struck teenager rather than a twenty-eight-year-old woman was vexing to her.

"Well, for the record, my name is Victoria Glenn."

"Victoria," he repeated, looking somewhat surprised.

"Yes, in honor of my paternal grandparents, Victor and Gloria."

Brad struck a thoughtful pose, his thumbs hooked over his jean pockets. Seconds later he clucked his tongue and shook his head with obvious disapproval. "Nice sentiment, but way too formal."

"Really?" she countered. "How unfortunate that my parents weren't able to consult with you on the matter."

"No problem," he said with an audacious wink. "At least not one that can't be fixed."

"You know, you're not only rude, you're downright presumptuous." She slid her hands over her hips to match his stance. "My friends call me Tori."

"Oh yeah. And what would you like me to call you? Never mind," he baited, without giving her the chance to reply. "We can decide about that later."

"There isn't going to be a 'later.' Kevin and I are leaving as soon as the interview is over."

"And that's another thing," Brad continued, as if he hadn't heard a word she'd said. "If you don't mind the observation, the kid looks a little on the young side for you."

"Kevin happens to be my brother," Tori explained, too thrown to think of a snappier comeback. "He lives with me. Actually I'm his legal guardian."

Brad gave her a wary-eyed stare, a look she'd seen before. It was an expression that declared, *That's nice, little mama, but I'm off to greener pastures.*

"You mean you're raising him and everything?"

"Right you are." *And with all the parental responsibility that comes with the package.*

"So . . . is that something you're doing all by yourself, or is there a husband in the picture?"

"No husband. No boyfriend. Just me," Tori answered.

"Good."

"Good? Why is it good?"

Suddenly he felt like a kid who'd been caught licking the frosting off the cake. What was he gonna tell her?—The less competition the better?—That she was drop down gorgeous and that his vocal cords were being ruled by wayward hormones? That would explain all of his stupid remarks. He was glad she wasn't married and even more surprised that she didn't have a boyfriend. A queen bee like her could have all the male workers in the hive.

Something warned him she wasn't the typical bimbo type he'd taken to hanging out with. It was starting to look like there was substance to this woman that went beyond her beauty. Maybe that substance was the very thing causing him to stumble all over himself trying to impress her. Women of intelligence weren't easily fooled. If it turned out she was smart—really smart, he could be getting in way over his head. He'd been burned bad enough to know that much.

"Why is that good?" she repeated, jarring him from his thoughts.

"Less work," he finally answered.

She looked puzzled.

Genius. That impressed her. "I . . . uh . . . less people for you to take care of is what I meant."

Was Tori supposed to decipher that too? For that matter, why should she bother? She was a small-town chiropractor . . . not some groupie. And this whole situation was definitely out of her realm. She wouldn't even have been here if the interview hadn't been so important to Kevin. Now she was trading barbs with this pompous rock star. He probably didn't even know what a chiropractor was.

"Look, could we back this tape up and start it over again?" Brad asked with a look of true contrition. "I was out of line before, and I'm sorry. Call it opening night jitters, but sometimes I just run off at the mouth."

There was no smile this time, just a hopeful expression that said forgive me. Tori knew she was softening, but still she met him with silence.

"Hmm, I'm not above groveling if it will get me off the hook."

His tone sounded sincere, maybe because she wanted to believe him. "Apology accepted," she finally said. "And by the way, there's blood on your collar. Are you all right?"

"I'll live, though it's probably a good thing my shots are up to date. That one girl came at me like a blitzing linebacker. It felt like she scratched my neck when I pulled her off."

"Why don't you let me take a look at it?" Tori offered.

"I doubt that's necessary . . . but if you really want to," he amended with a teasing edge to his voice.

"I do." Maybe it was the doctor in her reacting to a medical need. Or maybe it was something else.

"There's a washroom down the hall," he suggested, leading the way. A minute later he ushered her into the ladies' room. "The men's room is around the corner. Trust me, you wouldn't want to go there."

The situation was awkward, to say the least. He towered over her, and in order for her to examine his wound, he was going to have to sit somewhere.

As though he'd been reading her mind, he positioned himself on top of the one toilet seat in the small enclosure. Despite her obvious discomfort, Brad looked somewhat amused.

Wordlessly she moistened a paper towel with some warm water, stood in front of him and dabbed at the injured area. He flinched once, but his gaze remained fixed on her.

"There might be something useful in that first aid kit on the wall," he said.

Still silent, she reached for the white plastic box. Pay dirt! Bandages and disinfectant both.

"You're awfully quiet," Brad noted. "Which is it? You don't like musicians or you don't like me?"

"I never said either."

"So then you do like me?"

She swallowed. "I don't know you well enough to like you or dislike you."

"I can rectify that. For instance, I'll tell you something about myself that nobody else knows."

"And what would that be?" she asked, applying the disinfectant to his neck.

"I love long, curly hair on a woman. Especially when it's the shade of cinnamon that yours is. Soft. Silky. The kind of hair a guy could really enjoy running his hands through."

Tori's heart was racing like a panther giving chase. It had been a long time since any man had noticed the color of her eyes or paid attention to her hair. She couldn't help being flattered. Still, such a personal observation from him made her uneasy, and she didn't know how to respond.

"This is your cue to say something," he pressed. "Now you can tell me one of your secrets."

"You're right about this scratch," she finally said. "It isn't serious." But her reaction to him was, and she tried to keep her hands from shaking as she applied the bandage to his abrasion.

"That's not exactly a news flash, Tulip. I was hoping for something a little more insightful."

"Tulip?" she repeated, with a raise of her eyebrows.

"A name befitting one of nature's most beautiful creations," he explained, with the eloquence of a poet, "and my very favorite flower."

She recognized a load of blarney when she heard it, and she couldn't help but laugh out loud. Nonetheless, his impudent charm caused a slow spreading warmth to invade her face.

"I think we're about finished here," she said, careful to avoid meeting his gaze.

Brad stood and tipped her chin, forcing her to look up at him. "I was hoping that we were just getting started."

"I . . . I don't know what you mean."

"I think you do," he persisted. "I think that's why you're turning all red. Maybe you're just shy."

"It's hot in here, that's all," she stammered, pulling from his gentle hold. She was shy all right. She was especially gun-shy of relationships with men. Her track record in that department hadn't been good, and there was certainly no reason for her to believe her luck was going to change with a man like Brad Daniels; a man who could have his pick of countless women in numerous towns across the nation— and probably did. "Anyway, I have to leave now." Hurriedly she put the first aid kit back on the wall and headed for the door.

"What do you mean, leave?" Brad followed her out into the hallway. "You're staying for the concert, aren't you?"

"Actually no. I don't have a ticket, and neither does Kevin. He's planning on seeing your performance tomorrow night with his friends."

"If you had tickets, would you stay for the show?"

"Frankly I don't know too much about your music— other than it's loud. Kevin is your fan."

"Ouch." Brad gave her a wounded look. "What kind of music do you listen to?"

Tori thought for a moment. "Barry Manilow," she answered matter-of-factly.

"God!" His eyeballs rolled upward.

"No, Barry Manilow!"

Brad shook his head in seeming disbelief. "Give me a chance, Tulip. Do the words *new millennium* mean anything to you? Let me expose you to music as I hear it. I always reserve a small section of seats right up front. You and Kevin can both be my guests tonight. Afterwards I'd like it if you'd come backstage and meet some people."

"Well . . ."

"Say yes," he pressed. "You already know your brother wants to."

That much was certainly true. Kevin would never forgive her if she turned Brad down. Tori thought for a moment. What harm could it do to stay and listen to the concert? After that she'd go home to her patients, Kevin would be walking on air for the next week or so, and then life in Wheatfield would return to normal.

"That's really very nice of you," she conceded. "Kevin and I would love to be your guests tonight."

He flashed her a thumbs-up grin. "All right! Mike should still be with your brother in that backstage room. Why don't you catch up with them, and I'll make sure you get the tickets and the passes."

"Well then I guess I'll see you later," Tori said, turning to leave.

"That you will. Oh, and by the way," he called after her, "thanks for patching me up." Then she heard him mutter something under his breath that sounded a lot like, "Barry Manilow."

Tori smoothed the back of her rayon, print skirt, trying

to make herself comfortable in the cushioned, metal seat. There was still half an hour before the show was scheduled to begin. A blanket of gooseflesh covered her arms as she remembered the sweater she'd left in the car. Weather in late spring had a way of being unpredictable. Though if people continued to flood the aisles of the massive Pavilion as they were now doing, things were bound to heat up soon.

Spending most of her time in the suburbs, she'd forgotten how exciting Chicago could be and was surprised to discover that her enthusiasm was mounting. After all, how many women would have given their Godiva chocolates to trade places with her earlier in that washroom, alone with Brad? And now here she was, his personal guest.

The question was why? A warning went off in her head, reminding her about what had happened with Jack.

So what if Brad hadn't seemed put off by the fact that she was Kevin's guardian. What difference would it make considering he was only going to be in town for two nights? If Brad Daniels thought she was the kind of woman who was going to be another willing notch on his belt, it wasn't going to happen. Admittedly, all this attention was an ego boost, but she was smart enough not to take it too seriously.

In fact, the more she looked around, the more out of place she felt. She was starting to wonder whether she was going to be the only female there who wasn't wearing skimpy clothes and shoes that were guaranteed to provide her with lifetime job security. At least she wasn't the oldest one in the crowd, as she'd feared. There were a considerable number of thirtyish people, which made sense, since Brad was probably around that age himself.

Still, she couldn't help wishing she'd dressed more casually. But when Kevin had gotten the call, she'd barely had time to close up the office much less change clothes. It was a good thing her last patient had canceled or they never would have made it on time.

Where was Kevin anyway? He'd agreed to meet her at their seats, but he was already twenty minutes late. She smiled as she thought about his exuberance over this concert and for the opportunity to meet the band members. Kevin had been learning to play the guitar himself. She supposed he needed a hobby, though she would have been happier if he'd demonstrated as much enthusiasm for his schoolwork. Instead, music had been his main outlet since they'd lost their parents in that fatal accident nearly four years earlier. It had been a brutal time for both of them, and things were still difficult. She'd never planned on having to raise an adolescent while she was still so young herself. Neither had Jack for that matter. But there was no sense dwelling on that right now.

"Hey, sis!" Kevin called to her from the aisle as he made his way toward her.

"Where were you? I was starting to get concerned."

"Aw, Tori, that's your biggest problem. You worry too much. When are you going to loosen up?"

"Maybe after you're grown and on your own," she said, as he took the seat next to hers. "Till then you're my responsibility. And you still haven't answered my question."

"I'm more grown up than you think." Kevin shrugged, his dark eyes burning with intensity. "Mike was just showing me around. He's a nice guy."

"Did you get to talk to Brad anymore?"

"No. Remember, he promised an interview later," Kevin said. "But I saw him walking down the hall with you, and the next thing I know we've got the best seats in the house. Wanna tell me what gives?"

Tori shifted uncomfortably. "Nothing gives. He had a

little wound that needed some attention. The tickets are in exchange for my medical expertise."

"So that's all there was to it, huh?" Kevin grilled in a teasing voice.

He'd touched a nerve, and she could already feel the heat start up her neck. "What else would there be, Sherlock Holmes?"

"Hey, I was just asking," he said with an annoying grin. "Anyway, I'm sure not complaining. This is probably the greatest thing that's ever happened to me in my whole life. You know, if we lived in the city stuff like this might happen more often."

Tori folded her arms in front of her chest. "Haven't we been over this about a hundred times?"

"Wheatfield is boring. There's nothing to do there. They don't even have a music store or a movie theater. We're lucky we have a grocery store, such as it is."

"I know," Tori agreed with a heavy sigh. "But we are hooked into an excellent school system, and right now I think that should be your number one priority. Plus the air is clean, and there's not much traffic. I like that, Kevin. Besides, what about my practice? After all the time it's taken me to instill trust in the people I treat, am I supposed to pull up stakes and relocate? My patients depend on me."

"Your work is your whole life, Sis. You hardly ever go out. Don't you ever feel like playing?"

"Sure, I like to have fun, and there is a certain lure to the city. We can always visit though. After all, we are here."

What she hadn't added was that it was all those long work hours that were paying the bills for her student loans and her practice. She'd still been in school at the time of her parents' death. Graduating had been a financial burden as well as an emotional struggle. Although her folks had left her and Kevin with the house, it was sadly in need of repairs. People in Wheatfield weren't used to big city prices, and while her fees were reasonable, patients were often slow in paying. She could never refuse to treat someone just because they were unable to afford her services. But that was her problem, not Kevin's. The boy had had enough to handle in his young life without loading him down with her troubles.

Kevin looked like he was about to say something further when the opening band was introduced. They began to play, and while Kevin seemed to be enjoying himself, Tori hoped she was going to like Brad's music a lot more. Otherwise it was going to be a very long night.

Finally the music stopped, and after a short break the Pavilion darkened. The atmosphere was crackling with anticipation. In the distance Tori could see the faint parade of lit flashlights settling on various portions of the stage, causing a hungry murmur from the audience. Then total blackness. People began to scream and howl, and in the next instant white hot light illuminated Brad Daniels' face.

"One-two! One-two-three-four!" he exploded.

Drums and synthesizers and horns came to life to form the perfect background as he stood, swinging his guitar like a hockey stick. With a vengeance he gripped the microphone and began to sing.

The audience went wild, and Tori could feel the chill of excitement climbing up her spine. People were standing, clapping, singing, cheering and dancing at their seats, and she couldn't help swaying to the rhythm of the erotic sound. Some of the women were even crying.

Brad wore a sleeveless shirt, and his jeans were tight fitting—all the way down to his purple, snakeskin boots. From a chiropractic standpoint, his anatomy was enviable. But who was she kidding? Her awareness of those rippling arm and chest muscles was strictly lustful appreciation.

He moved swiftly and energetically, covering the stage with his aerobic performance, and the power of his voice touched the very core of her womanhood. When the song was over Brad took a moment to introduce each band member.

After several more numbers the Pavilion darkened once again, leaving only a small spotlight on Brad. Cigarette lighters flared across the aisles. The crowd stilled. He pulled up a chair and parked himself directly in front of Tori, but slightly above her on the elevated stage. He began to sing solo, a slow ballad accompanied by his acoustical guitar. A rush of feeling coursed its way through her body as she listened to his words . . . words about cherished values and loved ones . . . a longing for the past and wishes for a second chance. She couldn't help wondering if the lyrics had evolved from his own personal experience. The song tugged at her heart. His voice, gravelly as a stone quarry, yet laced with velvet smoothness, mesmerized her. Even in the dim light she could see his eyes were upon her.

Kevin playfully poked her in the arm, a sure signal that he'd noticed too. But she pretended to be oblivious.

With a wide grin and a devilish wink, Brad finished the song. There was no mistaking that the gesture was for Tori, and the crowd responded by whistling and roaring at fever pitch. Her face burned as she sank deeper into her chair, making a futile attempt to hide from his gaze. But that only gave him more to feed on.

"Maybe the lady will like this one better," he drawled, as he launched into another song, once again vaulting all over the stage.

"That must have been some wound you nursed," Kevin

taunted. "I think the guy has the hots for you."

"You're missing the show," Tori insisted with as much dignity as she could muster.

"Yeah, right," her brother howled.

The concert continued for the next hour and a half. When the last set was finished, Brad was drenched in a pool of sweat. The noise from the audience was deafening as people continued to clap, whistle and yell in a cheering rhythm for several minutes after his exit. "Brad! Brad!" they chanted over and over again. And while Tori would only admit it to herself, she too, was eagerly hoping for an encore.

In the next instant Brad's explosive voice could be heard again. It became clear that the performance was to continue, though he wasn't yet visible. The stage was covered with artificial smoke, and suddenly he appeared, having jumped through the billowing clouds. The audience was revved, and their response to him shook the very walls of the building. He sang two more songs, and then all hell broke loose as band members tossed drumsticks, guitar picks, their T-shirts and a number of other items at the spectators. Brad waited in the background until some of the furor died down, and then he surfaced with a handful of flowers. One at a time he threw the red carnations out into the crowd while females competed and screamed for his attention. When there was only one flower left, one single yellow tulip, he walked toward Tori and motioned her to stretch out her arms.

"Catch," he called, in a hoarse whisper.

Instinct made her obey his command. Caressing the soft petals against her cheek, she inhaled the heady scent of his gift. It wasn't likely the single tulip could have been part of his original act. He'd probably special ordered it, and his gesture made her feel like a princess. Even though she knew it was only a temporary fantasy, she was determined to let herself enjoy the moment.

"Thank you," she called back to him, as their eyes locked.

Then, with the rest of the band members, Brad walked off the stage for the last time that evening. The crowd was demanding still more. But when the lights went on, it was obvious the show was really over, and people began to leave the Pavilion.

Kevin tugged at her arm, and she turned to face him. "You know, Sis, for someone who doesn't get out much, you sure know how to make up for lost time."

"Oh yeah." She had to smile. There was no sense denying that she couldn't remember when, if ever, she'd had more fun. Certainly not in the last four years anyway. "What do you say we try and find our way backstage?"

Chapter Two

With passes in hand, Tori and Kevin were ushered into a crowded backstage room. There, along with an assortment of record-label representatives and other people, they waited for the band members to arrive.

Suddenly Mike Sweeney appeared, and a loud cheer of congratulatory celebration went up. Waving two bottles of champagne and grinning from ear to ear, he yelled, "Somebody get me a towel!"

Tom Mallone, the bass player, came in right behind him. "Happy to oblige, Michael," he shot back, tossing over the ceremonial piece of cloth. The table against the wall was loaded with a selection of cold cuts and salads, and the beer and champagne began to flow.

Tori turned to Kevin. "No alcohol for you," she warned quietly.

"I know," he acknowledged, with an upward glance. Notebook in hand, he immediately left her side for a spot closer to the action. A minute later he was caught up in conversation with someone.

Tori had to admit that so far he'd been handling this opportunity with a finesse that was a credit to his youth, and she was proud of him. He'd come a long way in the past four years, and it gave her a good feeling to know she may have had a little something to do with his progress. Despite his young age he seemed to fit right into this whole party scene and with these people.

Tori, on the other hand, took a deep breath and self-consciously scanned her surroundings. Clearly she was out of her element. Brad was nowhere in sight. In fact, she was beginning to wonder if he was going to show up at all. Maybe after that display during the concert, he was having second thoughts.

Other than her brief introduction to Mike, she knew no one. What she really wanted to do was go hide somewhere until her brother was ready to leave. But for Kevin's sake she would stick it out.

Her stomach growled angrily, and she realized it had been hours since she'd had anything to eat or drink. Gently she fingered the tulip, which she was still clutching in her hand. Then she carefully wrapped it in a tissue and tucked it into her purse before heading toward the buffet table.

"Tori," Mike Sweeney said, as she stood in the line. "Glad you could stay for the show. How did you like it?"

Before she could answer, someone came by with a tray of champagne. Mike grabbed two glasses and handed one to her. "Have some," he insisted.

She knew it wasn't a good idea to be drinking on an empty stomach, but she clutched the glass all the same. At least she'd have something to do with her hands.

"Thank you," she said, taking a small sip. Maybe it would help her relax. "The show was wonderful. I enjoyed it very much. I really appreciate your being so nice to my brother. This whole thing means a lot to him."

"Hey, Kevin's a great kid. But I know Brad wants to spend some time with him too. In fact, we talked about it."

"Really, where is Brad?"

"Right behind you, Tulip."

Tori's pulse quickened at the sound of Brad's voice, and she turned to face those piercing blue eyes. "How long have you been standing here?" she asked.

"Long enough to hear that you liked the show."

"Brad . . . some comments about your new solo. This is the first time we've heard it," one of the reps interrupted.

"Give me a few minutes, and we'll talk," Brad promised.

A second later a blonde woman in black stretch pants boldly brushed against him and linked her arm in his. "Looking good, Handsome," she said in a throaty voice. "Very good, indeed."

"Always nice to see you, Madeline," Brad said, immediately breaking her hold and flashing her a look that told her he was preoccupied.

"A girl can try," she muttered, sauntering off.

"Gotta mingle," Mike said. "Catch you later." With that he was gone, and Brad moved in alongside Tori.

"Are you as hungry as I am?" Brad asked.

"As a matter of fact, I'm famished."

"We can do a lot better than cold cuts, if you can wait about half an hour."

"Well it's getting awfully late," Tori said, looking at her watch.

Brad stepped up to the table, filled a plate with some strawberries, roast beef and cheese and handed it to her. "Here, this will take the edge off till we're ready to leave."

"We? . . . Leave for where?"

"My hotel of course. How else are you and I going to get the chance to talk?"

The idea was enough to double her heart rate. "Now wait a minute . . ."

"More like about twenty-five," he countered. "That should give me enough time to wrap things up here. After that—I'm all yours."

Add controlling to his list of character traits. Before she could respond, someone else latched on to his arm. A second later Brad was on his way to the other side of the room. The man was exasperating. *"All yours"* indeed. Her and about a million other women. If he thought she was going to fall for that line just to get her to go to his hotel with him, he didn't know who he was dealing with.

"Hey, Sis, how's it going?" Kevin asked, appearing at her side.

"Now that you mention the subject, I was just thinking we ought to be—going that is. It's pretty late."

"Tomorrow's Saturday!" Kevin reminded her with a stricken look. "I don't have school."

"No, but I have patients."

"Only till noon. After that you can take a nap," he bargained. "Didn't Brad tell you? We're invited to his hotel suite later on. Can you believe it? This is like a dream come true."

"I don't know . . ."

"Please, Tori," he begged, as she stood in thought. "I still haven't got enough info from Brad to write up the interview, and this is really important to me."

She hadn't seen such a spark of life in her brother since their parents had died. Were a few hours of lost sleep really that serious compared to Kevin's happiness? Besides, Brad had invited Kevin as well, so she supposed she would be relatively safe.

"We'll see," she said, leaving herself a measure of an out. But she knew that she was going to give in, and judging by the look of relief on Kevin's face, he knew it too.

"Thanks, Sis," Kevin said, before disappearing once again. The next several minutes seemed to drag on forever as Tori tried to blend in amid the roomful of rock stars and strangers. At best she was uncomfortable. On the other hand the thought of leaving with Brad sent a nervous surge of adrenaline charging through her.

"Excuse me," said a man, tapping her on the shoulder. Tori saw that he was tall with a beard and mustache and long, rust-colored hair. He wore dark sunglasses and had a professional-looking camera around his neck. "I'll bet you could use some real food to go with that champagne you're almost drinking."

Something about his voice was familiar, and she stepped back to take a more discerning look. The man was wearing baggy jeans and a corduroy blazer. "Actually the buffet's not bad," she retorted.

"But the atmosphere leaves a little something to be desired."

"Have we been introduced?" Tori asked, with a suspicious raise of her brow.

The man flashed her a teasing grin, exposing part of that famous dimple, which rendered his disguise a dead giveaway. "I was hoping you might remember me from the song I sang for you during the show. I know I remember you."

"I liked your song—a lot. And I especially liked the tulip," Tori added, with a shy whisper.

"Me too," Brad said, with a look that told her he wasn't referring to the flower he'd given her.

"So, why the disguise?" Tori questioned, breaking the spell. "Aren't you among friends here?"

"Too many, in fact. I'd still like to spend some time alone with you. If things go right, maybe we could slip out of this place unnoticed."

He'd triggered another pulse-pounding alarm. "Why with me?" she blurted. "I mean, forgive my skepticism, but it's obvious that a man in your position could have his choice of countless females in most any city . . ." She stopped speaking and looked down.

"Oh, I get it," he said. "A guy's gotta have a little something every night, huh? So you figure I'm just laying the trap for the kill?"

Shrugging her shoulders, she looked up at him once again. "Look, in a couple of days you'll be in some other town having this conversation with someone else. Does it really matter to you what I think?"

Brad let out a disgusted sigh. "You believe all that crap they print in the tabloids, don't you? You think I'm some sort of playboy. I didn't figure you to be the type who won't even let a guy plead his case."

Hmm. He certainly had a knack for stripping her defenses. She was going to have to be careful. It would be so easy to get carried away from reality with a man like Brad Daniels. "All right then. What is your case?"

"I just think people should be judged on what's truth and not hearsay. You can't know what that is until you get to know me. Is there any reason we can't spend some time together—talking and getting to know each other?"

"Won't that be difficult?" She deliberately softened her tone. "Your last show in Chicago is tomorrow night."

"Which is a long way off," he pointed out, tugging at his artificial beard. "All I'm asking for right now is the next few hours."

Sure, a quick romp in the sack, and then it's on to some other potential princess for the night.

"So why can't that happen?" he continued.

"Because we're complete opposites, Brad. Our lifestyles

don't match." *And because I'm never going to let another man do to me what Jack did.*

He folded his arms over the large expanse of his chest. "Whoa. Let's not get ahead of ourselves here. It's a little early for a marriage proposal."

That was a jolt. Of course he was right. All he'd really suggested was some conversation, and she'd responded by making a prize fool of herself. Embarrassed, she turned away from him.

"What are you afraid of?" he questioned, seeming oblivious to her humiliation.

She wasn't about to admit she'd been stripped of her self-confidence in the male-female relationship department. She searched hard for her voice and an answer that would redeem her foolish behavior. But the only reply that would surface seemed lame, even to her. "It's just that we're so different . . ."

"You're different," he emphasized. "Different from a lot of women I come in contact with. I could see that right off."

Wait a minute. She straightened her shoulders and faced him. That wasn't what she'd meant at all. The man had a way of turning the tables on her. "How? How am I different?" she challenged.

"For one thing I don't know too many women your age who would be unselfish enough to be raising a kid, especially one who isn't your own."

What? She took a step back. *That was a totally unexpected response to her situation.* "Kevin is my brother. He's family," she explained.

Brad wore an intense expression that was impossible for her to interpret. "I don't know much about your lifestyle yet. So I can't say how opposite it is from mine. But our value system might be a lot closer than you think. Are you brave enough to find out?"

Maybe it was the champagne gone to her head, making her think she might have underestimated the man after all. Would it really be so dangerous to spend some time with him? Maybe Kevin had been right when he'd said she ought to loosen up a little. Enjoy life more. As long as she stayed on her guard, what could the harm be in a little conversation?

Brad tapped his foot impatiently.

"What have you got in mind?" she asked.

"You and I are just going to sneak out of here quietly—without the usual limo, security guards or pomp and circumstance, and go back to my hotel. Mike will keep an eye on Kevin till this thing ends, and then they can meet us a little later. The kid will be fine."

"And how are we going to do this?" she wondered, her sense of adventure piqued.

"Did you drive here?" he asked.

"Yes, as a matter of fact."

"What kind of car do you have?"

"A Toyota. Tercel," she added, "if it makes any difference."

"Good. That's nice and inconspicuous. Give me the keys, and tell me where you're parked."

Along with the keys, she gave him her license plate number, then waited while he spoke to Mike Sweeney. Minutes later, minus the camera, Brad slipped his hand in hers. "Hold on to me," he instructed, leading her through a side room and to a doorway. She could have sworn she saw him grimace as if in pain, but it happened so quickly she wasn't sure. "One of the equipment guys is going to drive us in your car. All we have to do is meet him by the side entrance."

"That sounds easy enough," Tori said, taking short, quick steps.

"Except that it's not a straight shot out of the building. But if we can get through this door and down the hallway without being seen, we can probably make it out to the street."

Tori couldn't stop herself from dwelling on those two teenagers who'd attacked Brad earlier that day. She wondered what would happen if she and Brad were spotted. "Just one more question," she asked skeptically. "Have you ever tried this disguise idea before?"

"Yeah," he answered with a wry smile.

"Did it work?"

"That was two questions, Tulip. You're just gonna have to trust me."

The door was a heavy steel one, and Brad pried it open a crack to check the hallway. After deciding the coast was clear, he helped her through the opening. "Hmm," he said, "let's just hope everyone's gone home."

She fought the urge to tiptoe and whisper while Brad cautioned her to act natural. "We don't want to arouse any suspicions in case we do run into anyone." But she could sense that he was nervous too.

Hand in hand, Brad led her down the long corridor. As they rounded the last corner she could see a group of teenage girls huddled close to the exit doors. They were locked in conversation and, for the moment, seemed to pose no threat. "Just keep walking," Brad whispered confidently, as he smiled down at Tori.

The exit doors were still several feet away when suddenly one of the girls took notice and said something to her friends. One by one they looked up and began a more detailed study of Brad, until one of them screamed at the top of her lungs. "It's him, it's him!" she shouted frantically. "Look at his boots."

Brad muttered a curse. "This is what I get for trying to bypass security."

Tori tightened her hold on his hand.

He groaned, his arm stiffening as if he were in pain.

"What's happening?" Tori gasped, conscious of the fear sweeping through her.

"I forgot about my boots," he explained, sheepishly gazing down at the purple snakeskin. "They're kind of like my trademark."

"Wonderful disguise. Your groupies are headed right for us!"

"Hurry!" he shouted. "There's another way out on the other side of the building."

They ran as though they were in competition for the Olympics, but Tori's dress pumps were hardly conducive to speed. One of the girls was gaining on them, screaming all the way. Just as they reached the second exit the girl caught up with them and made a lunge for Brad, pulling the wig off his head. Despite his fake beard and mustache, the sight of his ebony hair was final confirmation of her teenage suspicions, and she began to weep pitifully.

"Run!" Brad commanded, maintaining his grip on Tori's hand. Her heart was pumping so fast she could hardly breathe. By the time they got to the street Brad was winded too, and she couldn't help noticing the beads of sweat on his forehead. The crying teenager had almost reached them, and the rest of the unruly mob was not far behind.

"Where the hell is Ray?" he shouted, over the sounds of honking horns and Chicago traffic.

"Probably still waiting by the first exit," Tori answered. She looked over her shoulder. For a brief second she wondered how she could have allowed herself to get into such a situation, but this was hardly the time to start analyzing. It was clear if they didn't get out of there immediately, someone was going to get hurt.

"Over there," Brad said, motioning to a cab that had pulled up to the curbside. They bolted toward it and climbed in. Brad reached into his pocket and waved a fifty-dollar bill at the driver. "We've got an emergency here!" he pleaded, "so could you hurry it up?"

Just then the sobbing teenager reached the taxi and grabbed onto the door handle. "Let go!" Brad shouted, struggling to shut the door while the driver began to inch into heavy traffic.

"Please!" the young girl begged. "I love you so much, Brad. Oh, please! Just an autograph. I would die for you!"

He swore quietly, relinquishing his hold. "Get in here, quick," he demanded . . . "before you get the chance to prove it!"

"What the Sam Hill is goin' on back there?" the driver yelled, slamming on the brakes. "And where the hell you want me to go?"

"Hotel Collins. Step on it!" Brad shouted back. "We're cool now," he assured everyone. "Everything's under control."

Under control? The driver pulled away with such a force that the three of them were temporarily pinned to the backseat, leaving the rest of the screaming teens at the curb. *Cool?* If he thought things were cool now, she'd like to know what he considered hot. *On second thought . . .*

For a few moments no one seemed capable of saying anything, including the bewildered girl sitting beside Brad. She had finally stopped her tears. After catching his breath,

Brad turned to her and broke the silence. "What's your name?" he asked gently.

"Jenny," she answered, her voice trembling with emotion.

"Jenny, how old are you?"

"Fourteen."

Brad let out a deep sigh. "Did you mean what you said back there about dying for me?"

"I'd gladly give my life for you," the girl insisted with conviction.

Brad shook his head. "A fourteen-year-old shouldn't have to lay down her life for anyone, Jenny. Especially not for someone you've never even met."

The girl tossed her long, straight brown hair over her shoulders and studied him for a moment. "But I do know you. I have every album you've ever made. I've seen all your music videos. I've read every magazine article ever written about you."

"Oh, and those tabloids always tell the unfailing truth," he said sarcastically. "Let me enlighten you. I'm just a flesh and blood human being with faults. Plenty of them too. And I don't want anyone—not anyone, idolizing me like I'm Superman. Do you understand what I'm saying?"

"But I love you," Jenny persisted, impervious to the point he'd been trying to make.

"Well if that's really true, then you won't lay the responsibility for your young life at my feet. It's too precious to place so little value on it."

The girl sat silent. One could only hope that meant she was digesting what Brad was saying.

"You and your friends could have been seriously hurt. In fact, that little stunt you pulled with the taxi could have gotten all of us hurt. And for what? My signature on a piece of paper?"

"Yeah," she confirmed. "That and the fact that they're all going to die when I tell them I shared a cab with you."

Brad slapped his forehead in exasperation. "Jeez, there's that word again. How many of them did we leave back there?"

"Six."

Brad looked at Tori and winked. "I guess I can't have six deaths on my conscience. You got any paper in your purse?" he asked, as the driver approached the curbside in front of the Hotel Collins.

"Sure," Tori answered, handing him a small scratch tablet.

"If you'll just turn the interior light on for a minute," Brad said to the driver, who was, no doubt, happy to oblige, having worked less than ten minutes for his fifty dollars.

Tori looked over Brad's shoulder while he scribbled *"Peace,"* plus his name, until he'd written the same thing on six separate sheets of paper. His handwriting was worse than a doctor's she thought, watching him pass the signatures over to the young girl.

Jenny looked at Brad with hopeful adulation. "Thanks. Thanks a lot. But didn't you forget about someone?"

"Oh yeah," Brad teased. "I'll have to see if there's any paper left."

"I hope you're going to say something more personal on mine," Jenny pleaded. "It would mean a lot to me."

"Uh . . ." For a few seconds Brad looked very uncomfortable. But then his familiar grin reappeared. "I'll do better than that," he promised, reaching for the wig that Jenny was still gripping in her hand. A moment later he'd written his signature inside on the label. "You keep the wig, Jenny. I need a new disguise anyway."

"Wow!" the girl said, pressing the treasured keepsake to her heart.

"Driver," Brad instructed, slipping additional money into the man's hand. "Before I get arrested for kidnapping, please take this young lady back to the Pavilion, where her friends are."

"Yes sir," the man answered, looking extremely pleased.

Once again the young girl began to tear up, and Brad placed a gentle kiss on her cheek. "You're the best," she said, as he stepped out of the taxi and went around to Tori's side to open the door.

"Behave yourself, Jenny," Brad called out as the taxi pulled away. Then he turned to Tori. "C'mon," he said, leading her across the street, away from the hotel.

"Where are we going?"

"Unless I'm mistaken, that's Ray over there with your car. He must have seen us and followed the cab."

"That still doesn't explain where you're taking me now," she said, as they climbed into the backseat of her own vehicle.

"Hotel Whittier," he said, loud enough for Ray to take action.

"I don't understand," Tori said.

"You didn't think I'd be stupid enough to let that kid know where the band was really staying, did you?"

Tori let out a sigh of confusion as she stared at Brad. His black hair was sticking straight up and was a striking clash with his phony red beard and mustache. He still had the glasses on, along with the baggy pants and purple boots. She'd been pretty impressed with the way he'd handled the situation with those kids. And yet at this point the man looked like someone whose character might be seriously questioned.

"You know, Brad. I just met you about six hours ago. And I'm already beginning to feel like a character in a television drama. Is your life always this exciting?"

"As a matter of fact," he answered with a chuckle, "nothing like this has happened since a year ago when some fans recognized me in a deli. The band actually travels with very tight security. And certain people are going to be very honked off when they discover that I split the backstage party. Mike and Ray are the only ones who knew I was going to pull this shot. Right, Ray?"

"Yeah," Ray confirmed, the irritation clear in his tone, as he pulled in front of the Hotel Whittier.

"Just drop us off right here, Ray. We'll be okay now," Brad said, as he swung around to Tori's side to open the car door for her.

She started to thank Ray, but was interrupted by a man wearing a formal red uniform.

"Good evening. May I help you?" the hotel doorman questioned, giving Brad and Tori a scrutinizing look.

"Thank you, but we're fine," Brad replied. Without hesitating, he locked his arm through Tori's and rushed her past the man into the main lobby.

Tori's stomach churned, and she told herself it was from the fright of being chased. But her inner voice warned that there might be other reasons for her reaction, and she could only speculate at what might be next on the agenda.

"Now what?" she asked.

"Now we get ourselves up to the twenty-third floor as soon as possible. The trick is to act casual."

Where had she heard that line before? Tori could hardly control the motion of her eyes drifting toward the ceiling.

Yet, as her arm remained linked with Brad's, for some reason that seemed to defy logic, she knew he wasn't going to let anything bad happen to her.

A quick scan for the nearest elevator allowed only seconds to appreciate the magnificence of the rich marble floors covered with Oriental rugs and the Oriental artwork scattered throughout the various walls.

"Over there," Brad said, pointing. "That one looks empty and available."

As they hurried over, a few people turned to stare at them. "Have you forgotten that you don't exactly look like one of their average, well-dressed patrons?" she whispered. "For that matter, I'm pretty underdressed for this place myself. Half these women are dripping in jewels and draped in furs even though it's a warm evening."

"You worry too much." He smiled at her reassuringly as they stepped into the waiting elevator. When they began their ascent, he leaned against the wall, arms folded in front of his chest. "Whew! I think we just might be home free."

"I hope that isn't a premature prediction that's going to be followed up by another near disaster," Tori said with a note of sarcasm.

"Oh yeah," he countered, straightening his posture. A devilish look came into his eyes. "What could possibly happen now?"

An engrossing assortment of answers silently surfaced. In fact her mind was running rampant with response to his magnetism and charm in a way that had been foreign to her for a long time. And the color she could feel searing her face was undeniable evidence of that fact.

"You're blushing again," he teased, with an intimate grin.

She didn't need him to tell her that. But as her cheeks

grew hot, so came the logic to cool her thoughts. Had she forgotten that she was a professional? Come morning, she would have an office full of patients to care for. In the meantime, she'd been acting more like one of Kevin's peers than his legal guardian, cavorting around with a rock star for heaven's sake! And nothing was going to change the fact that Brad had only one more show to do the following evening. After that he would be gone. What *could* happen next, indeed? Not much, assuming her brain stayed in the operative mode.

After what seemed like the longest ride in history, the elevator stopped. Brad looked up to make sure they were on the right floor, then did a quick check of the hallway before escorting her off. "Just around the corner now, and we'll be there."

Tori's knees were beginning to feel wobbly at the prospect, and had it not been for the fact that she would have to wait until Kevin arrived with others, she would have considered bolting. Right then and there.

"Here we are," Brad announced, sliding the key card in the door.

Her first reaction as she stepped inside was to take a deep breath; a gesture of relief and an attempt to calm her nerves at the same time. Her second reaction was to marvel at the opulent surroundings. The foyer led to a huge living room with plush velvet furniture and lavish accessory pieces in an Oriental motif. Beyond the living room she could see there was also a dining room with a long rosewood table and upholstered chairs. Everything about this place smacked of upper echelon.

"You know, you've hardly said a word since we got on the elevator. Is anything wrong?"

"No." Tori nervously cleared her throat. "Quite the

living quarters though," she observed, taking a seat on the luxurious gray sofa.

"There are two bedrooms. Mike has the second one. The rest of the guys are staying in rooms across the hall. To be honest," he explained, sounding almost apologetic, "this place is a little extreme for my taste. But the security is excellent . . . when we use it."

"Right," she said, under her breath. "Are we the only ones here?"

"So far. Does that make you uneasy?"

"The truth?"

"I would hope so."

"Yes, a little."

"I want you to relax," he said, pushing his thick hair back from his face. "I'm not Jack the Ripper. And for that matter, your brother and the rest of the guys will be here soon. Are you hungry?"

"Yes," she admitted. She'd been too uptight at the backstage party to eat much.

"I can call room service and have them send up some steaks, lobster—whatever you like."

"I'm not fussy."

"Hmm," he said, giving her a look that told her he'd sensed her discomfort at ordering such an extravagant meal. "How do you feel about pizza? I've heard Chicago has some of the finest."

"I love pizza. And there isn't anything I don't like on it, even anchovies. So get whatever kind you want."

"I knew it!" Brad slapped his thigh with a certain smugness.

"Knew what?"

"That you like anchovies. See, we've got more in common than you thought."

She couldn't help matching his smile with one of her own. "Anything in particular you'd like to drink?"

"At the moment I'd settle for a glass of plain ice water."

"Well, what do you know? I like water too. So much so that I never stay at any hotel that doesn't have it," he teased, pouring her some from the pitcher sitting on the coffee table. He handed her the glass, then walked across the room and picked up the phone. She thought she heard him tack a bottle of champagne onto the order, but she wasn't sure.

"Our food should be here in about half an hour," he said, after hanging up. Meanwhile there's some fresh fruit in that basket on the end table if you'd like. I'm going to take a quick shower and get the gunk from this disguise off me. Make yourself comfortable. I'll be right out."

Tori watched him disappear into the bedroom, his stride purposeful and with sturdy grace. She could almost envision him peeling off his clothes, item by item, from his boots and shirt to his baggy pants—right on down to his briefs. She wondered if they would be the skimpy, bikini type or maybe just the regular white jockeys. Or maybe he wore boxer shorts. The kind with funny designs on them. A moment later she heard the sound of running water. It occurred to her that Brad Daniels' naked body was as close as the next room, and suddenly it didn't matter what kind of underwear he wore, because all she could think about was what he would look like without any clothes at all.

Her heart began to hammer a foolish staccato, and she walked over to the fruit basket to steady herself. There was a nice assortment of oranges, pears, apples, peaches—bananas. Bananas! Nervously she paced the floor. It was time to put a lid on those lust-ridden thoughts.

It wasn't long before Brad stepped back into the room. "Hi there," he said.

Surprised, Tori turned to face him. "When you say quick, I guess you really mean it."

"Yeah, well I'm only this fast when it suits my purpose." His voice was low and seductive, like his snug-fitting jeans. His well-muscled shoulders shifted against his blue T-shirt until she thought they might burst right through the fabric. Freshly washed hair, still wet and unstyled, hung flat on his head, giving him enough of a little-boy quality to form a dangerously appealing combination.

Warning! Emergency alert! her panic button screamed.

"Why don't we sit over there and talk?" he suggested, pointing to the sofa.

"All right." But she waited until he was settled before she positioned herself a good five feet from him at the opposite end of the huge piece of furniture. Keeping her distance seemed the only sane thing to do.

Brad slouched down and stretched out his legs. "I don't bite. But hey, if you're comfortable . . ."

"I'm comfortable," Tori assured him.

He turned to face her. "So, tell me how you wound up being legal guardian to Kevin."

The question delivered a piercing stab as the horrifying memories came back to her. Of all the subjects they could talk about, why did he have to start with the one that was responsible for so much pain, both in her life and Kevin's?

Chapter Three

"Sorry, Tulip," Brad said, his eyes sharp and assessing. "Obviously the matter is personal. What would you like to talk about instead?"

Tori thought for a moment. "I guess I'd like to answer your question," she said softly, as surprised at her own words as Brad appeared to be. For some reason it was suddenly important to her that he know. Telling him, making him understand how it was with her and Kevin, would afford her protection right from the start. Before he or any other man could ever work his way into her heart again and then break it . . . the way Jack had.

"I guess I should begin by saying that Kevin and I live in the town of Wheatfield. It's a small tight-knit community where people band together. We were a close family too. Despite the fact that I was already thirteen when Kevin was born, I never viewed him as a hindrance to my teenage social development. I was always willing to baby-sit whenever my parents had to go out. When he got a little older, sometimes I used to let him tag along with me and my friends; once in a while, even on dates. So you see, when we lost our parents it was only natural for me to take over their role.

"My folks were both teachers at the same elementary

school that Kevin attended. Actually my father was the principal, and my mother taught fifth grade. You can imagine that a good education was high on their list of priorities, and they did their best to instill those values in us."

Tori paused for a sip of her ice water to chase down the painful lump that was beginning to form at the back of her throat, while Brad sat patiently, waiting for her to continue.

"Time went by, and before I knew it Kevin was in the sixth grade. I was still living with my family, finishing up my own education. But that's another story. Anyway, every year the school, along with all the neighboring schools, sponsored a math contest. Kevin didn't really want to be in it. In fact, he pretty much balked at the idea. But he was an honor student, and my parents knew that he could make a real contribution to the team if he would just put forth the effort. And they insisted on his participation.

"On the day of the contest I had the afternoon free, and I went over to the school to watch." Her voice broke, and she clenched her fists in an effort to regain her composure.

Brad inched closer to her, looking for all the world like he wanted to scoop her into his arms, but his hands remained at his sides.

"I was on the sidewalk across the street from the front entrance of the building when I spotted both my parents. School was just getting out. Ordinarily there were other teachers who were responsible for dismissing the children. But because of the contest that day, those people had other obligations. So Mom and Dad were trying to talk a stampeding herd of excited children into leaving the grounds in an orderly fashion.

"I could see Kevin in the distance at the other end of the playground. When he saw me he waved and shouted something that I couldn't hear. Then he began to run toward me."

Tori's voice broke again, and this time a tear trickled down her cheek. "Sorry," she said, swiping at her eyes with the sleeve of her sweater.

"I'm starting to think I'm the one who should be apologizing," Brad said, moving still closer to her. "If this is too difficult for you . . ."

"No, I want to tell you what happened," she insisted, swallowing hard. "There I was starting to cross the street with Kevin still on the other side in the distance. Mom and Dad were between us, along with several of the school kids." Tori took a deep breath and closed her eyes. "Out of nowhere came this car. I saw it jump the curb and head right into the crowd. Within seconds people literally went flying. I watched, horrified, as a child who was thrown right over the hood of the car landed near my feet. My mother's mangled body was found on top of another child she'd been trying to protect. My father . . . the blood . . . well, it was just too horrible to tell.

"The driver was a teenager who didn't even have her license yet. She'd come to pick up her younger sister. Apparently she'd been driving with one foot on the brake and the other foot on the gas pedal. Somehow she confused the two and lost control of the car. When she finally came to a halt, three children had been injured. Four people had been killed. Two children and two adults. My mother and father."

Through her tears Tori saw Brad shudder as he drew in a sharp breath. He placed his hand over hers and gave her a light squeeze. "What a nightmare," he said, reaching for a nearby box of tissues. He grabbed a few and gently traced the wet path down her cheeks. His kindness was comforting. Yet his gesture was distracting . . . and unsettling.

"Yes," she agreed, breaking the spell. "At times it still is, even though it happened four years ago. For Kevin it was even worse. You see, my line of vision was partially blocked by the car. But from where Kevin was standing, I'm afraid every vivid detail is etched in his memory. It's been a real struggle to put our lives back together."

"I can only imagine," Brad said sympathetically.

"Well," she added, forcing a smile. "We take one day at a time. I love my brother very much, and it's important to me to see to it that he gets all the educational advantages and opportunities he would have received if my parents had lived. It's my job to raise him the way they would have. And I take that responsibility very seriously."

Before he could respond, the phone rang. Brad jumped up to answer it. "Our pizza is ready," he said, once he'd finished talking to the caller.

There was an awkward silence. "I didn't mean to put such a damper on the evening, Brad."

"You didn't. Besides, I'm the one who asked."

There was a knock at the door, an odd, rhythmic wrap. "Just room service letting us know it's really them," Brad said.

A moment later the serving cart was before them. Brad took the lid off the elegant silver platter. A large, piping hot, thick, stuffed pizza lay waiting to be tasted. "I hope you still feel like eating," he said, with a look of uncertainty.

"I try to live in the present as much as possible. Right now that looks delicious, and it smells even better," she said, in an effort to change the subject. He began to section out a large piece on the elegant china. Carefully he set the plate on her lap and then proceeded to serve himself.

"I'd really like it if you would come to the show tomorrow night," he said. "That's if you don't have other plans."

"Well . . ." She hesitated.

"You could sit off to the side of the stage. Best seats in the house. It would mean a lot to me, my last night in Chicago and all."

"And where do you go from here?"

"Home for a short break. Then back on the road. We're on tour for most of the summer and part of fall."

Tori cut into her pizza and took a small taste. "This is fantastic!"

"It is," he agreed, having swallowed a bite that was easily three times the size of her own. "But you still haven't told me whether or not you'll be my date for the show tomorrow. Will you?"

His date? Was that what he'd just said? How was it that he could alter the beat of her heart so radically with just a few words? Well why not? It had been far too long since she'd had a bona fide date. Why couldn't she have a little fun for a change? As long as she didn't get carried away and allow herself to forget that he'd be gone and out of her life by the following night. She looked at him and smiled. "Yes. I'd like that very much."

"Well now, that calls for a champagne toast," Brad said, looking pleased. He got up from the sofa and took the bottle from the ice bucket. He struck a debonair pose while positioning his thumbs to remove the cork. A second later the cork flew out of the bottle at the same time he dropped it, sending it tumbling to the floor. "Ow, damn!" he yelled, grimacing as he held his left hand with his right.

"What's wrong?" Tori demanded with concern.

"Nothing!" Brad insisted loudly, his face coloring in obvious pain. "At least I think nothing." He reached for a nearby towel and began to wipe the spilled liquid out of the plush blue carpeting. "Sorry, I didn't mean to snap at you just now."

"Never mind about that." She joined him on the floor and grabbed the towel away. "Let me clean up this mess."

"It's strange," he explained. "During the encore tonight my hand started hurting, kind of a throbbing sensation. In fact, I wasn't sure I was going to get through the last song. After I quit playing my guitar the pain stopped, and I almost forgot about it."

"Until the merry chase scene," Tori cut in, wiping the last of the champagne from the floor. "When you led me by the hand through the halls of the auditorium, I thought I saw you wince a couple of times. I wondered then if something was wrong."

"Funny, I don't even remember."

"Not surprising, all things considered." Brad had moved to the sofa and was alternately forming a fist and flattening the palm of his hand. She put the wet towel in the bar sink and sat down beside him. "How do you feel now?" she questioned.

"My hand hurts, and it's starting to feel tingly. In fact, my whole arm feels kind of weird. I've never had anything like this happen to me before," he said apprehensively.

"I wonder if it has something to do with the way those girls tackled you before the show this afternoon."

"I don't think so." Brad cleared his throat, looking slightly embarrassed. "They weren't exactly going for my hand."

Tori suppressed the urge to smile, then picked up his left hand and began to examine it.

"Tell me where the pain is located." She moved her fingers up his arm toward his shoulder and neck, applying pressure to certain areas along the way.

"Every place you're touching," he said, taking a stoic

breath through clenched teeth. "I've got a concert to do tomorrow night, and right now I can hardly feel my fingers. How the hell am I going to play my guitar?"

"Tomorrow night is a long way off—as you reminded me before," she said reassuringly. "Stand up so I can get a better look at the back of your neck."

His thick eyebrows creased with worry. "Look, I appreciate your concern, but right now I think what I need is a good doctor. Know any?"

"As a matter of fact, I'm a chiropractor. An excellent one," she qualified. "So, if you have no objection, maybe I can do something to ease your pain. At least for the moment."

"You're a chiropractor?" he asked with surprise.

"Yes," Tori answered patiently, while reaching into her purse for one of her business cards. She was used to varied reactions when people first discovered her occupation.

Brad took the small piece of paper from her. As he studied it, his face tightened, and his luminous eyes darkened to reveal a strange uneasiness.

"Don't tell me you're part of a certain segment of our population who still equates chiropractors with charlatans."

"No . . . of course not," he answered without looking at her. "It's . . . it's just that you're kind of little to be a bone crusher."

Tori cringed. "I hope that was a joke. Gentle manipulation is usually what it takes to get the job done. And size isn't nearly as important as proper leverage. Besides," she maintained, "I'm a lot stronger than I look. Would you mind taking off your shirt?"

"Uh . . . I guess not."

His hesitancy was cause for Tori to wonder if Brad was fearful that she'd further irritate his injury. Something was certainly bothering him.

"Are you sure that's all you'd like me to remove?" he suddenly added, with a suggestive rise of one brow.

That was an abrupt switch in gears. "Positive," she answered, watching as he gingerly pulled the shirt over his head and threw it on a nearby chair. Something didn't add up here. Was that last remark a little macho cover-up for his possible distrust of her ability? If so, she was all the more determined to act like the professional she was, even if the sight of his muscular chest was making her insides churn. It was important that she gain his confidence.

"Hmm," she said, after silently deliberating for a couple of minutes.

"Hmm?" Brad repeated, turning to face her. "Now you do sound like a doctor."

"Actually, I think the problem is in your neck. Of course I can't be certain without X-rays."

His eyes revealed a skeptic glint. "Why would my hand be numb if the problem is in my neck?"

"Well, it's like this," Tori explained. "Your neck has seven movable bones called vertebrae. A pair of spinal nerves exit between each two vertebrae, and these supply the tissues of the neck and arms. If the vertebras become misaligned, which might have happened when you were attacked, they could irritate a nerve and cause pain in the shoulders, arms, or in your case, tingling and numbness in the fingers and hands."

Brad sighed. "How bad is the damage?"

"Well, I'm sure it can be repaired. Some pictures would give me better information, but unfortunately I don't carry an X-ray machine around with me. I keep that back at my office in Wheatfield."

"Wheatfield?"

"It's about an hour west of here. I work out of my home. But since we're here we can start by putting some ice on your neck. That will keep the swelling down and help reduce the pain."

A moment later Tori emerged from the bathroom with a makeshift ice pack in her hand. Brad was curled up on the sofa with his shoes off, looking very helpless. She placed the icy towel at the back of his neck as he sucked in a deep breath of air.

"Jeez that's cold!"

She took his plate and carefully placed it in his lap. "Try eating the rest of your pizza. That should take your mind off the pain for a while. Careful not to spill."

"Maybe you should hold that pack in place for me—just in case."

"Oh, I think you can manage to keep it there without my help," she chided playfully.

He feigned a wounded look. "Can't blame a guy for trying."

Tori gave him a self-conscious smile while picking up her plate to finish her pizza. The minute it reached her lips the hot, sticky cheese formed a string down her chin, and the sauce began to dribble.

"Napkin?" he offered, as she struggled for dignity. Her extremities were turning to jelly. Not only was the man well aware of it, his smug look told her he was enjoying every moment of her struggle. In what seemed like an eternity, she finally managed to clean her plate. Having done so, she decided her best defense was to stick to being *Doctor* Tori Glenn. At least she'd be calling the shots. She took one last sip of water and then stood.

"Okay Brad, time for a little trigger-point therapy."

"What's that?" he asked.

"It's the technique of pressing on certain points of the body in order to relieve pain. It's kind of like acupuncture, only there aren't any needles involved."

"Yeah?" His tone was skeptical. "You really think that will do any good?"

"Definitely. If you are having some sort of muscle spasm, this will open up the constricted areas and allow the blood to circulate more freely."

"So, what would you like me to do?"

Tori thought for a moment and then moved the coffee table away from the sofa. "Why don't you lie face-down, right here?" she said.

"Yes ma'am," he said, obediently doing as she'd asked. "But wouldn't you have more room to work if I were on the bed?"

The man had a point, but the situation would probably not be conducive to the professional front she was determined to maintain. "I think I'll get better leverage right here," she answered.

Tori placed his arms at his sides and then began to exert pressure, starting with a trigger point just below the occipital bone in the neck area.

"Ouch!" he responded.

"I'm not surprised that's sore. Only a few more seconds," she said, holding her finger in place. "The pain should be letting up soon."

"Yeah, it's better now."

She moved assertively but slowly, testing the strength and reflexes of his arms and hands, applying pressure to places along his shoulders and neck. Carefully she maneuvered his head downward to assess the compression on the nerve, treating the troubled spots and waiting for his responses. It was a trial and error procedure, compounded by the fact that it was difficult for her to deal with him as a patient, and not the remarkably handsome man that he was.

Finally she had done a thorough enough job to test the results. "Stand up, Brad. Tell me how you feel."

Slowly he rose from the sofa and faced her, rotating his bare shoulder. "I feel terrific. In fact, I haven't felt this good in months."

Tori was pleased. "Does that mean your numbness has cleared up?" she asked, reaching for his hand and pressing between the joints of his fingers.

Before Brad could answer, she was startled by a loud coughing noise coming from the entrance door of the suite. She turned to see Kevin staring at her with a look of surprise. Tori dropped Brad's hand as quickly as if she'd accidentally latched on to a cactus.

"Sorry, Sis," Kevin said with a shrug, digging his hands into his pockets.

Mike Sweeney stood right beside the boy and let go of a howling sort of whistle. "If you wanted privacy, man, all you had to do was say so. The kid and I can go across the hall. The party's just gettin' started over there anyway."

"You'll do no such thing!" Tori interjected, her breath quickening while her face grew hot. "It's late, and Kevin and I have to be leaving."

"But we just got here!" Kevin protested.

Brad stood in silence, obviously amused by the situation. Evidently he had no intention of correcting the erroneous impression that Kevin and Mike had gotten about what had been going on.

She shot Brad a frosty look and then repeated her earlier question. "How is the numbness in your hand?"

"Gone. You're a real miracle worker, Tulip. I'm going to

have to think of some way to repay you," he added, with a shifty grin.

Why did she feel as though she'd been caught with her fingers in raw cake batter? "Brad was having some problems with his neck and hand . . . and shoulder. I was just doing trigger-point therapy on him," she explained.

"That's right," Brad confirmed, with an innocent little-boy tone. But the look on his face conveyed devilish innuendo. "I haven't felt this good in months."

"Do you realize it's two o'clock in the morning?" Tori said, looking at her watch. "Kevin and I really do have to get going."

"Not on my account you don't," Brad said. "I can sleep late tomorrow morning."

"Yeah, Sis," Kevin chimed in. "Besides, I didn't get to finish interviewing Brad for the school paper yet."

"Sorry, but some of us have to get up with the sun," Tori insisted. "And my first patient is due in about six hours."

"Don't worry, Kevin," Brad apologized with a guilt-ridden look. "I promise you'll get your interview before I leave town."

"How do I get to my car?" Tori asked.

"Ray parked it," Mike explained. "He's across the hall. The kid and I will go find him, and then he'll take you two downstairs. Right?" he added, poking Kevin in the shoulder, as though they were both privy to some conspiracy to leave Brad and Tori alone. Before she could protest, the two of them were gone.

Brad walked Tori to the door. For the moment, she was no longer Dr. Glenn, and Brad wasn't her patient. There was no denying her attraction to this man, however unsettling the realization was. The awkwardness set in as she reached for her purse and sweater. *What to do now? What to say? Was he going to kiss her?* She could hardly look at him. Why hadn't she been graced with the social skills needed to handle situations like this?

With a glacial slowness he moved in on her, backing her against the wall. He stood, hovering over her petite frame with his hands on her shoulders. "I had a good time tonight," he said.

"Me too," Tori admitted, forcing herself to make contact with his electric blue eyes.

"The thrill of the chase, huh?"

"Assuming you mean the one that took place outside the auditorium?"

"Sure," he said, with enough tease in his tone to tell her that wasn't at all what he'd meant. "And thanks again for the therapy on my hand. I feel a lot better now."

"I'm glad I could help, Brad."

Her heart was pounding as he bent down and touched his lips to her forehead, then with tenderness he gathered her into his arms, resting his chin in her auburn curls.

The clean smell of soap and his freshly washed hair enveloped her as Tori returned his hug with a fervor.

"I'll talk to you before tomorrow night," he said, releasing her from his hold. He smiled warmly as he opened the door to the suite and led her out into the hallway.

Brad lay on the bed staring up at the ceiling. The luminous numbers on the nearby digital clock told him that the sun would be rising soon. Restless, he shifted onto his side and closed his eyes for the umpteenth time since Tori had left his suite. But he still couldn't get to sleep. Nor could he get the woman out of his system.

Who would have figured that the petite lady with her

shy, embarrassed ways would turn out to be a chiropractor? A competent one at that. It was amazing how quickly she'd gotten him out of his pain. She was a chiropractor! . . . And he'd been calling her "Tulip" all night like she was some kind of damn flower.

The first time in years he'd let himself go out on a limb by trying to make headway with a woman other than the bimbo type, and she turned out to be a doctor. He'd never scored too many points with the highly educated before, not even with his own family. Certainly not with women. The warning sirens were blasting, and he knew he was treading deep water here. If he had any sense at all, he'd step out before he got stepped on—again.

But the fact that he'd lain awake all night told him that logic was already starting to take a back seat to something a lot more powerful . . . and that's what scared him. He couldn't remember the last time he'd been so stirred up by a woman. He knew himself well enough to realize it wasn't just a physical thing either. It had taken a lot of restraint to plant that little peck on her forehead, when what he'd really wanted to do was kiss her in a way that would have been much more memorable. Though he didn't have to be booksmart to sense that Dr. Tori Glenn was the kind of woman who needed to take things slow and easy. It was too early to push any further than the way he'd playfully teased her in front of Mike and her brother.

That was the other thing. The kid. It had just about blown Brad away to hear Tori explain how she'd come to be Kevin's guardian. After that story about the way her parents had been killed, he'd wanted to take her into his arms and soothe her pain, kiss away her tears, make it all better; but she wouldn't have bought it. Too much the skeptic she was, and too early for such intimacy. Still he couldn't help but respect her attitude of responsibility toward the boy—and a twinge of envy for the closeness they shared. A closeness he'd never experienced first-hand with his own family.

Logic screamed for him to bolt. Maybe that's just what he'd do—after the closing Chicago concert. Any sooner and he'd be a real heel, especially after making such a big deal about her being his date and all. She already thought he was an irresponsible playboy.

The woman intrigued him and intimidated him at the same time. While intimidation was hardly a new feeling for him, he'd become a real master at hiding it. He supposed there wasn't any real reason he couldn't do it for another night or so. At least long enough to see whether Doctor Tori Glenn was going to be worth his painstaking effort. With that in mind he rolled over one final time before drifting off.

The sound of the alarm clock jolted him awake. No, it wasn't the alarm, Brad realized, groggy and disoriented from lack of sleep. It was the telephone. He hadn't left a wake-up call. Who would be phoning at 6:00 a.m. the morning after a concert?

Still on his back, he reached over the nightstand and fumbled for the handset in an effort to stop the irritating clamor. "Yeah," he answered, "this better be good."

"Bradley, Darling, I'm always good." The familiar female voice at the other end purred like a Siamese in heat, and Brad bolted upright in the bed.

"What the hell are you doing calling me at this hour of the morning, and how'd you get this number?" he demanded.

"Sweetums, you forget that I'm a journalist. It's my job to stay on top of things . . . so to speak," she added with a snicker of innuendo.

"Leona, I'm not in the mood for your games, and I know you got your little care package this month, so why don't we just cut right to the chase. What do you want?"

"My we're testy. Now is that any way to treat such a dear friend? Especially after the big favor I did for you last night."

He could feel the beads of sweat forming over his forehead as he dangled his feet over the edge of the bed, trying to calculate what his next move should be. Leona Farnsworth never did favors for anybody—unless she expected a big payback. And he could only hazard a guess as to what the witch was talking about now.

"All right, Leona, why don't you tell me what favor that was," he suggested in a voice that was far more controlled than his anxiety.

"If you insist. It has to do with the Celebrity Spotlight Column the *Chicago Press* runs. It is syndicated, so you should be acquainted with it."

"What if I am?"

"Well then you would realize that little gad about town you pulled off last night, in that crazy getup you wore, was quite a newsworthy stunt."

Brad let out a caustic laugh. "I take it you were at the Pavilion? Spying on me again? It's a pretty sad commentary when the American public has nothing more significant to read about than what I do with my free time. Still, I'm not sure what this has to do with favors, so why don't you enlighten me?"

He heard her sharp intake of breath. "Of course, Bradley. By the way, who's your new little nymphet? She doesn't seem like your usual type."

He ran his hand over his neck and could feel the vein that began to protrude whenever his anger was on the rise.

"That's none of your freakin' business, Leona!"

"Now don't get edgy. You can't blame people for wanting to know. After all you are in the limelight."

"My association with the lady is private. It has nothing to do with my music! So are you telling me we made the damned news?" Not that he cared about himself. He was used to all the press, both good and bad. But if someone had written something about Tori—before he could even get the chance to slide his foot in the door with her . . .

"Fortunately the woman who writes that column is a friend of mine. Though it wasn't easy, I was able to convince her that there were more noteworthy items to feature than that little fiasco you were involved in last night. Anyway, she owed me one. So now I guess that means you owe me one too."

Well now wasn't that a big surprise? "Yeah I knew it was too early to breathe any sighs of relief. I thought you told me you were going to be out of town this weekend. What's the matter, did you forget your broomstick and have to come back for it?"

"Bradley, it's that kind of rapport with a journalist that bodes badly when it comes to the concert review that will be appearing in the afternoon edition of the entertainment section. You really must have Michael fetch you a copy, but I can give you the highlights, since I wrote it."

His heart began pounding out that familiar cadence of dread.

"Even though Brad Daniels' gravelly voice was up to his usual high standards at last night's Pavilion performance, the band itself seemed to be missing a certain element of . . ."

"Mediocrity?" he exploded. "Is that what this is leading up to? Cause I'm beginning to get the picture now. Is this about that mindless fantasy of yours to become a rock star?—or what's worse, join up with my band?"

"Now, Bradley," she said, with a sickening coo, "that attitude really won't help further our relationship. Besides, you know I play better than mediocre guitar, and I've only asked you if I could accompany the band one other time."

"The first and last time, Leona. That's what we agreed on, remember? And here's something else you should remember. We don't have a relationship. Not anymore."

"Be that as it may, Darling, I'm sure you won't mind sharing center stage with me for a few numbers. So I'll see you at the sound check this afternoon. We'll talk then. Count on it."

Before he could say another word the dial tone was in his ear. "Shit!" he cursed, slamming the phone down. *Looks like another round for the ice diva,* the voice bellowed victoriously. For more than two years now she'd been leading him around by the balls, and there wasn't a damned thing he could do about it; more to the point, nothing he was capable of doing. Crime was out of the question. He refused to stoop to her tactics. He still had some integrity, and he wasn't about to let her rob him of the little that was left.

Chapter Four

"Be sure you alternate that heat pack with ice," Tori instructed. "You should be a lot better by the time I see you on Monday."

"Ten o'clock, right Doc?" asked Tim Gaines, Wheatfield's leading auto technician.

"Yes, and try not to abuse your knee over the weekend," she warned, before locking the door after her last patient for the day. It was unusual to finish earlier than noon on a Saturday, but she'd had two cancellations. It was just as well. She'd hardly slept the night before, and now there would be time for a nap and some extra primping in getting ready for her date with Brad.

Just thinking about him sent streams of gooseflesh down her arms. A lot had happened in the past twenty-four hours, and while she knew the idea of her becoming romantically involved with a rock star was absurd, she couldn't deny that she was attracted to him. His sexual magnetism and little-boy charm were a potent mix, making her wonder what she'd missed when he'd kissed her forehead instead of her mouth the night before. In fact, his move had really thrown her. She'd been expecting a real kiss—hoping for one, though she could only admit it to herself.

She closed the blinds, walked over to her desk to check her appointment book, then flicked on the office answering machine. Having her treatment rooms located at the back of her house was both a convenience and a hindrance, but it did save on the high cost of rent. It also made her instantly available to her patients and to Kevin. After all, his welfare and that of her patients were her top priorities.

She headed for the door that connected her office to the kitchen. In the distance she heard voices. Was her brother listening to the television? No, she decided, as the conversation became more discernible. Kevin was talking to someone—someone with a familiar, velvet huskiness in his tone. With a start, she realized it was Brad Daniels.

Why couldn't he have shown up after she'd had the chance to put on fresh makeup and style her hair? More to the point, what was he doing here? She paused and took a deep breath, trying to summon the courage to open the door, while Brad and Kevin continued to talk.

"So, were you born with a guitar in your hands?" she heard Kevin ask.

"Not exactly," Brad answered. "But by sixth grade I'd pretty much taught myself to play by ear, and I was doing my own songs."

"You mean you never had any lessons?" the teenager questioned, surprised.

"Well, I hung out with a lot of older guys. Most of them were into music, so I picked up a lot of stuff by watching them. And I'd listen to records and tapes to see if I could figure out the riffs myself."

"Wow!" Kevin sounded impressed. "Maybe you could show me something later. I'm learning guitar too."

"Yeah, sure," Brad said.

Tori realized that Kevin must have been working on his

interview with Brad for the school newspaper. Maybe she shouldn't interrupt.

"So then did you study music in high school?" Kevin went on.

"Uh . . . no, I didn't finish high school."

"You're kidding!" Kevin replied.

"Actually, I didn't have the chance to. By the time I was sixteen I already had my own band. We were gettin' gigs all over the place, and the money was good. The way I see it, you have to take your opportunities when they come around. Especially in this business," Brad explained. "I guess you could say I went to the school of on-site experience. I learned plenty that way too."

"I sure wish my sister felt that way," Kevin lamented. "She's always talking about the value of an education."

"To her, that's important."

"But so is music, at least to me. All Tori cares about is that I make good grades so I can get into the right college."

"Well, like I said, there are more kinds of education than just the formal kind. I did okay without a diploma."

"Okay! I'd say you did a lot more than okay."

Tori had heard just about enough. She should have known a man like Brad Daniels wouldn't share her value system. But the fact that he was now undermining what she'd been trying so desperately to instill in her younger brother made her bristle. At fifteen, Kevin was still a child, and it was obvious how easily swayed he could be if she allowed this to continue without interjecting her own opinion.

Her vanity was about to take a back seat to her agitation. "Good morning," she said, throwing open the door.

"Well hello." Brad gave her a smile that would melt an igloo in the middle of an Alaskan winter. She could feel a tingling in the pit of her stomach, but this was no time to become unglued. "I'm surprised to see you here," she said somewhat curtly.

"I called first," Brad explained. "I thought maybe Kevin and I could finish up the interview while you were working, since I didn't get much of a chance to talk to him last night. I did promise, after all."

The fact that he was a man of his word was starting to soften her. *Careful, Tori, you don't want to lose ground.*

"He brought some Italian pastries," Kevin added, pointing to the opened box of sweets on the table.

"That was very thoughtful of you," Tori said.

"There's a bakery right around the corner from the hotel," Brad said. "The band orders from them whenever we're in town. I couldn't resist."

At that point she would have liked nothing better than to forget the conversation she'd overheard. But it was still fresh in her mind.

"The cannolis are incredible, Sis."

"I hope you haven't been eating too many sweets, Kevin. You know how bad they are for you."

"Aw, Tori, ease up. Why don't you sit down, and relax for a while?"

"Yeah, please," Brad said, jumping up to pull out a chair for her.

Tori sat. "So, how is the hand?" she asked, turning to Brad.

"It feels great. I haven't had any problem since you worked on me last night."

"All the same, now that you're here, maybe we should take an X-ray just to be sure."

"Nope," he insisted. "I'm fine. Just fine. In fact, Kevin and I were almost finished, and I was wondering if you and I could . . ."

"How's the interview going?" Tori interrupted. "Did you get some thought-provoking information, Kevin? Something your teachers are going to be proud of?"

Brad chuckled. "This isn't exactly going to be a piece on pop psychology, Tulip. I was just telling the kid a little about how I got started, and how the music business works. I don't think it's the type of material that's destined to leave a lasting impression on the youth of America."

"Really?" Tori snapped. "Has it occurred to you that you might be underestimating your ability to influence your fans? Maybe you should think a little more carefully about what you say."

"Tori!" Kevin said, his face reddening. "What's the problem?"

"The problem is that I happen to believe that education is the answer to almost everything. Knowledge is power, and without that piece of paper called a degree, the doors to a lot of places stay closed."

"You were listening to us!" Kevin accused.

The silence was deafening. Brad ran his fingers over his chin while he appeared to be thinking about what she'd just said.

"I couldn't help it," Tori explained. "I was on my way in here, and I just caught the last part of what you were saying. I didn't really mean to eavesdrop."

"Your sister's right, Kevin."

"But you said . . ."

"What I said had to do with my particular situation," Brad broke in. "I got a few lucky breaks. Most people have to struggle for years before they gain any level of success, and even at that, you never know how long you're going to stay there. The industry is unpredictable. It doesn't hurt to have something on the back burner."

"But you told me before that when you set your mind on a dream, you have to be focused and not let anything else get in the way of that dream," Kevin said, with a stricken look. "How can I concentrate on a music career when I have to study all this other junk that I'll probably never use?"

So now Kevin was going to pursue a career as a rock star? This was the first Tori had heard of it.

"You could always take some music courses," Brad suggested. "Maybe you and your sister could work out some kind of compromise."

"That's an idea," Tori agreed, softening the tone in her voice. "Why don't we talk about it later, Kevin?" *When she could be alone with him to discourage him from all this foolishness, before he threw away his whole life and his chances for college scholarships.*

"You know, if you don't already have plans," Brad said, turning to Tori, "I'd really like to spend the afternoon with you. I've got some time before I have to get back to the hotel. What do you say?"

"What did you have in mind?" she asked, her agitation further fueled by her brother's announcement. If she could talk to Brad alone—get him to see her point—explain to him what a bright future Kevin could have as a doctor or scientist or any other number of occupations he might attain with his high grade point average, maybe then Brad could help Kevin see just how right she was.

"For starters, some lunch. And how about a trip to the zoo? The weather is perfect for it, and I understand Brookfield is one of the best."

The zoo? She hadn't been to the zoo in years, she realized with longing. When had she had the time? Well why not? All that walking around would give them a perfect opportunity to talk. "It will take me about half an hour to shower and change," she said.

"Great!" Kevin chimed in. "While you're waiting, Brad, I can show you my guitar."

A moment later Tori disappeared. She hurried through her shower, partly because she didn't want Brad to spend any more time encouraging Kevin's musical fantasy career, when that's all it would amount to. And partly she hurried because, despite her annoyance with Brad, something about him still intrigued her, still attracted her, still mesmerized her. She was about to go out with him on a date. Just the two of them. All alone. Together.

Once she'd turned the water off, she opened the bathroom door a crack to let the steam out. Quickly she threw on some jeans and a cotton top, then reached for her makeup bag. In the distance she could hear music. Bright treble notes, and deep resonant bass sounds. The kind of music that could only be played by someone who truly loved the instrument. The chords coming from Kevin's acoustical guitar sounded almost magical, and she threw open the door to hear better. Brad must have been showing him some of those so-called riffs.

Then the music stopped. "That was good, Kevin," Brad said. "I'm really impressed."

Despite the heat of the day, Tori felt a chill run up her spine. Had she heard correctly? Had that really been her brother playing guitar? How could he have gotten that proficient without her even taking notice?

Fifteen minutes later Brad and Tori headed out the door. Brad was wearing a T-shirt and jeans—and normal gym shoes. He'd borrowed Kevin's White Sox hat, and with his sunglasses he actually looked fairly inconspicuous.

Maybe they'd get lucky and nobody would recognize him, though Tori still felt a twinge of apprehension at the thought. The minute they reached her driveway she saw the taxi with the driver.

"The guy who drives for us took the van this morning for some band business. So taking a cab seemed like the quickest way to get out here," Brad explained.

"I'm sure the meter's been running the whole time. Why don't we just take my car to the zoo?" Tori suggested. "Besides being less conspicuous, it makes more sense in case we're forced into a fast exit. Though I hope we at least get to see the gorillas."

"Good idea," Brad agreed. He took a minute to say something to the driver, and then the taxi was gone. "He'll be back here around four o'clock. That should give me plenty of time to do the sounds checks for tonight."

"It might be easier if I drive," Tori offered, motioning him toward her Toyota Tercel. "Unless you've got some kind of macho hangup about it."

"Who, me?" Brad smiled. He almost looked relieved as he opened the car door for her, then swung around to the passenger side.

"I haven't been to the zoo in years," Tori admitted, pulling out onto the street. "I'm actually kind of excited."

"That makes two of us—on both counts."

She drove in silence for a while, edgy because she was alone with Brad and acutely aware of his masculine appeal. Then they exchanged small talk, which made her even more anxious because she knew she wasn't going to relax until she'd had her say about Kevin. Finally there was no getting around it any longer. "You know Brad, before we get there I'd like to talk to you about my brother."

"I'm listening."

"It's just that . . ." *How could she say it in the most diplomatic way?* "It's just that last night when I told you about how my parents were teachers and all—I thought you understood how important it is to me that Kevin gets a proper education so that he can have the right future."

"And you know what the right future is for him?" Brad tugged on his seatbelt and shifted positions.

"Kevin is an honor student. He takes the most accelerated classes and still he gets *A*'s. He could be a scientist, or a brain surgeon, or . . ."

"What if he doesn't want to? What if he doesn't even want to go on to college?"

"He's gifted. He has to go to college or all that talent will be wasted. Don't you see that?" she insisted. "It's what my parents had planned for him. And now that I'm responsible for him, it's up to me to see to it that it happens."

"What about Kevin's plans?" Brad challenged, as Tori stopped for a red light. "For that matter, what about his musical talent? In case you haven't noticed, the kid plays an above-average guitar. If he keeps on practicing, he'll only get better."

"Kevin is a child. He doesn't even know his own mind yet. He's too young to be making decisions that are going to affect his entire future. But he listens to people like you. He idolizes you. If you're going to feed him a line about how you made it without even a high school diploma, he's going to believe it. And it's going to be all that much harder for me to control what he does."

"That wasn't a line!" he said, in a blaze of defense, and she watched, as a vein in his neck became more prominent. "The light is green."

Tori stepped on the gas pedal and continued down the street.

"I happened not to have graduated from high school. I don't shout it from rooftops, but I'm not ashamed of it either. I had a chance to do something that makes me happy, and I took it. I'm no rocket scientist, but I earn a decent wage. In fact, my accountant thinks I make a damn good living! What's more, I make people happy. Some people anyway," he qualified.

"But that doesn't mean that Kevin could be lucky enough to achieve your level of success—in any career, without schooling," Tori shouted back.

"You heard me tell the kid it couldn't hurt to have something else to fall back on."

"You didn't say it with conviction."

"Hey, I'm not his father!"

His words stung. Not just because she'd heard them from Brad, but because she'd heard them before—from Jack.

"That doesn't mean I wouldn't like to be his friend," Brad added. "But it's like I told that girl yesterday, I'm not a role model for today's youth. I'm me. I don't pretend to be anybody else. Besides, it's just a little early for me to be as involved in this situation as you are."

She was shaking now. This conversation had gotten way more confrontational than she'd intended. She spotted a convenience store and pulled into the parking lot. Then she turned off the engine and faced Brad. "I'm sorry," she said. "It really was unfair of me to put you in that position. And I didn't mean to imply that what you do isn't important. It is. In fact it was important to me last night in a way that I didn't even know it could be."

Brad's expression softened. "So what are you saying?"

What was she saying? "I guess I'm telling you that I'm very confused." *Confused about a lot more things than she was willing to admit at the moment.* "Sometimes I'm not sure what's right when it concerns Kevin. I want to be a good parent to him, but it's a huge responsibility. I'm not always prepared for some of the stuff that comes along with raising a teenager. Especially since he's a male. Females think differently."

"Yeah, well maybe what you have to do is let go of the reins a little. I can see where you're coming from, but there are some things you've got to understand about a fifteen-year-old guy."

"For instance?"

"First off, the kid does have a mind, or he wouldn't be pulling all those *A*'s. Second, you've gotta be willing to listen to what makes this kid tick. If you really listen—you're gonna hear. That'll go a long way in helping you figure out what to do when you don't automatically know."

Those cobalt blue eyes of his were searing a path to her very soul now, and what he'd said made more sense that she cared to admit. He reached over and gently touched the side of her face. "You gotta learn to loosen up a little. Figure out when it's okay to bend the rules. Start enjoying your life. Cause when it comes right down to it, you're gonna find out that there's only a limited amount of control you can have over most situations anyway."

"Well," Tori conceded, "I suppose I'll have to give some serious consideration to your advice."

"Maybe you should try and figure out what else is confusing you," Brad said, his eyes still fixed on hers.

Again she could feel that strange tingling in the pit of her stomach. The man had a way of zeroing right in on her innermost thoughts, and she knew he was going to pursue the comment she'd made about the importance of his concert performance. Unless she could quickly divert his attention.

"Suddenly I'm hungry," she announced, starting the engine and pulling back out onto the street. "There's a fast food place up the street a bit. Want to stop for burgers on the way?"

"Sure," he said, with a look that told her maybe she'd won this round, but only because he'd let her.

"Tropic World is that way," Tori said, pointing to the exhibit just west of the South Gate.

"Hmm, I don't know about that line. It looks kind of long."

"So far nobody seems to recognize you," Tori whispered.

"All right, let's give it a shot. We can't have you missing the gorillas. But if anything even starts to get weird, we head for the nearest exit. Agreed?"

"Of course."

Together they stood among the crowd that consisted largely of parents who were distracted by their small children. That was a lucky break, Tori thought. Still, as the line moved forward they spoke quietly to each other for fear someone would pick up on Brad's voice. But people seemed pretty much oblivious to their presence. Probably because no one would be expecting to see Brad Daniels at the zoo, certainly not without a full entourage.

Finally they'd reached the entrance. "Here," Tori said, grabbing one of the printed guides and handing it to Brad. "This will tell us what we're seeing."

"Uh, no," Brad said, putting it back on the pile. "I'd rather watch the animals than the printed page. I wouldn't want to miss anything."

"Suit yourself." Tori shrugged and decided maybe he was right. Maybe it wouldn't hurt to try a little spontaneity. They walked beneath covered waterfalls and trees and various kinds of foliage, through the simulated rain forests of three continents. Birds roamed free, tame enough to approach people. Best of all, the animals were in an environment not unlike their natural habitat, instead of being locked up in cages.

"I could just stand here and watch them all day," Tori said, as they approached the gorillas.

"Don't you wonder what that big guy is thinking?" Brad pointed as one large creature with expressive eyes stared back at them.

"Maybe he's wondering why we don't go in there and join him for some lunch," Tori said.

"If we did that, we might end up being part of his lunch."

Tori laughed. "I'm not sure, but I think gorillas are vegetarians. All the same, I guess if we're going to see anything else we'd better get moving."

"So far, so good," Brad observed, as they went north to the Elephant Arena. There was a group of spectators gathering while two of the keepers were doing a demonstration with one of the elephants. Tori started to move in closer, but Brad grabbed her hand and held her back. She met his gaze, and in that split second a surge of electricity ran up the length of her arm. She swallowed hard. Even under his sunglasses she could see his flirtatious wink. "I'm not sure it's a good idea for us to plant ourselves in the middle of that crowd."

"Right," Tori agreed. But he was still hanging on. Not awkwardly, not possessively. Yet as his large, muscular hand blanketed hers, she felt secure. It had been a long time since she'd held hands with a man, and the fit was perfect—dangerously perfect.

"What have we got here?" Brad asked, as they walked toward an indoor display.

"Looks like the Australia House. Want to check it out?"

"Why not?" Brad said, as they approached the entrance.

Tori pulled back to read the warning sign: *Brush tailed Rat Kangaroo Bat Crossing: Bats are flying free in exhibit. Bats will not bite.* "On second thought . . ."

"What's wrong?"

"Read the sign," Tori instructed. "I don't think I want to go in there."

Tori watched Brad as he studied the wall. Was that an extra splotch of color on his face? Did that mean he was nervous too?

"What's the problem?" he asked once again.

So he was going to do a little macho cover up. Well two could play at that game. "All right, if you think it's okay. But you go first," she insisted.

"If it weren't safe, they wouldn't allow people to go inside." Without any further hesitation, he opened the screen door and led the way.

"It sure is dark in here," Tori said, tightening her hold on his hand. "And quiet."

"I'm surprised nobody else is in this building," he added.

All at once, several of the bats started flying overhead. Tori gasped and buried her head in Brad's chest while he covered her protectively with his arms. "Jeez, you think they'd give people some warning!" he yelled, as he whisked her out the door and into the closed-in exit way.

"Oh sure, like you didn't read the sign," she said with playful sarcasm. "You just wanted me to get spooked so you could get me in a compromising position." She was clinging so closely to him she could feel the rapid beat of his heart against her ear.

"And what if I did?" he asked, in a voice that courted her senses with persuasiveness.

He coaxed her hands to his shoulders so that she had no choice but to look into his face. Then he bent down to brush the hollow of her throat with his lips. Teasing, testing, torturing her with a wanting for much more. She could feel the tips of her breasts hardening, and she pressed against him so that he could feel them too.

The mild scent of aftershave mingled with his warm breath, and the combination drugged her with desire. His breathing grew labored until his lips pressed against hers, gently covering her mouth. But her response was eager, and a second later the kiss deepened with a touch that was far more urgent. All too quickly it was over, leaving her shaken and trembling. And wanting more.

"We'd better get out of here before somebody comes along," Brad said, with a look of great satisfaction.

You're getting in way over your head, Bad Boy, the voice warned. *You bluffed yourself out of this one, but next time you might not be so lucky. Tori Glenn is one smart cookie, and she's bound to catch on sooner or later.*

He couldn't take his eyes off her; windblown curls, pink embarrassment painted all over her cheeks, and that puckered up smile that told him she felt too shy to look directly at his face. It was a look that said she was smitten. That was probably the only thing that had saved him—this time. Trouble was, he was smitten right back.

It had been a long time since he'd let himself feel anything for a woman like what he was starting to feel for Tori. A rush of bad memories came flooding in to remind him why he ought to be putting on the brakes right now.

"So, where to?" Tori asked, as they walked out into the bright sunlight.

Good question. He looked at his watch. It wasn't that late yet. But suddenly he needed time to distance himself from the situation. Time to think.

And time to figure out what the hell he was gonna do about Leona. She'd be waiting for him when he got back to the Pavilion, and he hadn't even had the chance to warn the other guys yet. They'd all been asleep when he'd left the hotel, and Mike Sweeney was gonna be crazed.

"Maybe we ought to start heading back to your place. I wouldn't want to get hung up in traffic."

"All right," she said, turning in the direction of the South Gate.

Did she have to be so agreeable? He couldn't seem to stop his hand from gravitating toward hers, and once again they were locked together. *Clever way you've got of creating distance,* the voice badgered.

"You never did tell me about your family or where you live," Tori said, in the car on the way back to Wheatfield.

Brad shifted uncomfortably, uneasiness pricking at his chest. He hated the subject, but knew she'd bring it up sooner or later. "There isn't that much to say," he answered. "I've got two parents. I'm the youngest of three kids, and I grew up in Boston."

"I'm surprised you don't have the tell-tale accent."

"Occasionally it slips out, but I try to keep it at bay. Just good discipline, I guess." *Some people would call it rebellion.* "Anyway, once I was out on my own I decided to get a place in Worcester. I live in a quiet neighborhood, which is a nice contrast from the type of life I lead."

"Really? Where is Worcester?"

"It's only about an hour's drive west of Boston."

"What about your family?" Tori quizzed, stopping for a red light. "Where are they?"

"My parents still live in Boston. My brother and sister are both married now, but they live in the area too."

"Oh, so when you're in town you can see them all. They must be very proud of you."

Brad sighed deeply as Tori continued to drive. "Actually no. The fact is, I'm more or less considered the black sheep of the family."

"I don't understand," Tori said, surprised.

Brad folded his arms in front of his chest over the tight restraint of his seat belt. "Well, it's like this. My dad is a heart surgeon—a damned good one at that. He's very well respected in the community. Mom is a real-estate tycoon. Jason, my brother, is the family attorney. And Courtney, my sister, followed in dad's footsteps. She's an internist. So you can see I came from a family of high achievers."

"They don't consider the music business a respectable profession?"

"They don't consider it a profession at all. They regard it as a major cop-out. Kind of like the way you'd see it if Kevin made the same choice," he added.

Tori took her eyes from the road for a second to glance his way. It was long enough for him to see that he'd struck a nerve with her. "I never meant . . ."

"Look," he interrupted. "I wasn't comparing your relationship with Kevin to mine with my family. So don't go getting your knickers in a knot. I came along at a time when my folks thought they were finished having babies. They'd already groomed Jason and Courtney for high-powered careers. But I was raised, for the most part, by a nanny because my parents were too busy maintaining their social statuses to take much of an interest in anything I did."

"I'm sorry," Tori said.

"Well don't be. I gave up a long time ago on trying to win their approval, or anyone else's for that matter. I am who I am. People either like me or they don't. That's the way it is."

So matter of fact, the voice blared. *Think she'll be convinced?*

Tori looked stricken. "Does that mean you never see your family?"

Careful now, Bradley. You wouldn't want her to know how easily you bruise. "We see each other. We're all very polite—until we go our separate ways. It's the pretense of the perfect family unit. But I haven't got time to be upset over it. I'm busy these days too." *Liar!* The voice threatened to shatter his eardrums.

"Well now that you're all adults, maybe you could sit down with them and . . ."

What'd I tell you? She's not gonna let this thing go. She wants to fix something that can't be fixed. "As I said," he interjected, with a tone that cautioned, *drop it!* "Things are fine just the way they are."

The silence was overpowering, and Tori seemed agitated as she continued to negotiate the heavy traffic. He supposed he owed her an apology for being so short, but what if she took it as a license to probe further? Then what would he tell her? That over the years he'd done—and was still doing—just about everything but stand on his head and spit wooden nickels to get his family to pay some attention to him. Though he knew they would consider his accomplishments trivial in comparison to their own achievements.

Still, he'd showered them all with gifts, sent them tickets to his concerts, remembered them on every important occasion. He'd all but begged for some love and affection. But from childhood on, he'd disappointed them with his bad grades, his willful behavior, and by not living up to the standards of the Daniels name. They never failed to let him know that he was an outcast. And that's all he'd ever be to them.

"Anyway I like Massachusetts," Brad finally said. "Did I tell you I have a summer home on Cape Cod?" *That's good. Change the subject.*

"No you didn't. Where is it?"

"Provincetown, only about a half hour flight from Logan International Airport in Boston. It's an old Victorian on the far East End, overlooking the ocean."

"The ocean," Tori repeated, with a certain longing in her voice. "It sounds wonderful. I haven't been to the ocean in years."

He wanted to scoop her up in his arms and carry her off to his beach house right then and there. Imagine being marooned with the beautiful Tori Glenn. *Doctor Tori Glenn,* the voice emphasized. "It's peaceful there. It's where I go when I want to drown out all the city sounds and escape the hustle of my tour schedules." *It's where I go to get away from the pressure of trying to pretend I'm like everyone else, and the pain of knowing I'm not.*

"I guess we all need a place like that sometimes. For me there is no escape house. So I just have to go inside myself," Tori said.

"Maybe we could escape to Cape Cod together sometime," Brad heard himself say. "I'll bet you'd love it." The words had just tumbled out before he could stop himself, and now she had come to a stoplight and was looking at him like he was some kind of shining knight on a white horse. *Too late to take it back now, genius.*

"I'll bet I would," she said, softly. A second later she accelerated.

They were almost back in Wheatfield, and for that he was grateful. He'd had enough serious talk for a while. Before long it would be show time. Between Tori and Leona, he just had too damned much racing around in his brain. If he were going to be in any kind of shape to stand in front of an audience, he needed to get into his performance state of mind. "Care if I turn on the radio?" he asked.

"Go right ahead," Tori said.

He found a station with some light jazz and then put the seat back some. He must have fallen asleep the moment he shut his eyes.

"We're home," Tori said, gently shaking him awake, and turning off the motor of her car.

"What? Hmm—I didn't mean to crash on you like that," he mumbled, rubbing his eyes to pry them open.

Tori smiled. "I'm glad you caught a little cat nap. You couldn't have gotten much sleep last night." Of course, neither had she, but she wasn't about to admit it.

The sound of a car engine caught her attention, and in the rear-view mirror she could see the taxi driver pulling in right behind them. "Just in time," she said.

Brad reached for her hand. "Listen, Tulip, I had a really great afternoon. But you've done enough chauffeuring for the day. Kevin's riding to the concert with his friends tonight. I already checked it out with him. So I'm sending a car for you. Can you be ready by six o'clock?"

"Well sure, but you don't have to . . ."

"I want to," he interrupted, touching his finger to her lips. "After the show, you and I are going out on the town. So wear something pretty, and I'll see you in a few hours."

A wink and a smile later he was gone.

Chapter Five

"Turn up that friggin' bass, and give me more highs on the keyboard! Don't make me beg!" The order had come from Chet Harper, and by the look of things, he wasn't in a good mood.

As it was, Brad had arrived at the massive Pavilion half an hour late for the sound check, and he'd been hoping the guys from the crew would have things set up already.

"Where have you been, man?" Mike Sweeney asked. "I thought we were going to get some rehearsal time in here, but we can't get the mix to gel yet."

Aside from being the finest keyboard player Brad had ever worked with, Mike was also his best friend. They'd known each other since grade school, though Mike was a couple of years older, and they were the only two original members of the band.

"Believe it or not, I went to the zoo, but we can talk about that later. Right now we've got more pressing problems."

"I'll say," Mike agreed, his eyes widening to take notice of the lanky, redheaded female in the skin-tight black leather pants and spandex top. Leona Farnsworth had just come barreling through the center of the stage with her guitar at her side. "What the hell is she doing here? Shouldn't she be off stirring her caldron or something?"

"Bradley, Darling," she said, "aren't you the picture of health and good looks? I only watched you from a distance last night, but up close I can see that a Florida tan really agrees with you."

Brad could feel the hairs at the back of his neck standing on end while his skin prickled with agitation. The sound crew continued to work with the other band members, motioning to each other and communicating across the massive area through headphones and mouthpieces. Other than Mike, no one appeared to be taking notice of the scene that was unfolding. At least not obvious notice.

Still, Brad gave a twisted little smile and linked his arm with hers, pulling her off to the side to a more private spot. "You can't just come marching in here like you own the place, Leona. I thought I made it clear that you aren't going to be on stage tonight—not with this band anyway."

"What a pity," she retorted. "I would hate to have to spend a Saturday evening trying to track down my friend Celia—you know the one who does the Celebrity Spotlight Column. Your little escapade last night is, after all, still timely." Her chestnut eyes were flaring daggers. "Now who was that woman you were with . . . Tori Glenn, I believe? No, I should say Doctor Tori Glenn."

He sucked a deep breath and let go of her arm, fearful that in his mounting rage he might lose control and hurt the woman. "Lower your voice!" he demanded, with a contained whisper. "Sound travels around here."

She batted her eyelashes with the skill of a high-priced call girl. "Oh, Bradley, I was so looking forward to this concert."

"I'll see to it that you get front row seats!" The words

had come from his mouth, but the voice was shouting louder. *You really want to call her bluff? . . . Just when you seem to be scoring a few points with Tori? You know this witch means business. She's already done her homework.* If Leona took it in her head to badrap Tori, there was no telling what kind of damage might be done.

"Hey Brad," Chet called, from several rows back. "We're just about set up here if you want to get started on rehearsal."

Brad glared at Leona. Then he looked over at Mike Sweeney, who was standing with his arms folded over his chest and eyeballs rolled upward. It was a pose that demanded to know, *How could you let this happen again?* He would try to reason things out with Mike later, but for the time being there seemed to be only one thing Brad could do.

"You're gonna have to do a check on one more instrument," Brad yelled out to Chet. Then he turned to Leona, who flashed him a coy smile of victory. "Take your guitar out of the case and get set up," he ordered.

Tori emerged from the shower and began to style her hair. A change was in order, and she swept one side back from her face, fastening the thick curls with a barrette/comb. Her crystal earrings would lend the amount of sophistication she was striving to achieve.

Meanwhile Kevin was blasting his stereo with Brad's latest CD. "Did you do your homework?" she shouted into his bedroom.

"Most of it," he answered.

Five hours ago "most of it" wouldn't have been good enough, but after considering what Brad had said earlier, she decided to let the matter ride. After all, it was only Saturday, and Kevin still had Sunday to finish up.

Sea green crepe, she reasoned fifteen minutes later, after having changed three times. The flowing, ankle length dress with matching crocheted jacket would emphasize the green in her eyes. She slipped on a pair on taupe heels and made a final check in the mirror. Not bad, she thought.

"Hey Sis, have you seen my jeans jacket?" Kevin asked, appearing in the doorway of her bedroom. As she turned to face him, he did a double-take, and let out a long whistle. "Wow!"

Tori smiled. "Does that mean you approve?"

"Brad's going to flip. He's already got the hots for you."

I hope so. "What makes you so sure?"

"I've got eyes. I've got ears too," he said, raising his eyebrows up and down to bait her.

"Specifically? . . ." Tori pressed, feigning her sternest tone and face.

Kevin laughed. "I see the way he looks at you—it's a guy thing. Besides, he never stops talking about you all the time he's around me."

"Well . . . what does he say?"

"Nothing mushy if that's what you want to know. Just stuff. Why don't you ask him if you're so curious?"

"Why don't you go downstairs and take your jeans jacket off the clothes-line?" Tori said, attempting to drop the subject. "I washed it the other day."

"Thanks, Sis," Kevin said. "I'll wear it tonight."

"Are you set with your ride and all?"

"Mark's dad is driving. He'll be picking us up around six."

"And you'll be home . . . ?"

"As soon as the concert's over and we can head out of traffic. Brad already told me he wouldn't be sticking around the Pavilion for very long. Something about a hot date," he said with a snicker.

"Is that right?"

"He promised we'd stay in touch though. So what time is curfew for you, Cinderella?" he needled.

"Curfew for me is whenever I get back," Tori snapped.

"Touchy, aren't we?"

"You just remember who's in charge, Kevin. I don't need any flack from you tonight."

"Sorreee," he emphasized, walking off.

So was she in fact. She knew Kevin had only been teasing. And if they'd been closer in age, she supposed she would have accepted his razzing good-naturedly. But the way things were with the two of them she often didn't know whether to be his mother or his sister. If she were going to maintain any degree of control, there was a fine line as to what was acceptable behavior from him and what wasn't.

Still, she hadn't meant to be so irritable, and she felt a twinge of guilt—along with some anxiety, as she noted the time on the digital clock. The limo would be arriving soon. Although she was dressed and ready to leave, her insides were pretty much churning.

A lot had happened between her and Brad that afternoon. She closed her eyes to relive the kiss they'd shared at the zoo. It had been everything she'd fantasized—and more. It was a kiss she wouldn't soon forget, and her adrenaline surged as she thought about what it might be like to make love with him. A man who played guitar as skillfully as Brad was a man who knew exactly what to do with his hands. She'd already had a little demonstration to prove it.

But the attraction went well beyond the physical. Brad was an intensely creative man who appeared capable of tempering his passion with common sense. And he did have a handle on her situation with Kevin, at least concerning her fear of failing as a parent.

Yet from what he'd told her, she was beginning to understand why Brad seemed so impressed with her relationship with Kevin. She had the feeling that family acceptance and especially parental acceptance were a lot more important to him than he'd been letting on. Oh, he'd delivered a convincing enough speech—if she hadn't gone looking beneath the cracks and sensed his pain at being abandoned by the very people who had given him life itself.

And while it was true that she'd also been abandoned by her parents, they had loved both her and Kevin. Of that she was sure. She and Kevin had been able to extend that love to one another. She wondered if Brad had ever allowed himself to truly love someone or if he'd allowed someone to love him in return.

Maybe he was trying to embrace the whole world as his family. That would explain his charismatic performances and the fact that his fans were so devoted to him. But they provided an exterior sort of adulation that wasn't an adequate substitute for the real thing. Tori had the distinct impression that with Brad, a person could get just so close. Despite what he'd told her, there were many more things he'd left out. Important things. It was clear that Brad Daniels was a man with barriers and secrets.

So why should it matter to her anyway? This was going to be his last night in town, and it really was for the best. All of this daydreaming about his attributes wasn't going to erase the fact that they were all wrong for each other. His lack of regard for higher education and his free-spirit lifestyle were in direct conflict with her philosophies of discipline and structure. All of Brad's charm and magnetism notwithstanding, that fact wasn't going to change. She really did need to plant that in her mind and keep it there. *Have fun on your little date, Tori. But don't take anything too seriously. That way you won't get hurt.*

The sound of the doorbell made her jump. Calm. Be calm, she told herself as she walked toward the living room. Kevin had already let the driver in, and the two of them stood talking in the foyer.

"If you're hungry, there's some leftover pasta salad in the refrigerator," she said to Kevin, after acknowledging the man Brad had hired to chauffeur her to the concert.

"We're grabbing some burgers on the way," he said.

"Have fun tonight, Kevin. Maybe I'll see you there."

"You too, Sis. And relax," he called after her, as the driver opened the van door for her to get in.

From the moment Tori had arrived at the Pavilion, she'd been given the VIP treatment, so much so that she felt like a celebrity herself. Though not quite comfortable with the situation, she had to admit that such status was exciting. While hundreds of people were lined up outside, no doubt hoping to get a close look at the famed lead singer, she'd been personally escorted to a small room backstage to be with Brad.

She wasn't alone more than a couple of minutes before he arrived, closing the door behind him. And even though they'd only been apart for a few hours, the sight of him sent a jolt of electricity coursing through her veins. He gazed at her in silence for what seemed like an eternity; his eyes probing like laser beams through her very core. She couldn't help being somewhat in awe of him when he flashed her that heart-thudding grin. "You look incredible," he finally said. "Like some kind of princess out of a fairytale."

"I was hoping you'd like the dress," she said, suddenly feeling too shy to look at him.

"It's more than the dress. It's the whole package.

You're exquisite—inside and out."

His words had forced her eyes to meet his. What did he really know about her insides? Could he read her mind—as well as her heart? "That was a very nice thing to say, Brad. Thank you," she responded, as she studied the look of sincerity on his face.

"I meant it, Tulip. I'm happy that you're here. Unfortunately I'm not gonna be able to spend too much time with you till later on. There are a few things I gotta do before the show."

"I'm a big girl," she said. "Just tell me where I'm supposed to sit, and I can take care of myself."

"First things first," he said, moving closer to her. She felt the pressure of his hands as they wrapped around her waist, drawing her nearer still. He bent down until the whisper of his breath against her cheek made her tremble. Then he lightly pressed his lips to hers. She heard herself whimper as his touch triggered a much stronger desire, and she circled his back with her arms.

A second later there was a knock on the door. "Time's gettin' tight, man," a voice yelled out.

He jerked away from her. "Hold that thought until after the show," he said to Tori.

Frustrated, she took a deep breath and bit down on her lower lip. Brad took her by the hand and began to pull her along. "Come on," he directed, with a sudden edginess to his voice. "I'll show you where you'll be sitting. You'll have a great view."

A few moments later she was situated along the side of the stage with two other women, whom Brad quickly introduced as friends of the band. "See ya later," he said, as he went rushing off. She wondered if he had a case of preshow jitters.

"Good luck," she called after him.

Tori turned to the two women, and the three of them began to talk. She learned that Sherry had been dating Mike Sweeney for nearly two years and that she lived in another state, but had flown in to be with him for the weekend. The second woman was someone who had just met one of the guys from the crew and, in fact, it wasn't long before she disappeared with him.

Talking to Sherry had given Tori some insight on what it might be like to be in a relationship with a rock star, and she realized that on some level, whether she wanted to concede to it or not, she'd been fantasizing about being in that situation with Brad.

All the while, roadies were working at setting up the equipment on the stage. Every now and again she caught a glimpse of Brad. Clearly he was busy, but he did pause once to wink at her, and she could feel her pulse quickening as she smiled back at him.

Then she noticed the tall, thin woman with straight hair the color of fire-engine red. Her tight-fitting outfit was attention-getting enough to make Tori wonder whether she was a performer, maybe a backup singer. Though Tori would have remembered seeing her onstage the previous night. For the moment the woman was locked into a discussion with Brad, so maybe she was associated in some way with the Pavilion.

Tori tried to stay focused on her conversation with Sherry, but her eyes kept gravitating to the shapely redhead, and to her consternation she found herself curious to know what this woman's connection was to Brad.

"So Sherry, what do you do when you're not traveling around the country to be with Mike?" Tori asked, all the more determined to keep her mind on present company.

"I run a health food store," Sherry answered. "Vitamins, herbs, homeopathic remedies—the whole nine yards. I know it's a controversial topic that has a lot of doctors in an uproar, but you'd be surprised at how many people are seeking alternative answers to their medical health problems."

Tori gave a smile of acceptance and understanding. "You have no idea how happy I am to hear that. I'm all for mixing traditional and alternative health care for the patient's best advantage. In fact, I'm a chiropractor."

A look of distrust flashed over Sherry's face, making Tori wonder if one of them had misunderstood the other. "Aw, oh," Sherry muttered quietly, "here comes trouble."

Tori turned around and was startled to see the redhead standing over her. "You must be Tori," the woman said, extending her right hand. "Brad has told me all about you," she added, in a voice that dripped so much sweetness, Tori's warning antenna shot upward.

"Really?" Tori answered, shaking hands, while at the same time scanning the area for Brad. He was nowhere to be seen. *How much could he have told the woman, considering the length of time Tori had known Brad? On the other hand, she'd trusted him with some of her most private emotions. Had he shared them with this stranger? And who was she?* "That's funny. He hasn't mentioned you to me."

The woman blanched, and Tori immediately regretted her rude response. What if she was Brad's sister or something? "I'm sorry," she said. "I only meant that with all that's been going on—Brad's preparation for the concert and everything, he really hasn't had time to introduce me to many people. But I'm very happy to meet you."

Tori's apology was met with momentary silence while the woman appeared to be deciding about its sincerity.

In the meantime Sherry cleared her throat. "Tori, this is Leona Farnsworth," she explained. "Leona is a reporter for the City Beat."

"Oh." Tori brightened with a smile of relief. Although for a journalist, the woman wore a lot of flashy makeup. "You must be here to review the concert."

"Actually no," Leona said. "I'm afraid I might even be the subject of someone's critique tonight. You see, I'll be playing rhythm guitar right next to Brad. It's a little sideline I'm attempting to cultivate."

"Oh," Tori said again. And for some inexplicable reason her antenna went on the rise once more.

"Well, I just wanted to come by and say hello. I'm sure we'll be seeing more of each other later on," she added. "Hope you enjoy the show." With that, Leona Farnsworth turned and sashayed back toward center stage, leaving Tori with the distinct feeling that the woman could, indeed, be trouble.

"That's interesting," Sherry commented with unmistakable sarcasm.

"I take it she doesn't normally play guitar with this band?" Tori questioned.

"No, and the one other time that she did, Brad complained of a migraine for two days after. I remember because I spent that particular weekend with Mike. He told me he hoped that was the last time he had to share the stage with the witch."

"Really?" Tori said, with a raise of her eyebrows. "Evidently Brad doesn't share the same sentiment."

"I'm not so sure about that. In any case, watch your back with that one," Sherry warned.

"Why?"

"I can't honestly say with any kind of certainty. I can

only tell you that Mike can't stand Leona. She was on the scene before I even met him or Brad, and neither one of them is talking. I have a feeling it has more to do with Brad than with any of the other band members. But Brad's a very private person, and Mike never betrays a confidence. It's one of the reasons I'm so crazy about him, yet sometimes I'd like to strangle him with all of his secrets."

Tori knew the feeling. "Yes, I sense that Brad keeps a lot of things under wrap."

"Actually I can't blame him. Nobody wants to live in a fishbowl, but his lifestyle is sure conducive to it. You really like him, don't you?" Sherry asked.

"He's nice, but it's not like we know each other that well," Tori hedged, slightly embarrassed.

"I have a feeling you will," Sherry said.

"Why do you say that?"

"Because I see the way he looks at you, and the way you look back at him. I've been to a lot of concerts in the past two years. Brad doesn't hook up with many women. And the ones he has dated haven't been invited to sit up on the stage during his performances. The man likes you."

Tori didn't say a word, but she was unable to keep the grin of pleasure off her face.

Soon after, someone came on stage and announced that the opening band had been cancelled. The noise from the audience was deafening as people chanted and clapped, anxious for Brad and his band to appear. Brad went directly on stage, not waiting for an introduction. The crowd was wildly appreciative—rowdy but not destructive. He seemed to have a shrewd knack for taming his audience while keeping their excitement at a high level.

Leona Farnsworth stood several feet away from him, playing her guitar and for the most part, blending in as background accompaniment to the rest of the band.

By the time the band had been performing for forty minutes the crowd's enthusiasm was at its peak. Young girls were screaming, and periodically one of them would try to jump on the stage to hug Brad. But they were always stopped by security people. One girl threw a bouquet of flowers at him, and he stopped singing long enough to go over and kiss her hand in response. The young teen almost fainted.

Tori found herself enjoying the show every bit as much as she had the night before. She understood Brad's need to interact with his fans. He was a man to be shared, at least during his concerts. But the fact was he'd been communicating with her throughout the show with little knowing looks, reminding her that at least for the moment, she was his date. He would flash her that infectious grin, and even from twenty feet away she couldn't miss that sexy cavern in his right cheek. Every time his gaze met hers, her heart turned over in response.

By the same token Leona seemed to be keeping a watchful eye on Brad's interaction with Tori, and suddenly her performance tactics began to take a sharp turn. Changing her stage position, she moved in much closer to Brad—as if she were competing with Tori for his attention. Her guitar playing became more intricate while her body language radiated blatant seduction. She seemed to be flirting with Brad as well as her instrument, almost as if she were trying to upstage him. Though even to the untrained ear, Tori could see that Leona lacked the musical skills to pull it off, and she wondered what was going on.

Whatever he'd been expecting, Brad's professional response to Leona was credible enough for the crowd to think it was all part of the act, and Tori herself wondered. In fact, she was so taken in by his magnetism that she failed to notice what was happening with his performance—until Sherry alerted her. Little blunders at first, missed chords, obvious to the band members, but so adroitly covered over, the audience hadn't seemed sure. Then the mistakes became more apparent, until even the crowd began to mutter.

When it became evident to everyone that there was a problem, Brad said something to Mike Sweeney. Then, with an indisputable grimace of pain, he walked off the stage. From what Tori could surmise, the problem was more complicated than Leona Farnsworth.

"Folks!" Mike Sweeney announced. "We need to have a short intermission, and then we'll be back in full swing!"

"You hope," Brad muttered loud enough for Tori to hear.

She felt momentary panic, as he approached her. "What's wrong?" she asked.

He was sweating profusely, the color drained from his face. "I can't feel my guitar strings. My hand is totally numb!"

"I knew we should have taken an X-ray this afternoon," Tori groaned.

"That's not gonna help me now. I've got a crowd waiting! What am I supposed to do?" The man was like a volcano on the verge of erupting.

"The first thing you're going to do," she ordered, with soothing reassurance, "is calm down. You need to control your state of mind the way you control those people out there."

"Please! Can't you do something?" he demanded.

Her message wasn't sinking in yet. She lowered her voice and slowed her speech in an effort to make him mirror her.

"I am going to help you, Brad, the way I did the other night, but you have to do your part. Is there somewhere we can go where there's a sofa or table?"

"There's a sofa in the dressing room."

"On the way there I want you to take slow, deep breaths. Don't talk. Just breathe," she commanded.

Mike was right behind them. So was Leona Farnsworth. "Do you need help?" she questioned.

"We can handle this!" Mike answered. "You stay backstage with the rest of the band!" He spoke with such force that Leona backed off and left them. The look of relief on Brad's face all but shouted *thank you.*

By the time the three of them reached the dressing room she had her own audience of security people and promoters, wanting to know what was going on.

"Give us some space," she insisted, ushering everyone out except Brad and Mike. "It would help if I had a towel."

"I'll get one," Mike said.

A moment later Brad lay on his stomach, his face over the towel, which Tori had fashioned into a makeshift pillow. She knelt at his left side and began placing her fingertips over strategic pressure points on his neck.

"Ow!" was the only thing Brad could manage to say.

"Take it easy," Tori soothed. "We're going to do the same thing we did the other night. I think I can at least get you out of the woods enough to finish this concert. Are you game?"

"Whatever you say, Tulip!"

She worked swiftly, carefully monitoring Brad's responses. Then she helped him turn onto his back and placed her hands on the other side of his head, putting a gentle upward traction on his neck. "That should help take the pressure off the nerve," she explained.

"Wow!" Brad said, after about ten minutes. "I've got feeling in my hand again! It hurts, but I can actually feel my fingers."

"Boy, that's some pretty amazing stuff you're doing." Mike's eyes widened in astonishment.

"Give us about five more minutes, and we'll have him back on stage again," Tori promised.

The second half of the show went well. Even Leona seemed to be staying in the background. The band performed for an extra half hour, in addition to the time they'd missed during the unplanned intermission. Brad played impeccably and was rewarded at the end of the evening with a lengthy standing ovation. Tori felt swollen with pride at his accomplishment, and pleased with herself that she'd been able to help him.

When the show ended, the band members came running off the stage. Brad was the first to reach her with a big hug. "That's two I owe you now," he said, declaring his gratitude.

"Way to go, Tori!" someone else shouted.

"Great work," another voice rang out.

It was nice to be appreciated. "How are you feeling?" she asked Brad.

"Kind of like I've been hit by a runaway train. But I'll live."

"That's what I was afraid of."

"That I'll live?" Brad questioned, his eyebrows raised.

"No, silly. That you're still in pain. We really need to treat your injury in a more thorough way."

"I'll be fine," he assured her with a smile that looked forced. "And besides, I promised you a night out on the town."

"I'm sorry, but I'm going to have to decline that offer, Brad."

"Why?" he demanded.

"Because you're hurting, and as your chiropractor, I can't, in good conscience, sit back and pretend nothing's happening. You need treatment."

"Well, what do you suggest?"

"Let's go back to my office in Wheatfield. I can take care of you there."

Brad grumbled and did some sort of macho shuffle, but the pained expression on his face told her she was going to get her way on this round. Indeed, he turned to say something to one of the roadies.

"You win, Tulip," he admitted, a few moments later. "That glass-tinted van you rode here in is waiting outside for us. If you can stand all the hype, my security people will get us back to your place."

Chapter Six

An hour and a half later the driver turned onto Tori's street. It was already close to 2:00 a.m., and Brad looked exhausted. On the way to the van they'd been intercepted by a mob of screaming fans, and even though security was tight, Brad had insisted on stopping to at least sign some autographs and talk with the people. To the casual observer who fell for his act, Brad was upbeat and energetic. But once they'd reached the van, he hadn't said more than about five sentences during the whole trip. Tori could see that he was suffering.

"What time is your flight tomorrow?" she asked, as the driver turned off the ignition.

"Not till noon," Brad answered.

"Why don't you spend the night here then? We have a spare bedroom. You'll get more rest that way, and I can give you another treatment before you leave."

"That's really nice of you—if you're sure."

"It only makes sense," Tori said. But she wasn't terribly certain that it did. She could already feel the increase in her heartbeat. "After all, it's so late." She was thankful that at least Kevin would be home by now. Even though he was probably sleeping, the fact that he was in the house would insure that things with her and Brad wouldn't get out of hand . . . probably.

Brad had come with his guitar and an overnight bag, which he'd kept in the van in case of emergency. The driver carried them into the house and then left. "Why don't I show you where you'll be sleeping," Tori whispered, picking up his suitcase.

"I'm not an invalid," Brad insisted, firmly. He grabbed the suitcase from her.

"I'm well aware of that!" Tori emphasized in a louder whisper. "I'm just determined to keep it that way."

Brad eyed her and grinned, handing her back the suitcase. "Spunky little thing, aren't you?"

"When I have to be. And keep your voice down," she chided, as he followed her down the hallway. "Kevin is sleeping." But as they passed the open door to his bedroom, it was obvious that Kevin wasn't sleeping. In fact, he wasn't even there.

"Oh my gosh!" Tori said, "he should have been home long before us."

"Now don't get tense," Brad reassured. "He's a teenager, and it's Saturday night."

"I know how old he is!" Tori said, no longer whispering. "What if something happened?" She continued the trip down the hall until she reached the spare bedroom, where she dumped Brad's overnight bag on top of the bed. Wasting no time, and with Brad on her heels, she then hurried to the kitchen.

"My answering machine is blinking," she noted, and pressed the playback button.

"Tori," she heard Kevin's recorded voice. "I'm spending the night at Mark's house. His dad had some car problems on the way home, and we had to get a tow. So Mr. Andrews doesn't have a car right now. Mrs. Andrews works the night shift at the hospital and she'll bring me home in the morning. Don't worry, everything's fine. If you don't believe me, call me at Mark's. But not too late. His dad has to get some shut-eye. Hope you had fun tonight."

Tori breathed a sigh of relief. "Well, at least I know he's safe."

"What—you're not going to call and check out his story?" Brad teased.

"I trust Kevin. Besides, it's two o'clock in the morning. What purpose would it serve to wake everyone up?"

Tori's relief was short-lived as it dawned on her that it was indeed late. She and Brad were all alone—in her house. And this wasn't the time to be questioning whether or not she'd done the right thing by inviting him to spend the night. All she could do now was to act like the professional she was. "Follow me," she said, leading him toward her treatment area.

When they reached the waiting room, she directed him to a chair and handed him a questionnaire. "I'll need to know your medical history," she said, as matter-of-factly as she could. "While you're filling this out, I'm going to get out of these clothes and into something I can work in."

"Something a little more comfortable, huh? Need some help?" he asked, with a daredevil grin.

Gone, for the moment, was his look of pain. It had been replaced by the brazen and ever so appealing expression that continued to turn her knees to jelly. She could already feel herself starting to color. Well, she wasn't about to let him get away with it—at least not without putting up a good fight.

"I'm here to help *you*," she emphasized, in a tone designed to let him know that she was the doctor, and he was her patient. Before he could respond, she turned and left.

By the time she returned, she'd dressed the part and had regained her professional confidence. She was going to need it if she was going to solve Brad's problem. She couldn't help noticing that his cocky expression had been replaced by one of apprehension, and she wasn't sure whether it was because of his pain or because he was nervous about the treatment. "How are you doing?" she asked.

"Uh . . . I couldn't fill out these forms because I seem to have misplaced my glasses. I probably left them back at the hotel. I only need them for reading, so I don't wear them much."

"Oh, well that's not a problem," she said, taking the papers from him. "I'll just ask you the questions and write down the answers myself." When they were finished, she checked his posture, examining his spine and testing reflexes and joint motion to help make an accurate diagnosis. Then she took his vital signs. "Aside from a slightly elevated pulse and your obvious pain, I'd say you're in pretty good shape," she announced.

"You're in pretty good shape yourself," he teased, with an appraising gaze.

Once again butterflies danced in her stomach. *He's leaving in the morning,* the voice warned. *Get anymore involved with him, and he'll be taking your heart along with him.*

"A couple of cervical X-rays should tell us the rest of the story," she answered, pretending she hadn't heard his remark.

A while later, Brad sat shirtless in the treatment room as Tori spoke. "It's pretty much as I suspected," she explained. "When the bones in the neck move out of their normal location, they get stuck, so you can get restrictions where the nerve and blood vessels pass through. In other words the nerves get pinched, and that's why you're experiencing the numbness and pain. I believe we can eliminate your problem by restoring the normal motion and position to the vertebrae. You should be feeling a lot better in a few days or so."

"Great, let's get started," he said.

"All right. I want you to lie facedown on the table with your arms hanging loosely down to the floor."

When he did, she positioned her hands on the sides of his head. She could immediately feel him tense. "I've never been to a chiropractor before," he admitted.

"The best thing you can do is relax and trust me, Brad. The calmer you are, the easier it will be for me to treat you. What scares some people is the cracking noise they hear. It will sound a lot louder to you than to me. But don't let it upset you. It's all perfectly normal. Are you ready?"

"Go for it."

"Take a deep breath," she instructed, "and then let it all out. That's it," she coaxed. Quickly she made the adjustment.

"Ahh!" he exclaimed.

"That was good! Tori said. "We got a nice movement. Are you okay?"

Brad thought for a moment. "Yeah, I guess I am. That really didn't hurt much at all."

"Good, because I'm not finished. Now take another deep breath like before, and let it all out. Come on, loosen up."

As soon as he complied, she made the adjustment. Again she met with success. "I wish all of my patients were this cooperative."

"You'd be amazed at just how cooperative I can be," he retorted. The implication was one she couldn't afford to dwell on. She still had work to do. "Turn over on your back," she instructed.

When he did, she positioned herself behind him, holding his head from both sides. "Relax," she urged, and then quickly completed her last adjustment.

"Yow!" he exclaimed. "I heard fireworks that time."

She massaged his neck for a moment. "You'll be all right. In fact, I predict you're going to be fine. Take your time getting up from the table."

Brad sat, looking kind of dazed for a moment. Then he stood, stretching his arms and shaking his hands. "I do feel better," he said with a grateful smile.

"We'll do this again in the morning," she said.

Brad looked at his watch. "It's pretty much morning now. It won't be long before the sun comes up."

"Well, fortunately it's Sunday. So I won't have to get up at the crack of dawn. Of course, I'll be up early enough to give you another adjustment and drive you to the airport. What time . . . ?"

"I don't expect you to . . ." he said, without letting her finish.

"I want to," she interrupted right back. "In fact, it's a shame you can't stay longer because you'll really need more than two treatments. Though I could call around and try to set you up with a good chiropractor in Massachusetts. That is where you'll be going, right? What time do you think we should be leaving here tomorrow?" She was on a roll now—couldn't seem to stop the words from falling out the sides of her mouth. "I suppose Kevin might want to go along for the ride," she added, without even waiting for Brad to answer her questions. But it was better than crying. And damn it, she was on the verge of tears. Though she could only admit it to herself, she didn't want him to leave. But she'd known all along that he would.

The feel of two hands on her shoulders made her stop. "Take a breath, Tulip," Brad said softly, towering over her.

She wouldn't look at him. Couldn't. She be lost in the liquid blue of those eyes. But his hand slid under her chin, lifting her face to meet his gaze. From somewhere in her throat came a little sound as she tried to swallow. Then he lowered his head. She moved to meet him, and his mouth covered hers in sweet exploration. His touch made her body come alive with a yearning that she hadn't felt since—since the last time he'd kissed her. A yearning that she knew would be best unmet, and suddenly she tensed. She'd sworn to herself she wasn't going to be his one-night stand. Yet that's exactly where this situation was heading.

As if he could read her mind, Brad pulled back. The moment was awkward, and the spell was broken. "You know," he said, "I promised you a night out on the town, and you didn't even get dinner. You must be starving."

Tori had been so agitated she hadn't even thought about food. But now that he'd brought it up, she realized just how hungry she was. "Why don't we go into the kitchen and see what we can find?" she suggested.

"Allow me," Brad insisted. A few moments later he motioned for Tori to sit at the kitchen table while he rummaged through the refrigerator and the cabinets. "I make a pretty mean omelet when I'm put to the test."

"Other than eggs, I'm not sure I have the makings," Tori said.

"I'm betting that you do. That's the fun of spontaneity. You never know what surprises might be ahead."

In a short while he'd whipped up a meal that looked and smelled fit enough for a gourmet restaurant. "This is delicious," Tori said, tasting the first forkful. "I never would have thought of throwing in carrots and olives. Where did you learn to cook?"

"It may be an old cliché," Brad answered, "but necessity really is the mother of invention. The band used to do a lot of traveling by tour bus. In the early days we couldn't afford to eat out all the time. So we'd take turns cooking on the road. Actually it was kind of fun, and it helped pass the time."

Tori tried to stifle a yawn as she checked the clock. As tired as she was, she didn't want to fall asleep. She wanted to savor these last precious hours with Brad before he went walking out of her life.

"I've been thinking," he said. "At the risk of sounding presumptuous, I don't really have to get back to Massachusetts until Tuesday. So you'd be doing me a big favor by letting me stick around for a few days."

Instantly she was wide awake as her mouth flew open.

"I could mow the lawn or something to earn my keep."

"Or possibly I could keep you slaving away in the kitchen," she joked.

"So, what do you think? This would give us a couple of extra days to straighten out my neck problem, and maybe I won't have to hook up with a new chiropractor."

"I think it's a great idea," Tori said, trying to contain her jubilation. "I'm sure Kevin will agree."

"Then it's settled. I guess what we both need now is some sleep."

"You go on." She stood and began clearing the table. "I want to clean up these dishes. I hate waking up to a mess."

Brad put his hand over hers to stop her. "It's not your mess, Tulip. It's mine. I promise I'll clean it—as soon as I've had some rest. Can you live with that?"

This business of bending the rules and ignoring structure was interfering with her routine. It was going to take some getting used to, but she was beginning to see that there were some fringe benefits to the concept. "Yes," she answered, facing him squarely. "I think I can live with that."

"Excellent," he said, with a smile of great satisfaction.

Brad kicked the sheet off his body to feel the gentle breeze from the open window in Tori's spare bedroom. The air was warm, but not warm enough to keep him from sleeping. It was the voice that continued to badger him; the voice that kept him from getting a proper night's rest.

So, Bradley, this is how you create distance? You invite yourself to spend the next few days with the good doctor—in her own home yet. You know she doesn't want to be involved with you. That's why she went all rigid the last time you kissed her. She's got you pegged. She's only being nice to you cause she feels sorry for you—cause you're in pain. She's got the cure. Her interest is purely professional.

"Shut up!" he muttered under his breath. *Great, now I'm talking to the walls.* But it wasn't true. He wouldn't let it be. He'd make her fall for him the way he knew he was starting to fall for her. Maybe. What if she already had, and she was afraid of getting hurt? . . . Like he was. *Wishful thinking!* Yeah? Well the signs were there, if he hadn't misread them. Hell, when they'd started talking about his flight home, she'd looked like she was gonna cry. Maybe she was hiding things too. Things like her fears—or her pain. What if someone had hurt her the way he'd been hurt?

He'd given her such a great pep talk about spontaneity and bending the rules. Risk taking. That's what it was. *"Stick your toes in the water, son, the rest of the body usually wants to follow."* That's what his father had always told him. Had the man been right?

He'd gotten his feet wet. Gotten a taste of what a relationship with Tori would be like. Wasn't she worth the risk of going the whole distance? Yeah, he decided. Maybe the time had come for him to take his own advice.

The smell of freshly brewed coffee drifted into the bedroom, and Tori sat up in bed. Thumbs bore marks in her temples as she tried to ward off the headache that had come from too little sleep. Was it any wonder? What had she been thinking when she'd agreed to let Brad stay with her for a few more days? A few more days for him to instill himself into her life and her heart . . . and then walk out.

But it was what you wanted. Admit it. Subconsciously you helped make it happen. So now deal with it. If she could learn to enjoy the moment for what it was—just the moment—maybe she could handle the inevitability of their separation when the time came. Maybe that was part of all this spontaneity business that Brad kept spouting. She threw a matching robe over her short, satin nightshirt and made her way into the kitchen.

He hadn't noticed her yet. True to his word, Brad was busy cleaning up last night's mess. So she watched quietly while the well-muscled, shirtless man with the tousled hair padded around barefoot, washing dishes and scrubbing pans. He was humming a catchy little melody, and she wondered if he'd written it himself. She could only marvel at the fact that this super star, who'd brought the entire house down with his performance just twelve hours earlier, was now cleaning up her kitchen like he owned it.

Finally he sensed her presence and turned to face her. "Hi there," he said, his eyes traveling the path from her face to her sleepwear. "I made coffee."

"Thanks," Tori said, appreciatively. "I think I'm going to need some."

"I know what you mean. I didn't get much sleep myself."

"Were you in pain?" she asked.

"No, the arm feels pretty good. I guess I was just kind of restless."

"Me too," she admitted.

Brad poured the steaming liquid into a mug and handed it to her as she sat at the kitchen table.

"Are you hungry?" Tori asked.

"You must be kidding, after the meal we put away before we went to bed. That was only a few hours ago."

Tori smiled. "I'm still pretty stuffed myself." *Well great. Now that we've covered all the trivia, what shall we talk about next?* She shifted uncomfortably in her chair. Suddenly the satiny robe seemed much shorter than she'd remembered. And it wasn't doing a very adequate job of covering her legs. Once again his gaze moved downward, and once again he had her quivering like jelly. She took a sip of her coffee and prayed that she would think of something to say that sounded halfway intelligent. "It looks like a nice day. Is there anything special you'd like to do?"

"Just being with you is special enough," he answered.

She took another swallow of coffee. But it collided with her elevated pulse as it reached the back of her throat, and dribbled out of her mouth. Now she had coffee dripping down the front of her robe. "Wonderful!" she chastised herself. She jumped up to get a washcloth from the sink and began dabbing at the stain.

"I'm glad you agree. I like a woman who responds with enthusiasm."

"Hmm?" Tori glanced over at Brad to see his deepening grin.

"Need some help?" he offered.

The man was incorrigible. "You know I . . . uh . . . I'm not really awake yet," she said. "I think I'll go take a shower."

"The offer still stands."

"Which offer is that?"

"I'll be glad to help."

That did it. He'd reduced her to the likes of a stammering, blushing teenager who couldn't even look him in the eyes. And just to complete the picture, she heard the sound of the key in the lock of the kitchen door. Kevin was home.

He entered the room and saw the two of them standing there; Tori in her wet and now partially transparent sleepwear, and Brad clad only in jeans and whatever he wore underneath them. The look on Kevin's face said it all, but he summed it up in one word. "Whoa!"

"Mornin', Kevin," Brad said with total composure.

"I didn't expect to see you here, Brad. Sorry if I walked in on something."

"Your sister and I were just trying to decide what we were gonna to do with the rest of the day."

"Brad is here because he's still having a problem with his neck and hand," Tori broke in. "He's going to be spending a little time with us so that I can treat him."

"Are you serious? I can't wait to tell the guys!"

"Hold it," Brad said. "You can't let anyone know about this, Kevin. Well you can," he amended. "But I hope you won't. I'm just layin' low for a while till my hand gets better, and I'd really appreciate some privacy. Besides, if people find out I'm here because of an injury there's no

Once Upon a Secret

telling what kind of rumors might get started about me or my career—or your sister. Catch my drift?"

Kevin thought for a moment. "Oh. Sure," he said. "Then I guess it'll have to be our secret. But this pretty much blows me away. I thought you were supposed to be on tour."

"I am. I have to leave for Massachusetts on Tuesday."

"So . . . have you been here since . . . the end of the concert?" Kevin asked. The question was worded with as much discretion as he seemed capable of mustering, but the implication was clear enough to Tori.

"Brad spent the night in the spare bedroom," she said, flustered. "What was left of it anyway. The night, I mean. After I gave him a treatment, we stayed up so late talking that neither one of us got much sleep. Which is the reason I was clumsy and spilled my coffee. I need a shower. So if you two will excuse me . . ." That was about as much of an explanation as she was able to offer. Without waiting for any more questions, she turned and left the room.

"Boy, what's wrong with her?" Kevin asked. "She's as jittery as a smoker who's run out of cigarettes."

"I figure your sister's afraid you'll think there was some sort of hanky-panky goin' on here last night."

"Was there?"

"Weren't you listening when she explained the situation?"

"That was her side of the story." The kid was wearing a grin that smacked of challenge.

"That was the story," Brad emphasized.

"But you do like her, don't you?"

"What if I do? Would that be a problem for you?" Not that he was asking for permission.

Kevin's grin had been replaced by a face that was firmly

set in thought. "Not for me. Just don't turn it into one for Tori. Okay, Man?"

"What do you mean?"

"I wouldn't want to see her get stomped on—again. She might look tough, but inside she's one big marshmallow. No offense meant," he added.

So—the Tulip had been burned. That would explain her fear of getting involved. "Well thanks for the tip, Kevin. And for the record, I don't stomp on people. No offense taken."

Once again the kid wore a smile. "She likes you too."

"Did she say that?"

"She didn't have to. She's my sister."

Obviously Kevin approved, and Brad couldn't help smiling in return. "When I need a social director to run interference I'll let you know. In the meantime, why don't you go get your guitar, and we can jam a little while she's gettin' ready."

A moment later Kevin was back. "Wanna trade?" Brad offered, taking his custom, hand-made acoustic guitar out of its case.

"You'd let me play your VanLear?" Kevin's eyes were wide with surprise.

"It's the only one I brought. My electric one is already in transit."

"No, I mean you'd actually let me play your guitar? VanLear has a reputation for being one of the finest there is. There aren't even that many of them around."

"It is a great instrument," Brad said, handing it over to Kevin. "I really appreciate playing it after some of the brands I started out on."

"Wow." Kevin lightly brushed his hand along the highly polished lacquer finish, examining the aged rosewood. Brad's initials stood out in an abalone inlay. "This is awesome!"

And it was, especially compared to the old beater Kevin played. Brad remembered what it had been like when all he could afford were pawnshop seconds. He'd been far too independent to go to his family and ask for financial help. No, he'd been determined to show them he could make it on his own. And he had. For that, at least, he could be proud.

"So let me hear you strum a few chords," Brad said.

"Are you sure?"

Brad nodded, and Kevin began to play. But he'd lost the self-assurance he'd played with the day before. The sounds were tentative, as if he weren't even sure his fingers should be touching the strings.

"Look," Brad said, after a couple of minutes. "The guitar is beautiful, but it's not that fragile. You're not gonna break it by playing it."

Brad began to strum Kevin's guitar. The tone was a stark contrast to his own VanLear. But the tune played was a spirited blues number that was one of his favorites. "Like this," he coaxed, as he showed Kevin the chord progressions.

It wasn't long before Kevin was lost in the music. Not only had he picked up on what Brad had taught him, but he was improvising. The kid had potential.

After several minutes they stopped playing, and they both glanced up at the sound of zealous clapping. "I'm impressed," Tori said. "You two play wonderfully together."

And she looked wonderful. A simple green T-shirt and jeans, but she filled out her clothes in all the right places.

"Brad's not only a great musician, he's a great teacher!" Kevin said.

That was the paradox of the decade! But Kevin seemed happy, and Tori was impressed. Not a bad way for a guy who'd had such a restless night to start his morning.

"Thanks for the compliment, but I'm not sure I'm the one who deserves the credit here, Kevin. You catch on pretty quick."

"Still, it was nice of you to let him play your guitar," Tori said, "and to show him those . . . what do you call them? . . . riffs?"

Brad laughed. "Yeah, riffs. So, have you decided what you'd like to do today?"

"Aside from giving you an adjustment, I was wondering if you'd like to go for a bike ride. The Prairie Path isn't too far from here, and the weather is nice. We could have a picnic lunch."

"That sounds like a great idea, except that I don't have a bike."

"You could borrow mine," Kevin offered.

"Tell you what. Why don't you hang on to my guitar while I'm gone? I won't be bringing it with me anyway."

Kevin's eyes were wide with excitement. "Thanks, Brad!"

"It's a deal then. It won't take me long to shower and get ready."

Brad disappeared, and Tori turned to Kevin. "Have you had any breakfast?" she asked.

"I grabbed a sweet roll at Mark's."

"Not very nutritious."

"I can always eat later. Right now I want to write down those progressions before I forget them. Then I want to practice. It's not every day a guy gets a chance to play a VanLear guitar, let alone one that happens to belong to Brad Daniels."

Yes, but what about your homework, Kevin? The old Tori would have bristled and bubbled over trying to make her point, but the new Tori was going to have to be more cautious before she spoke.

"I don't blame you for being excited," she said, with a gentle smile. "It's been quite a weekend for you."

"For both of us," he added.

"Yes. So how is the interview for the school newspaper coming? Isn't that due pretty soon?"

"Good point, Sis." His look switched to one of concern. "It doesn't have to be finished until Tuesday, but I do have to work on it today. I've got all my notes. It's a matter of getting them organized. Don't worry, I'm not going to screw it up."

"No. I'm sure you won't. Opportunities like this don't come along every day."

"You can say that again."

"Of course, opportunities for scholarships don't come along every day either. I wouldn't want to see you blow your chances for one of those."

"Meaning?"

Kevin had immediately switched to the self-defense mode, and she was going to have to proceed carefully if she wanted to avoid an argument.

"I just want to make sure you get all of your homework finished, Kevin. Because it's *all* important," she emphasized.

"Don't you think I know that? Can't you ever trust me to decide what my priorities ought to be? Do you always have to be on my case, Tori?"

"If being on your case means looking out for your best interests, then I guess the answer is yes! Until you're mature enough to decide what those are, it's my responsibility."

"I've made the honor roll every time except for the last report card!" he exploded. "I mess up once, and you're on me like white on rice. I'm fifteen years old for crying out loud!"

"My point exactly. You're the child, and I'm the adult. It's my job to keep you in line and on track until you're grown enough to do that for yourself."

Congratulations, Tori! You handled that with finesse, didn't you? You just said all the things you were determined not to say . . . and more.

Kevin glared at her, his eyes burning with hostility. Cautiously, he laid Brad's guitar back in its case, then locked it. "I know it's Sunday, Tori, but I'm not in the mood for one of your sermons!" With that he picked up the guitar and went storming out of the room. Seconds later she heard the thunderous slam of his bedroom door.

"Wonderful," she muttered under her breath.

"What was that all about?" Brad asked, as he emerged from the hallway.

"Old habits die hard. We got into another discussion about his homework."

"It sounded like more than a discussion to me. I could hear the shouting all the way from the bathroom—with the door closed. Want to talk about it?"

"I just don't like to see him neglect his school work, especially not now. His grade point average could mean the difference of whether or not he gets a scholarship. If he doesn't get one, we may not have enough money to send him to the right college."

"So you let him know that unless he gets into the right college, he won't be meeting your standards? That he won't be worthy of your love?"

"Certainly not!" She was indignant at the thought. "This has nothing to do with my love for him."

"Does he know that?"

"Well, of course he . . . I assume he . . . I . . ." *Confound it! Why did this man always have to play Frisbee with her?*

"That control thing works both ways, you know. Did it ever occur to you that your brother might be fighting the same battle?"

"What do you mean?"

"Maybe the issue for Kevin isn't about his future. Maybe it's about who's controlling his life right now. You know; you say black, he says white. Kids reach an age when they think their parents don't know anything. Maybe he's just trying to show you who's boss."

"So, in other words, I can't win."

"I didn't say that. But I do think you're gonna have to change your strategy."

"You know, for someone who doesn't have any kids of his own you sure seem to understand an awful lot about them."

"Maybe I just remember how I felt when I was his age," Brad said. "Anyway it's always easier to tell someone else what to do when you're on the outside looking in."

She looked at her watch. "I know it's getting late, but would you mind if I try to straighten this out before we go? I hate to leave things like this."

"Take your time. In fact, I'll see what I can do about throwing together some food for that picnic."

Tori smiled. "You're a prince."

"I'm glad you're beginning to realize that," he said, flashing her a wink that made her skin tingle.

A moment later Tori knocked on Kevin's bedroom door, but there was no answer. "Please let me in, Kevin," she said. "I'd really like to talk with you."

Still, she was met with silence.

"I promise, no more lectures."

The door to the bedroom opened slowly, and then Kevin cracked a cautious smile as he saw the white napkin Tori was waving. "I come in peace," she reassured him.

Brad's guitar lay in the opened case on the bed. "It truly is a beautiful instrument," she said, sitting next to it, fingering the polished wood. "And it sounds wonderful. I can see why you enjoy playing it so much."

Kevin kept a prudent distance, standing at the other end of the room. "Can you? Can you see how much music has come to mean to me?"

"I'm beginning to, Kevin, and I think it's good."

"As long as it's always on the back burner and not at the forefront of my life," he finished for her.

Tori took a deep breath and whispered a silent prayer that the right words would come. "Kevin, when Mom and Dad died, you were very young. While it might not seem like it to you, I was too. I wasn't prepared to take on the job of being a substitute parent to an adolescent. I'd barely grown up myself, but that isn't the issue.

"The point is that the only blueprint I had for stepping into their shoes was the map I thought they'd laid out for you. They raised me to believe that education was the key to life, and I've tried to raise you the same way. Because it's what I know, and it's what I thought they would have wanted for both of us. I'm not convinced that it's wrong either, though I can see I've made a lot of mistakes in my approach to this whole thing.

"But know this much, Kevin. Whether you think so or not, all of my actions are based on the fact that I care very much about what happens to you. You're a part of me, and I love you. Nothing . . . nothing," she emphasized, "is ever going to change that. I'll always be there for you no matter what you decide to do with your life. Count on it."

Her brother was listening with a whole new intensity. "It means a lot to hear you say that, Sis. I love you too. I know you've made sacrifices for me, and I'm grateful. But there comes a time when a guy has to make his own decisions about his future."

"You're right," she said. "While I'm not sure this is that time for you, I do respect your feelings. So I'm going to try to let go of the reins a little. That doesn't mean I'm going to let you run roughshod over me though."

Kevin smiled, walked over and enveloped his sister with a big hug. "Thanks, Tori."

The two stood embracing in silence until Tori added, "It's going to take some patience on both our parts."

"Speaking of patience, haven't you kept Brad waiting long enough?"

"Yes," she agreed. "I'm not sure what time we'll be home, but since you're so independent, I know you won't have any trouble scrounging up something for dinner in case I'm not here to fix it."

"No problem. I can always order a pizza." He laughed, aiming a pillow at her on her way out the door.

Chapter Seven

Brad and Tori had been bike riding for about an hour when they decided they were hungry. "There's a small clearing about two minutes up ahead. We can stop and have our picnic there," Tori suggested.

"Hope you like peanut butter and jelly sandwiches," Brad said, as they spread the blanket across the small patch of greenery. "It's all I could find."

"That's because I'm low on groceries." She grabbed the paper plates and napkins and methodically began doling out the food. "I usually shop on Saturdays. In fact, I'm behind in my housework, but with all that's been going on, my routine has taken a back seat to . . ." Tori stopped mid sentence.

"What's wrong?" Brad asked, sitting beside her.

"I just started listening to myself, and I'm beginning to see what you mean about my lack of flexibility. The fact of the matter is, I have enough food in the house to last at least another week. Granted, it's not the stuff we usually eat, but we can certainly make do. The housework will always be there. As for the peanut butter and jelly, I like it fine. Thank you for putting it all together."

His gaze was fixed on her, bringing all of her senses to

life. "So are you telling me you're not sorry for the way you've spent the past few days?"

Tori swallowed hard. "I wouldn't have traded this weekend for all the groceries in the store."

Those eyes of his were flickering with intensity. "The weekend's not over, Tulip. When it is, there will be lots more of them to come."

Are you saying this doesn't have to end when you leave on Tuesday? Because you are, I'm not sure I can afford to let myself believe you. "Potato chips?" she offered, reaching into the tote bag. *Much safer to change the subject than to risk asking a question to which she wasn't sure she wanted to hear the answer.*

"So, how did things go with Kevin?" he asked, taking her cue. *Relief! The spell was broken.*

"Pretty well, I think. I stayed away from the topic of his grades. Believe it or not, the fact that he missed the honor roll last quarter didn't upset me nearly as much as the reason why."

"Which was?"

"He simply wasn't trying. He wasn't turning in his assignments. He stopped caring about his schoolwork. That's what worries me. I can't fault anyone who tries and fails. But like I said, I didn't get into that. I simply tried to make him understand that I love him no matter what he does. And I do. You were right, Brad," she admitted. "I'm not really sure he knew that."

A shadow of tension touched his face. "I'm glad you told him then. It's important for the kid to know he's needed and loved—and that he has value. No kid should have to grow up thinking he's worthless."

She knew instinctively that Brad was no longer talking about Kevin. He was relating his own childhood experience, and she longed to quiet his pain. "You seem to have a clear understanding of the situation. I really appreciate your input."

"Glad I could help," he said. *Bet I could help in other areas too—if you'd learn to trust me. But every time I start to get close, you push me away.* "It's clouding over. Is it supposed to rain?"

"I don't know," Tori answered, looking up at the sky. "The weather around here can change pretty fast. You think we should start heading home?"

"No, not yet," he said. "It's peaceful here, away from crowds and phones . . ."

"And patients," she finished. "Although I did bring my pager along."

"Guess I hadn't noticed. Do you always wear it?"

"Pretty much. I'm the only chiropractor in town. People need to know they can depend on me to be available when they have an emergency."

Now that he knew he could be competing with the damn beeper, he'd have to work faster if he were going to make any headway with this woman. Tuesday was just around the corner.

"Tell me something, Tulip."

"What's that?"

"Who hurt you? Who squeezed the life out of your spirit?"

He had her attention now, and he watched as she stiffened and her face turned a vivid scarlet.

"Who said that anyone did?" she flared. "Did Kevin say something?"

Kevin had only confirmed his suspicions. "You don't have to be a genius to see that something keeps you contained. Some life experience of yours has taught you to hold back. If we're gonna get to know each other better—and I hope we are—I need to know what I'm up against. Can you trust me enough to answer my question?"

She gave a shrug of resignation. "It's a pretty humiliating story."

"More humiliating than admitting that you're the family outcast?" *That your own parents don't love you and never wanted you.*

The embarrassed look on her face turned to one of compassion as the subject volleyed back to him. But that wasn't what he wanted right now. "Tell me, Tulip. Tell me what happened."

She turned away from him, and in that moment he thought he'd lost the momentum. Then in a surprise move, her shoulders heaved, and she looked directly into his eyes. "I was engaged to be married at the time my parents were killed. Jack was going to be a chiropractor too. We had big dreams and plans to start our own clinic once we graduated. We were going to be partners—in business and in life."

"Did you love him?"

"Yes, I really did. That's why it hurt so much when it didn't work out."

"What made it all come apart?"

"Well, the one thing we hadn't planned on was children. At least not right away. Of course with Kevin in the picture, I became an instant parent. Jack couldn't handle that. It pretty much cramped his style. I mean, things were rough enough with the two of us trying to get through school. Then when my parents were killed, I had to deal with all that emotional turmoil and grief."

"I take it he wasn't very compassionate."

"Well at first, he tried to be supportive, but it wasn't a

situation we could get through in a month or two. Grieving takes time. After a while, his patience wore thin. I was no longer available to go out with him on a moment's notice. I had responsibilities in addition to my schoolwork. Plenty of them. Jack couldn't understand why I had to put Kevin's needs first. Eventually the relationship began to deteriorate.

"But the real clincher was when Jack started dating Alicia. At that time she was my best friend. Alicia was also studying to be a chiropractor. I got behind in my studies for a while, so the two of them graduated before I did. A month later they married each other and moved to another state. As far as I know they set up the practice that he and I were going to start. I guess they're living happily ever after now."

Brad took her hand and placed it in his, trying to soothe her wounds with a gentle stroke. "I'm sorry he hurt you like that. I am. But it was his loss. Not every guy feels that way about kids. Some guys actually think that the family unit has real value. I respect what you've done. I have nothing but admiration for the loyalty and love you've shown in order to preserve your family."

"You really mean that, don't you?" Her green eyes were pleading for yet further confirmation, and it was clear to him that Tori Glenn, the woman, was not nearly so self-confident as Doctor Tori Glenn, the professional.

"Damn straight I mean it!"

"Even with all the mistakes I've made?"

"Who doesn't make mistakes? How else do we learn?"

Just then the clouds opened up, and it began to rain. "Aw oh, I was afraid of this," Tori said, scrambling to get the remains of their picnic back in the tote. Together they folded the blanket. "I have a heavy sheet of plastic in the saddlebag on my bike. Maybe it will keep us dry until some of this blows over."

Brad took the plastic and quickly threw it over their heads. "Well, I have to admit," he said, as they huddled beneath its shelter, "sometimes it pays to do some advance planning."

The air turned colder, and Tori shivered as chill bumps appeared on her arms. "I don't have a jacket or I'd give it to you. But maybe we could improvise," he added with a suggestive raise of his eyebrows.

She studied him silently, and then with a shy smile that told him she was taking the bait, she reached for his hand. He wanted to envelop her, gobble her up like Thanksgiving dinner. But instinct told him to hold back—let her call the pace until he was sure where she was going. Without letting go, she turned herself around so that her back was now nuzzled up against the front of his body, and his arms were blanketing her with his warmth. And that wasn't all that was heating up. The back of her head lay against his shoulders, and her hair smelled like the first apples of the season—sweet and tart.

In a bolder move, she leaned into him until her rear was right up against male hardened flesh that now threatened to defy the confines of his jeans. "Oh, Tulip," he whispered, caressing the side of her face with his cheek. His hands went from her slender waist to her breasts, circling the pointed tips right through her cotton top. With a shudder, her breathing became more rapid.

She reached inside of her jeans to pull her shirt to the outside of the waistband. A clear signal that Brad's hands were heading in the right direction; underneath her top and over the satin thin fabric of her bra. Her moan was brief as she turned to face him, raising the shirt up to offer better access. Her bra was transparent enough to expose the creamy perfection of two well-rounded breasts, and he could hardly wait to eliminate the final barrier. If only that damn plastic weren't restricting their movements.

"It stopped raining," he heard her say from somewhere. By the time it registered, she'd already thrown the plastic to the ground.

Yes! his mind was shouting.

And then "Oh, no!"

Oh, no? What did she mean?

"Darn."

"What's wrong," he asked.

"I'm being paged," she said, reaching for the device in her pocket.

"I didn't hear anything."

"That's because it vibrates."

That's not all that was vibrating. "What a concept. Are you sure it was your pager?"

Tori glanced upward and grinned. "Unfortunately. I'm sorry, Brad, but we're going to have to head back," she announced, after checking the display. "This is Mr. Farley's phone number. He's elderly, and he took a nasty fall last week. Luckily he didn't break his hip, but he's been in pain from the whole ordeal. He's the kind of man who suffers in silence, so I know he wouldn't be calling me on a Sunday if it weren't an emergency."

His loins were pleading with her to ignore the pager, but he knew she wouldn't—and that she shouldn't. In spite of himself, he admired her dedication.

"All right, Tulip. But just think of this as a chapter in a book—to be continued."

It was close to six o'clock when Brad and Tori walked into the house. Kevin had left a note on the kitchen counter, which Tori read aloud:

"Did the first draft of the interview, practiced on the awesome VanLear!—even finished my homework. Felt caged after that, so I went jogging with Mark. Be home by dark.

Kevin

P.S. Brad, someone named Leona Farnsworth phoned looking for you. I didn't want to blow your cover, but she seemed to know you were staying here. Said she would call back later tonight."

Brad could feel his body tightening as his adrenaline level began to rise. So the ice diva had already tracked him down. It galled him that she'd had the nerve to call Tori's home, but he knew he had to stay cool.

"It looks like that talk we had took hold," Tori said, regarding Kevin's note.

"The kid's been busy, I'll give him that."

"Leona Farnsworth," Tori added, with a slight edginess in her tone. "Isn't that the reporter who moonlights as a musician in your band?"

"Only occasionally," Brad answered, feigning as much aloofness as possible.

"Well, excuse me a minute," she said, dropping the subject. She headed straight for the telephone to make arrangements to see her emergency patient. "I'm sorry," Tori apologized, after hanging up the phone. "But I'm going to have to treat this man, and it could take some time. He'll be here soon. After that I need to work on you. How are you doing?"

"To tell the truth, the arm's a little stiff from the bike ride, but it's not bad."

"You look tired, Brad. I hope we didn't overdo it. Maybe you should lie down for a bit."

"I'll be fine. In fact, while you're with Mr. Farley, I've got a couple of things to take care of myself. You don't mind if I use your phone, do you? I'll be happy to reimburse you."

"There's an extension in the guest room. Please make yourself comfortable, and I'll try not to be too long," Tori said, as she headed toward her office.

Brad went straight to the phone. He knew Leona's number by heart, but his hands were shaking as he dialed.

"Hello," she said.

"Who told you I was here?" he demanded, without even identifying himself.

"Bradley, you really must try to stop underestimating my talents. I'm a reporter. I earn my living tracking down facts and information."

"You don't need to remind me of that," he said bitterly. "Although it's a pretty liberal use of the word *earn*. You had your rendezvous with the spotlight. What the hell do you want from me now?"

"Darling you mustn't be so cruel. I only called to see how you were feeling. You were in pretty bad shape by the end of the concert. I was worried about you."

"Spare me, Leona. What's this really about?"

"Like I said, Bradley. It's about your health. How's the hand?"

"Just peachy. Look, your concern is touching, but does that about wrap it up?"

"For now," she said.

"Good. The next time you're looking for a progress report, why don't you try checking out the *National Meddler*. Their writers are on a par with you." Without giving her the chance to respond, he carefully hung up the phone.

He'd wanted to slam the receiver in her ear, tell her not to sic her bloodhounds on him or Tori ever again, or else he'd . . . *What? What are you going to do?* He knew better than to threaten the woman. She thrived on challenge, and it only made her more volatile. He'd done the best thing by staying as calm as he could. No sense in letting her know how much she'd rattled him. *You might have won that round,* the voice taunted, *but she'll be back. When you least want her. She'll be back.*

Mr. Farley had been in bad shape, and Tori was glad he'd been able to reach her. While he had far more range of motion by the time she was finished treating him, he was still slow in getting around. Slow and talkative. Ever since he'd lost his wife, the poor man had more time on his hands than he knew what to do with. And Tori hadn't had the heart to rush him.

But now that he was finally gone, and she'd locked the waiting room door after him, she was disappointed to realize that the night was half over. Her precious time with Brad was slipping through her fingers like sand through an hourglass. The only good thing was that she'd scheduled a light patient load for tomorrow, and with some luck she'd be able to spend a good part of her day with him.

A rush of warmth flashed through her as she remembered their encounter in the park. "To be continued," he'd said. There was no telling where it would all lead. She was wildly attracted to the man. There was no denying it. He was impulsive and exciting, yet there was a responsible side to him all wrapped up in one package . . . a package that drew her to him at the same time it frightened her.

But she knew that he would be leaving soon. Once he was gone, there was a strong likelihood that she'd never see him again. And on the slim chance that she would, realistically, what kind of relationship could she hope to develop with a man who was on the road for as much time as Brad?

... A man females swooned and fainted over ... a man who could have his choice of countless other women, once he tired of her. Brad was married to his music and all the hoopla that went along with the fame and adulation from his fans. Maybe he didn't even realize it himself, but she could feel his exhilaration during a performance. Who could blame him? Why would he give up any part of it for her?

For that matter, she had her own profession to weigh. She was a small-town chiropractor who considered the welfare of her patients to be of the utmost importance. In order to care for them she would have to be available—and well rested. A concept that required the type of discipline that didn't blend too well with Brad's lifestyle.

Yet here she was, admittedly fantasizing about some kind of future with him. In the short time she'd known him, he'd managed to capture a part of her heart that no one else had—not even Jack. Despite whatever happened from this point on, she was already in too deep not to feel the inevitable pain of his absence. So maybe having him for only a little while was better than not ever having had him at all. Maybe he would leave her with memories that would comfort her enough that she would have no regrets.

If only it were easier to let go of the controls—if only she could throw caution to the wind, as the saying went. If she'd been a little more flexible with Jack, maybe she wouldn't have lost him the way she had. But Jack was out of the picture, and that was no longer the issue. Surprisingly, the thought of him married to Alicia barely fazed her anymore. Brad was another matter. The mere idea of making love with him sent a current of electricity racing through her.

She walked from the office to the main part of the house.

In the distance she could hear music. A few chords, some singing, but nothing was connected. As she got closer to the living room it became clear that Brad was composing a song. She was anxious to be with him, yet at the same time she didn't want to interrupt his train of thought. He was working, and she respected that. So she held back, stayed near the kitchen and listened quietly.

After a while she heard more music; his voice, his guitar, but the sound was different. He had tape-recorded the song, and now she was hearing the finished product. "I like it," she said, unable to resist walking into the room.

Brad looked up and smiled. "It needs some work, but it's got potential."

"Do you always do your composing with a tape recorder?"

"Mostly. It's easier than having to stop and try to write things down. This way I can be more spontaneous. It lends itself to better creativity. At least it works for me."

Ah, yes. The magic word again. Spontaneity. "Are you at a point where you can take a break? We need to go to work on your neck."

"Yeah," he said, rolling his head in a circular fashion. "The muscles are kind of tight."

Together they walked back to her office. Within minutes it was obvious that Brad was in worse shape than she'd thought; no doubt from having over-extended himself on the bike ride that day. She couldn't help feeling guilty, after all, it had been her idea. Moreover, it was getting increasingly difficult to treat him without becoming . . . involved. But she was determined to maintain the doctor–patient stance while he was in her care, at least during the adjustment. Of course, with Brad the innuendoes flew, though she made the pretense of ignoring them. It was the only way she could do her job properly. Getting him well was her main priority.

It was late when they finished, and as they headed out of the office Tori began to feel a bit light-headed. It occurred to her that she'd been running on sheer adrenaline for several days, and that her supply had finally run down. She literally was exhausted.

"I'm starving," she announced with a yawn, "but I'm not sure I can stay awake long enough to eat, let alone cook."

"How about we order carry-out?" he suggested, "assuming there's a nearby restaurant open."

"Chinese?" Tori questioned, looking at her watch.

"Fine with me," he said.

A moment later they were in the kitchen, and she tossed him a menu.

"Uh . . ." He held the menu at arm's length and studied it.

"Oh, I forgot you don't have your glasses. Tell me what you like to eat, and I'll let you know if they have it."

"I'm not fussy, surprise me."

Maybe I'll do exactly that, Brad Daniels. In a way that has nothing to do with Chinese cuisine. But the fact of the matter was that she was so tired she could barely focus on the words in front of her. By the time she'd placed the order, Kevin had come home.

"I hope you're hungry," Tori said. "We're having egg rolls, hot and sour soup and cashew chicken—as soon as it's delivered."

"Great," Kevin said. "I'm going to get to work on finishing up that interview. So call me when the food gets here," he said, on his way to his room.

In the meantime, Brad took Tori by the hand and led her

into the living room. "Sit with me," he insisted, guiding her onto the sofa. "You look drained."

"I am," she admitted.

"Yeah, well one good turn deserves another." Brad reached for her feet, swung them over to his lap and began removing her shoes and socks.

"What are you doing?"

"What does it feel like?" he answered, massaging her foot.

Tori smiled, resting her head on the pillow at the opposite end of the sofa. "Like a little bit of heaven."

"You know, you work too hard."

"The hours come with the profession," she said. His hands began to work their magic, while she closed her eyes to let the tension flow out of her body.

"Those certainly are a pair of multi-talented hands," she murmured.

"I'm only gettin' started," he whispered.

The implication in his tone was clear, as a slow tingling feeling started to warm her. The sensation was absolutely drugging.

The next time she opened her eyes, the room was dark. It was three a.m., she realized, as she lay there alone, curled up on the sofa with a blanket over her. Tori sat up slowly and turned on the nearby lamp. She'd fallen asleep! How could she have done that when all she'd really wanted to do was spend the rest of the evening with Brad? Disappointed, and half disoriented, she sauntered into her own bedroom to spend the rest of the night.

Chapter Eight

It seemed the weather near Chicago had a way of changing fast. Brad wiped his brow with the bottom of his shirt and headed for the kitchen sink. Jeez, this place was a sweatbox. It was too early in the day for a beer; maybe some water would help. He knew Tori couldn't afford to air-condition anything but the patient area. But what he couldn't understand was how a person could even breathe in this kind of humidity, much less function.

Then again he supposed that attitude fell right in line with his whole style of life. It was all in what you got used to. Money talked. He turned on the faucet and let the water run till it felt cold to the touch. Not that he hadn't come by his luxuries the hard way. He'd paid his dues. Maybe he hadn't gotten his education in the formal sense—like she had. But he certainly was schooled in the knocks of the business. That was what counted, not all this highfalutin, honorary degree crap from some ambassador type institute, in order to prove to the world that you had an IQ. *Feeling a bit intimidated by the lady doctor, are we?* the voice taunted.

Where the hell had he put those glasses when he'd cleaned up the kitchen the other day? Impatiently he searched the cabinets till he found what he was looking for.

And why the hell was he so damned agitated? Just because Tori was a proponent of higher education, it wasn't like she was out to prove that she was smarter than he was or somehow above him. She didn't even have a clue about his problem. He was sure of it.

Ice. A few cubes from the freezer into the glass and maybe he'd cool down some. Besides, she respected him. Yeah, and maybe it was more than that. He'd mesmerized her the other night on stage. He could tell. He could always tell when a woman was caught up in his act. Only this time it hadn't been an act. He might have had the chance to convince her of that if he'd been able to spend more time with her the day before—if her professional life hadn't gotten in the way.

Not that he didn't admire the way she cared for her patients. But she was wearing herself out. That had been obvious last night when she'd fallen so sound asleep on the sofa, he hadn't had the heart to wake her.

He looked at his watch. It was almost noon, and he knew she'd only scheduled patients for the morning. She'd be coming through the doorway soon, and then, hopefully, he'd have the rest of the day to spend with her. Maybe they could start with lunch in some nice, air-conditioned restaurant.

In the meantime—what was that dripping noise he kept hearing? He checked the faucet to make sure he'd closed it all the way. But that wasn't the problem. A quick look through the bottom cabinets and the mystery was ended. Water was fast seeping from the pipes under the sink, soaking both the cabinet contents and the kitchen floor.

"Wonderful, just wonderful," Tori declared, arriving in time to scan the damages. "I need another plumbing bill like I need an extra appendage."

"Oh yeah," Brad teased. "Sometimes I wonder whether another arm or something might come in handy. Think how flexible I'd be with my guitar." Hmm, judging by the frown on her face, she'd seen his attempt to humor her feeble at best. Time to try another tactic.

Hunched over with his head underneath the sink to better assess the problem, he spoke again. "Not to worry, Tulip. Plumbing emergencies are my specialty. I'll need to get a few parts though."

"You can fix this?" she asked. Her voice was heavy with doubt.

"Hey, it's just a leaky pipe. I noticed the wiring on your garbage disposal looks like it's in bad shape. Might as well take care of that too."

He stood in time to see her eyes roll upward. Before she could say another word he cut in. "Is there a hardware store around here somewhere?"

"Yes. There's one in town. It's only a couple of miles away."

"Good. I'll take a trip over there while you mop up this water and get all that stuff out of the cabinet. I'll need some working space."

"Really, Brad, this is awfully nice of you, but I don't expect you to spend the entire afternoon taking care of my plumbing problems."

Now there was an idea with potential. And he fought to steady the tightening in his lower region. "You underestimate me. With any kind of luck I'll have this whole mess fixed an hour or so after I get back. We'll still have the rest of the day to do whatever. So if you'll just point me in the right direction, I'll head out."

"Straight down this road six blocks, and make a left. Go past two lights, and you'll run right into the place. Take my car," she said, throwing him a set of keys from a hook on the wall.

He hesitated, setting the keys back down on the counter. "I think I'll just borrow Kevin's bike again. I could use the exercise."

She gave him a puzzled look. "But what about your hand?"

"The hand is fine," he said, on his way out the door. And it was. Sooner or later she was going to figure out that he didn't have a driver's license. But when that day came, he could always chalk it up to the drawbacks of being on the road half his life. He'd say it expired while he was out of town, and he hadn't been home to renew it. In the meantime, bicycling was healthy—if you didn't have to pedal in ninety-degree weather. He'd be lucky to make the trip without getting heat stroke.

The temperature wasn't helping his nerves much either. Not that he didn't know what he was doing. As a teenager, he'd once spent an entire summer working for a plumber. Still, this wasn't Brad's arena, and he couldn't help wishing Tori weren't going to be standing over him to undermine his confidence. She wouldn't do it intentionally. It's just that he'd gone and made such a damn big deal out of his own expertise. It wouldn't be like he'd have a manual to fall back on if he forgot something. He could feel his jaw stiffening and his muscles growing tense. No, if that happened he'd just fall flat on his face, like he had so many times in school as a young boy.

Well, you're a man now, and this isn't school. What you're feeling is performance anxiety, the same kind you feel before every single show. Things always turn out okay. No reason to think this will be any different.

When he got back the door was unlocked, the floor was

dry, and the cabinet had been emptied and cleaned. "Anybody home?" he called out.

"Be there in a few minutes," Tori answered from the bedroom down the hall. "I'm changing my clothes."

"Take your time. I just need to know where the main shutoff valve is for the water."

"In the basement, next to the water meter."

He ran downstairs, but when he made it up to the kitchen again, she still hadn't appeared. Whether she showed up or not, it was time for him to get to work. His stage was set, and he inhaled with newfound self-confidence.

On his back with his head halfway under the sink, he began to remove the old water cock.

"Hi there," he heard Tori say a moment later. Her voice was smooth as liquid silk. Apparently she'd calmed down some. The faint scent of lilac soap was wafting up his nostrils, telling him she was freshly showered and in close proximity.

"Hi there yourself," he answered back, distracted by the sight his peripheral vision was hinting at. Was she wearing shorts? Might be worth it to scoot down a little to find out, he decided, shifting his body. While his hands were busy with the parts underneath the sink, his eyes were now drinking in a more ample view of the body parts in front of him. Yeah, those were definitely shorts, and they were hiding a lot less leg than the skirts and jeans she usually wore. As his gaze traveled up the long, lithe creamy expanse of her skin, he fought the urge to reach out and touch her. And that wasn't the only urge he was fighting. *Careful, Brad. You're a little sweaty to be thinking such thoughts.*

"So . . . what exactly has to be done, and how can I help? she asked.

"I guess you can grab this cock while I get to work on

the nipple," he answered without missing a beat, holding the defective part out to her.

"Excuse me?"

The elevation in her voice was jolting, and it was then that he realized how she might have interpreted his words. He slid out from under the sink and immediately banged his head in the process of sitting up. "Son of a . . . !" he started to curse, but caught himself.

"Are you all right, Brad?"

"Fine. I'm just fine," he answered rubbing his forehead and looking up at her. He couldn't help noticing the heightened color in her face. So she had misunderstood.

"Uh . . . this is the valve that shuts the water on and off from underneath the sink," he explained awkwardly, setting the part on the floor. "It's called a water cock."

"Really?"

Had he detected a flicker of a smile on the woman, or had it just been controlled skepticism? Once again he maneuvered his body beneath the sink and began to work. To his annoyance, the heavy ache of male hunger set in. All it had taken were just those few seconds he'd had to glance up at her. But they'd been enough to plant the image of Tori's seductive green eyes and that reticent blush of hers firmly in his head. Together they were a volatile combination.

He removed the old nipple, and a moment later he was back standing on the kitchen floor. "Now what did I do with that pipe thread compound?"

"Is this it?" Tori took the tube from the paper bag on the table.

"That's the stuff," Brad answered, unable to avert his gaze from the front of her T-shirt. He wondered whether she was wearing a bra. If she was, the fabric was much too thin to hide the hardened tips of her breasts.

"Knead before using. Apply to male thread," Tori read the directions on the label.

No problem. He'd like to do some extensive kneading before applying to his male . . .

"You say this goes on something called a nipple?" she questioned, jarring him from his fantasy. Her confusion was obvious.

"See, the pipe thread compound goes on the outside of the male nipple, and then it gets screwed into the T-shirt in the wall that goes to the sink."

"The T-shirt?"

His anxiety level rose a few more percentage points. "Uh . . . I meant the tee fitting." Was this a test of his technical capabilities or was this going to be a test of his physical endurance? Either way, he was in trouble.

Tori handed him the tube and watched as his fingers began to work with the contents. But his eyes were fixed on her. They were blazing cobalt now as he stared with such a piercing intensity her veins began to tingle. The tension in the room was thicker than the humidity in the air, but it wasn't about a leaking pipe. Her pulse quickened as she remembered his kiss and the touch of his hands on her body, and the feelings he'd stirred in her . . . feelings that had been dormant far too long.

Her inner voice screamed with turmoil. Nothing about this made sense. She wasn't the type of person to fall head over heels for a man in such a short amount of time, much less a rock star. They couldn't even agree on the necessity of an education. She was small-town family values; he was big-city playboy. Never mind that he'd tried to convince her otherwise. The signs were there, and if she had any sense left she'd pay heed.

He worked quickly, spreading the compound over the

part in his hand. He'd called it a nipple, and he handled it with such dexterity that she couldn't help wishing that his hands were on her own . . .

"Won't be long now," he assured her, flashing a smile that would thaw a glacier in the middle of Antarctica. Seconds later he was on his back, his head under the sink again.

Even through his jeans she could see how long and muscular his legs were. And as her eyes wandered farther up the length of his body, she noticed something else the heavy denim was unable to hide. A jolt of wanting shot through her.

But her feelings for Brad were more than physical. In just a few days he'd managed to tug at her heartstrings like no other man had, not even Jack. Despite Brad's apparent lack of regard for the system with all of its rules, he did seem to have a code by which he lived. And unless he'd done a complete snow job on her, he also had integrity.

"Once I get this cock screwed in tight . . ."

Be still my pounding heart! Was he muttering to her or to himself? Tori wondered.

"Gotta turn the water back on," he said, heading down to the basement.

Moments later he stood with her at the kitchen sink, washing his hands and splashing cold water on his face. They both crouched down on their knees to look at the pipe.

"You fixed it!"

"You're surprised," he said, facing her.

"No, grateful. You've saved me from a big plumbing bill, and I'm grateful to you, Brad."

"Considering that you rescued my career and my pride the other night with your doctoring skills, I wouldn't even begin to call us even. Besides, I still have to clean the P trap and fix the garbage disposal."

"Looks like we have a mutual admiration society here," Tori joked self-consciously.

"Looks like it might be a little more than that to me." His voice was husky now, and he was staring again, his blue eyes so magnetic she could hardly catch her breath. If he winked at her, it would be all over. She'd soften like putty in his fingers.

There was a moment of electric silence before his hands spanned her waist, drawing her against him. With feather-like sweetness his finger traced her lips, taunting her until she throbbed. When she could hold out no longer, she pushed his hand away to feel his kiss. His mouth was warm and demanding as a soft moan of pleasure came from her throat. Then he seized her in a deeper way, nudging his tongue against her lips until her mouth opened to meet him in sweet, lengthy exploration.

Still on their knees, Tori could feel the beat of his heart pounding against her chest as her breasts began to fill with need. Clinging to each other, their breathing grew labored.

Finally he broke the kiss, moving his hands slowly down her back under the waistband of her shorts and untucking her top. He slid his hand inside the front of her shirt and caressed her over the satin of her bra, making her tremble with hot desire.

He pulled her shirt up and over her head, gazing at her with a look of scorching intent. She knew that if she and Brad made love right now, she'd be saying goodbye—and that he'd break her heart when he left. But she could analyze this into oblivion. In truth, it was already too late. She was totally drawn to him, and if she denied the moment, she might never get another opportunity.

He didn't fumble when he reached for the front hook on her bra. A second later his hands and mouth were over her naked breasts. His tongue flickered in a slow, sensuous rhythm. When both nipples were marble hard, he sucked greedily, sending fire through every nerve in her body.

The time for deciding was over. Her response was shy but at the same time certain as she felt the force of his male length against her stomach. Her hands reached under his shirt, sliding first over the muscles of his back, and then on to circle the dark curling hair of his chest. A moment later his shirt was gone, and it was time for a bolder move. In quiet trepidation she unzipped his jeans and put her hand over his briefs to feel his arousal. With a sharp intake of breath he took her hand in his. "Ease up a minute, Tulip."

"What's wrong?"

"I just want to know that you're sure. Because I want you to feel as good about this as I do."

"I'm sure," she answered, nuzzling his chest with her face.

"What time does Kevin get home from school?"

Kevin, she thought with a start, checking her watch. She'd completely forgotten about her brother. "He's not due for another hour, but sometimes he comes home early."

Brad's look was fiercely possessive as he began to finger her auburn curls. "I want you. I want you bad. But we're not going to do this in five minutes of paranoiac frenzy, waiting for the kid to come home and find us here on the floor. I want this to be slow and easy . . . fast and hard . . . wonderful . . . thorough . . ."

"And totally unforgettable," she finished.

"What about your bedroom?"

"No good. That's the first place he'll look when he doesn't see me. On the other hand," she said, slyly placing her hand in its former position, "he usually doesn't disturb me when I'm in the patient area. I'll leave him a note, and we can go there. Besides it's much cooler."

"It won't be for long, woman. Not if you keep touching me like this."

Minutes later they were in one of the treatment rooms, both of them still bare from the waist up. "Take your shoes and socks off and lie down on your back," she coaxed, motioning him to the padded table. "I'll give you a massage."

"This isn't going to be more of that pressure-point therapy that feels so good when you stop?"

"Not at all," Tori answered, once again unzipping his jeans and guiding them toward the carpeted floor. "In fact, I hope this will feel so good you won't want me to stop."

Brad took everything off but his briefs and stationed himself on the table as she tuned the radio to some soft music. She wasn't Doctor Glenn, the chiropractor, when she reached for the massage oil and began to apply it to the spaces between his toes. She was a woman who was trying very hard to let go of her inhibitions, a woman filled with desire, and anxious to drive this man crazy with pleasure.

Gently she stroked each toe, up and down, as though she were touching another part of his anatomy. Judging by the look on his face and a certain noticeable swell, the friction was having a positive effect. In silent rhythm she went on to massage the arches of his feet and then up his calves and onto the insides of his upper legs.

"You do have a way with your hands," he whispered hoarsely.

"Why, thank you," she said. It was funny how he could make her feel shy, yet daring, all at the same time. "Turn over on your stomach."

When he did, she began to work her fingers down his

neck and onto his shoulders until she could feel the warmth escaping from his body.

"How about letting me make you feel as good as I do right now?" he offered.

"Oh, but I'm not finished." There was no way to still the wild beating of her heart as she slid her hands under his briefs and pulled them off. He was totally unclothed now, and her eyes were riveted in appreciation of the rear view. Bravely she positioned herself on top of him, straddling his thighs just below his buttocks. Then she laid her face against the small of his back and planted butterfly kisses just under the curve of his spine.

"Oh, Tulip," he groaned, arching his hip. His voice was thick with excitement.

She trailed her fingers in circles of delight over the backs of his knees, at the same time letting her long, curly hair spill over his rear in a tickling fashion.

"Whoa! That's it," he said, bolting upright, causing her to slide to the end of the table. "Unless you want this to be over before it starts."

"No, I'm in no rush," she said playfully.

He turned to look at her, his body radiating potency. The man was devilishly handsome.

"Good. Now it's your turn." A second later he stood in front of her, unzipping her shorts and gazing hotly at the pink, satin bikini pants she wore underneath. He put his hand inside them, and then his fingers found her most intimate spot. With great skill he moved within the liquid warmth, causing pulsing waves of pleasure to surge through her.

"Be on top of me, Brad," she pleaded. She shuddered as he straddled her belly, pressing up against her to feel his hardness.

"I want you!" she cried out. "But I don't have any . . ."

He silenced her with his kiss, then reached for his jeans to pull his wallet out of the back pocket. He slipped the condom on quickly and without comment. Standing before her, he stripped off the last of her clothes.

"You are so lovely," he gasped with heated passion, staring at her nakedness.

Whether she was or not, he made her believe it. That made the moment less awkward, caused her to feel a little less vulnerable.

She smiled up at him and then touched the side of his face with her own. He was clean-shaven with just enough skin texture to tickle her cheek. His hands began to work their magic, heating a path up and down her body. Tori molded to him, her breasts thrusting against his chest, his rigid length causing an aching need between her thighs.

"Be inside of me," she moaned.

Gently he eased her down onto the table, his body blanketing hers. She ran her palms over the hot flesh of his back, his waist, his hips, until he let out a tormented groan. Once again claiming her mouth, his tongue entwined with hers in urgent passion. Suddenly she felt the power of his smooth length within her—slow and easy at first, until her hunger flared with savage need. Then faster and harder. Tori arched toward him, and in sweet abandon she matched his thrusts with deep upward and downward motions. Wrapping her legs around him, she drew him closer to feel the explosions of physical ecstasy.

When the tiny convulsions turned into wild tremors, her breathing became a series of fragmented cries. She clung to him, wishing the rapture would never end. With a shuddering sigh, Brad called out her name, holding her tightly and rocking against her until they could move no more.

Chapter Nine

Someone was in the waiting area. As Tori lay naked and snuggled in Brad's arms, the sound of footsteps could be heard outside the treatment room. "I think Kevin is home!" she whispered in a panic.

"I thought you said he never comes back here when you're with patients," Brad muttered quietly.

"I said *usually*." She jumped off the table and reached for her clothes.

Both of them scrambled to get dressed, and when they were, Tori cautiously opened the door a crack to peer out. "Is that you, Kevin?"

"Yeah. You working on Brad?"

In a manner of speaking. "Uh huh."

"Good. I was hoping you'd both be here. I've got my interview typed up, and I thought you guys might want to take a look at it."

"I'll tell you what," Tori suggested. "We're not quite finished yet. Why don't you wait for us in the living room? We'll be out in a little while."

"Okay. I just wanted to make sure you two didn't leave before I got the chance to see you. I knew you had a light afternoon."

"That was close," she said, with a sigh of relief once Kevin had left.

"It was incredible!" Brad said, sweeping her into his arms.

Tori smiled. "I was referring to the situation with Kevin. Now that I've told him I'm adjusting you, that's just what I intend to do."

"You already have." He grinned with devilish innuendo.

"You wicked man," she teased, grabbing him by the hand. "Come on, we're changing treatment rooms. I need to play doctor for a while."

"Hmm, a game with definite potential."

"Brad Daniels! I'm serious." Though she didn't need a mirror to know that the look on her face didn't convey it. She couldn't help it that she was beaming from their lovemaking, and it was going to take all of her concentration to give him a proper treatment.

Kevin was in the kitchen by the time they'd finished.

"What happened in here?" he asked, checking out the plumbing parts and cabinet contents which were scattered around the room.

"Just a little flood. No big deal," Brad explained, looking at the clock. "But we are behind schedule, and I'm still not finished with the repair job."

"Sorry," Tori apologized.

Brad flashed her a knowing grin. "No you're not."

He was certainly right about that. Still, she shot him a look that demanded silence on the subject. Kevin wasn't stupid, and if they weren't careful he would figure things out. It might have been an old-fashioned concept, but Tori believed in setting a good example.

"Here you go," Kevin said, tossing the typed interview over to Brad.

"Why don't you give that to me. Brad doesn't have his glasses with him." Tori took the pages from Brad and started to read aloud. *"Lack of Formal Education Is No Detour to Rock Star's Fame!"* the headline began. Her reaction was immediate; a slow, silent bristle. Of all the lead-ins Kevin could have used, he'd chosen to emphasize the very subject that all three of them seemed to be at odds over. Even Brad looked ill at ease as he shifted around in his chair. Tori continued to read the interview, which covered the two weekend concerts, the selection of songs, and a few pertinent details about each band member. But the main focus on Brad seemed to center on the fact that he advocated the school of *"hands-on experience"* as his top educational choice for achieving success in the music industry. In fact, Kevin had cited a number of incidents to further illustrate that point.

As she read the last sentence she made a silent vow to bite her tongue before speaking. Apparently she wasn't the only one because for several awkward seconds there was silence. "It's written very professionally, Kevin," she finally said, with as much of a smile as she could force.

"You mean that?"

Choose your words cautiously. "Yes, I do. You did a great job."

"And . . . ?" he pressed.

Kevin knew her well enough to sense there was more on her mind. Brad had yet to say a word.

"And, nothing."

Kevin gave her a look that told her he knew better, though he let it go. "What did you think, Brad?" he questioned.

Brad stretched his legs out in front of the chair and with a slouch, crossed his arms over his chest. "Well, I'm no literary critic. My publicist usually takes care of things like this. But as far as I can tell, everything you quoted me on was accurate."

Kevin seemed satisfied with that answer. "Great. Then I'm off to Mark's. We've got a baseball game later, so I'll be kind of late."

"Not too late," Tori called, as he headed out the door. "It's a school night."

With tension thick in the air, the last thing Tori felt like discussing with Brad was the interview. Not while she still felt so euphoric from their lovemaking. It was a feeling that had wrapped itself around her like a comforter, and she wanted to savor it for as long as possible.

"So," she asked, without quite looking into his eyes, "is there anything I can do to help finish this job?"

"Not really. Tell you what though. I've been promising you dinner in a nice restaurant since we met, and it's yet to happen. Since it's my last night here, why don't we try for tonight?"

Her stomach tightened at the reminder. "I know a little place along the Fox River in St. Charles. The tables are kind of secluded, and I don't think anyone will bother us. How about if I make reservations for seven o'clock?"

"That should give me plenty of time to finish this project and get cleaned up," he said.

"All right. I guess I'll go get ready myself." With that she headed for her bedroom.

With a creeping uneasiness she sensed there had been an abrupt change in Brad's disposition. It wasn't so much what he'd said, it was what he hadn't said or done. He seemed to be going through the motions, but only moments earlier he'd been all hands and intimations. The nervous fluttering of self-doubt pricked at her as she rummaged through her closet for something to wear to dinner. Something for her last night with the man who now owned a large portion of her heart.

Brad finished repairing the garbage disposal and stared at the leftover mess. The reality of it all was a stark contrast to the fairy-tale afternoon he'd shared with Tori. He'd impressed her by fixing that leak. He could tell. Plus he'd saved her the high cost of a plumber. For a short while, he'd felt like a big shot, or at least worthy. And that had given him the confidence he'd needed to take it a step further. Making love with her had been everything he'd imagined. In fact, better. They'd made a connection; one that had brought out a touch of daring in her that had surprised him—overwhelmed him.

More than anything he'd wanted to follow her right into the bedroom for a repeat performance. The smell of her hair, the touch of her hands, the feel of her lips; he'd felt drugged with her essence, and he couldn't wait to just plain be with her . . . until the kid had shown up with that damned interview.

Now he was starting to wonder if this whole thing with Tori hadn't been a big mistake. He'd seen the look on her face when she'd read the quotes he'd given Kevin. Quotes that had been far too accurate, and not very impressive to the ear. If the interview had upset her, how would she react if she knew the whole truth about him? He wasn't sure he wanted to find out. He'd dealt with the humiliation of that kind of rejection before, and he was no glutton for punishment.

The problem was, he'd fallen for the woman. Big time. Maybe he was even starting to love her. *But not enough to trust her!* the voice blared. Not yet, anyway. *So, Coward, what are you gonna do? She already thinks you're a love 'em and leave 'em kind of guy.* Maybe she was right. Maybe that's exactly what he was. *Thanks for the memories, and now I think I'll pick up my marbles and go home.*

Could he do that without even giving her the chance to show him his fears were unfounded? In his heart he knew she wasn't the kind of woman who would have made casual love with him, especially not after the way she'd been burned herself.

But feelings could change with circumstances. Given the way she felt about education and all, would he ever measure up to her standards? No matter how high on the charts he climbed, no matter how many music awards he won, nothing he would ever do could match the importance of what she did—of the way she could heal people. The fact was he didn't know whether he'd ever be able to totally trust another human being again, especially not a woman. Yet he'd given Tori a measure of his trust. He'd opened up to her more than anyone else since the days of Leona Farnsworth. Because, whether he liked it or not, he was in this thing up to his elbows. He could end it all with his flight home to Massachusetts. But could he really do that to her? Could he do it to himself?

Tori stood in the ladies' room at the restaurant dabbing at tears, combing her hair and freshening her makeup. Dinner probably would have been delicious if she'd taken the opportunity to enjoy it. As it was she'd barely tasted the food, her mind focused on the fact that Brad would be leaving her in the morning.

She had, however, indulged in a glass of wine that would have been far better metabolized on a full stomach. The wine had made her weepy, though at least she'd waited until she was alone before she let herself cry. And now she had a nasty headache. *Doctor heal thyself!* She pressed at a few trigger points over her eyebrows, but there wasn't time to do much more. Brad would probably be sending a posse to look for her if she didn't get back to the table soon.

Neither of them had said much during dinner, and the conversation they'd had certainly wasn't of the caliber of two people who were connected; two people who, only hours earlier, had shared an experience of incredible lovemaking.

Why should she be surprised? She'd known all along that this was inevitable, but she'd made the decision to be with him anyway. So why couldn't she behave like a grownup, savor the memory, and suppress the loss?

Possibly she wasn't as sophisticated as a modern day woman needed to be in order to handle this sort of thing lightly. Because she was the type of person who only engaged in lovemaking with someone she truly loved.

Once again tears began to trickle down her cheeks. At this rate, she would never settle down enough to go out there and face the rest of the evening with Brad. She grabbed a tissue and blew her nose. *All right, Tori, that's it. Enough with the self-indulgence.* Maybe she couldn't have him for a lifetime, but she could try to make the best of the few hours they had left.

"You okay?" Brad questioned, pulling the chair out for her as she returned to their table.

"Fine," she lied. "Why do you ask?"

"You were gone for quite awhile."

"I'm sorry. I hadn't realized. I guess I was . . . primping. It's nice along the river front," she said, deliberately changing the subject. "Want to take a walk?"

"Sure."

The night was perfect; the wind calm and the temperature mild enough so that she didn't need a sweater. The soothing noise of the water emanated romance, and the moon provided just enough glow to light their path. So why didn't he take her hand? Only a few hours earlier they'd been so close. How could they have gotten this distanced? The frustration was enough to make her want to yell. But instead, she could feel herself struggling for composure again.

"You know . . ." she started.

"Hmm?" He was looking at her now, expecting her to finish her sentence.

"I want to tell you how much I enjoyed . . . our afternoon together." *There, was that evasive enough? Was she cool enough? It wasn't like she'd said, "I want you to know how very special our lovemaking was to me." No, she wouldn't use that word.*

"Well, uh, that goes for me too," he said. But he wasn't grinning or winking or flirting—or convincing.

"I also want you to know I'm not promiscuous!" she blurted. *Where had that come from?*

That seemed to get his attention because he stopped walking to face her squarely. "I never thought you were. Why would you feel you had to tell me that?"

"Because . . . Because when you think of it . . . if you think of it . . . I just want you to know that it meant something to me. That it wasn't just something I decided to do in the heat of the moment."

"What do you mean, 'if I think of it'? You don't think I'll remember what we did? What we shared? You don't think it meant something to me?" he asked, with an indignant look.

Tori looked down, biting hard on her lower lip, trying to control the emotions that kept threatening to spill out.

"I . . . guess I figure that there have been lots of women in your life." *And now I'm just one more number. Just like I swore to myself that I wouldn't be.*

"Let me tell you something, Tulip." His eyes flashed defensively. "I've been in this business since I was sixteen years old, and I'd be a liar to say that I've never taken advantage of the fringe benefits, especially when I was younger. It's a known fact that certain women like to hang around rock musicians. But even then I wasn't what you'd call indiscriminate.

"I'm not gonna tell you I've lived like a monk for the past several years. Though I'd like to think I've matured some since the days when I first took to the road. To be blunt, with the exclusion of this afternoon, it's been a hell of a long time since I've been intimate with anything but the palm of my hand." Tori could feel herself blushing at his admission, but he went right on talking. "With the AIDS crisis and all, I can't afford to be involved in one-night stands. Besides, I think it's wrong to use people."

"Does that mean you plan to stay in touch with me after you get on that plane tomorrow?" she challenged.

"Maybe I should be asking you that question. It almost sounds like you're telling me you were saying adios to me this afternoon. Is that what this is all about? Is this like a 'Dear John' talk?"

"That's ridiculous!" she flared angrily. "You know, you have a real talent for turning the tables on a person! You're the one who's leaving."

With his hands on her shoulders he stood towering over her. "On a plane! The interesting thing about airplanes is that they can fly round trip. In between times, there's the telephone. There are ways two people can communicate—if they want to." He moved his arms from her shoulders to wrap himself around her.

"I do want to," she said, surrendering to a crush of feelings as she leaned into him for support.

"So do I, Tulip! So do I," he admitted, in a voice husky with emotion.

He settled his mouth on hers, kissing her with a drugging sweetness. Then she felt a wild surge of pleasure as the pressure of his lips increased. She clung to him until finally, with a seeming reluctance, he pulled away. "Hello," he said, breaking into that familiar grin.

Not goodbye, but hello. It was a greeting that made her warm with a feeling of security, even if it was only for the moment.

"Hello yourself," she answered back, burying her face in his muscular chest.

"You know I'll have breaks in the tour. I want you to come visit me at my home on the Cape. You and Kevin. Summer's just around the corner, so he'll be on vacation from school."

"That would be wonderful, Brad. But I've never been gone from my patients longer than a couple of days. I'll have to try and figure something out so that I can get away."

"Damn straight you will. All work and no play make Tori a very exhausted doctor. That's no good for you or your patients."

"You have a point. I'm going to miss you terribly."

"I'll come back to Wheatfield as soon as I can. You'll see. We just need to give ourselves some time to work this thing out."

"Time to work it out." Well, that wasn't exactly a heartfelt promise of anything specific. But he hadn't closed the door either.

"I'd like that, Brad. I like knowing that you're still going to be in my life."

"What do you say we head back to your place then?" he suggested in a tone that was heavy with implication. He took her by the hand and led her toward the parking lot. "The night's not over yet."

"Good idea." Her pulse raced at the thought of making love with Brad again, and she could hardly wait to be in his arms. But the headache was making her queasy as well as emotional. If she were going to be in any kind of shape to participate in such intimacy, she might do well to close her eyes for the ride back. Maybe a short nap would make all the difference.

"You know what?" she said, reaching into her purse for her car keys. "I think you'd better drive us home. I'm not feeling too good, and if I close my eyes for a while it might help."

"Uh . . . sure," he said, sizing up the situation and taking the keys from her. "You're not getting the flu, are you?" In a nurturing gesture he felt her forehead, checking for fever. He'd realized during dinner that she'd been upset, and he'd noticed she hadn't eaten much.

"No, I don't think so. It's probably just a tension headache . . . partly caused by drinking that glass of wine on an empty stomach. That will teach me."

"Not to worry, Tulip. We'll have you home with an ice pack before you know it." After all, it wasn't like he'd never been behind the wheel of a car. He knew how to drive. Still, as he opened the passenger side for Tori to get in, he broke into a nervous sweat. He had no driver's license, and if anything went wrong . . . No, he wasn't going to sabotage himself with negative thinking. He would just be very careful, and everything would be fine.

"I'll get you to Route 64, and from there it will be a straight shot," she said. He adjusted the mirror, turned the key in the ignition, fumbled a bit looking for the headlights, and then pulled out of the spot onto the road. All systems were go, and it wasn't long before they made it to the main highway.

Tori settled back in her seat, and seconds later her eyes were closed. Out like a light she was. All the better he supposed. He'd leave the radio off. He needed to concentrate on the road, on the signs and their shapes. But he was all right. Once again, he reassured himself that everything was under control.

In about fifteen more minutes they'd be back at Tori's place. In fact, he even knew the street they had to turn on. He wouldn't wake her until he had her safe in her driveway.

And then he spotted it. Clearly. As he looked into the rearview mirror, he could see a squad car behind him. With a sharp intake of breath, his adrenaline level began to rise. His eyes flew to the speedometer. No, he wasn't going over the posted limit. *So what if there's a cop behind you. It doesn't mean he's following you.*

Brad glanced over at Tori. She was still asleep. *Turn, dammit! Turn!* Silently he willed the squad car to disappear down one of the side streets. There was a yellow light up ahead, and he slowed down. Why was it that he and the squad were the only two cars on the road? The light turned red, and he came to a complete stop. The longest light in history, he decided, as he drummed his fingers impatiently over the steering wheel. After an interminable amount of time, the light was finally green.

He stepped on the accelerator, and the cherry, rotating beacon of light made him check the rearview mirror again. "No," he said, and muttered an oath. A knot of fear formed in his stomach, and his heart felt like it was lodged in his throat. *It can't be! What'd I do?* With another deep breath he pulled off to the shoulder of the road and parked under a street light.

"Are we home?" Tori murmured.

"Stay put," he said, as he got out to talk to the officer who was stationed behind him.

"Sir, I'll have to ask you to get back in your car," the official ordered.

Brad put his empty hands in front of him. "Please, could we talk out here? I don't want my date getting upset."

The older man looked like he was going to say no, but as he stepped out of the squad car, he seemed to have a change of heart. "Do you know your taillight is out?"

"Oh. No, I didn't. The car belongs to my date, but I'll certainly see to it that it gets fixed."

"I'll need to see your driver's license, Sir."

Right. Instantly his mouth went bone dry, and he could barely get the words out. *Throw yourself at his mercy, and pray he has a heart.* "I don't have a license."

"You mean you don't have it with you? Or do you mean that it expired?"

"No, Officer. I'm saying that I don't have a license at all. And it would mean a whole lot to me if my date didn't have to find out about this."

The officer rolled his eyes upward. "You understand that it's illegal to drive without a license?"

"I know, and I didn't mean to break the law. But my date wasn't feeling well, and she asked me to drive. We haven't known each other too long, and this won't score many points with her, if you know what I mean. So do you think we could keep this our little secret, Man? Please!" he heard himself beg.

"Do you have any identification with you?"

"Yes. Yes, I do," Brad said, pulling out a card with his picture and some other pertinent information.

The officer looked at the card and then again at Brad. "You know, you look kind of familiar. Like one of those rock and roll poster people my daughter's got hanging in her room."

Great. All he needed now was some bad press to go along with this situation. "Uh . . . well they say everyone has a twin somewhere."

Brad watched apprehensively as the older man took out a pad of forms and began writing. "I'm just going to give you a warning ticket about the taillight. As long as you promise to get it fixed," he added.

Brad let out a sigh of relief. "Thank you, Sir."

"Look, son," the officer continued, "I'm afraid I can't let this other thing go. I'm going to have to run you into the station."

"You're arresting me?" he asked, breaking into another sweat. He glanced over at Tori, who was anxiously peering out the window.

"Sorry. I'll try and make this as painless as possible, but I have to do my job."

Within minutes Brad was handcuffed and seat-belted into the back of the squad car. He hadn't even had the chance to say anything to Tori. Not that he knew what that would be. As he sat there, the officer went over and spoke to her. Brad watched as she took something out of the glove compartment, and then she got behind the wheel of her car.

"Your girlfriend is going to follow us down to the station," the officer explained, as he got back into the vehicle. "I told her that you don't have your driver's license, and that we have to run a check on you. I'll leave any further explanations up to you."

"I appreciate that," Brad said. Not that it could begin to erase the humiliation he was feeling right now.

The ride to the station seemed to take forever, though in reality it was probably only about a mile away. On the drive over, scenes from Brad's early childhood kept on flashing before him; images of an embarrassed school boy at the blackboard in front of the whole class, unable to complete the work that was expected of him, sounds of laughter as the kids made fun of him, taunting him for his stupidity.

"Are you all right?" Tori said, as she jumped out of her car the moment they reached the station. She looked even more upset than he was.

"Fine, Tulip," he reassured her. "I'm sure we'll be on our way in a little while."

But the little while turned into quite a while. It seemed that even in small towns they had their share of unlawful activity, and things at the station were busy. Brad phoned his attorney, who spoke to the officer in charge. But by the time they completed the paperwork and Brad posted bond, it was well after midnight.

True to his word, the officer had carefully avoided letting Tori know exactly why Brad had been arrested. In fact, she'd spent the entire time waiting for him in the lobby. But for the small amount of face it had saved him, he still felt like a criminal. Not only that, he'd been given a court date and would have to appear back here in about a month. He wasn't even sure yet how that was going to affect his tour dates.

"Sorry about all this," Brad apologized, as he and Tori got into her car. He took his seat on the passenger side.

"You're sorry! I'm the one who's sorry. I knew about

that stupid taillight, and I forgot to have it replaced. Then I had to go insist that you drive. I couldn't feel worse about this, Brad. And on your last night here. It's all my fault!"

"Not quite," he soothed, rubbing her shoulder. "I'm the one who let my license expire. One of the consequences of being on the road so much, I guess."

"Well, it's been some night for both of us," she said, pulling back out onto the road. They drove the rest of the way home in relative silence.

Chapter Ten

One thing was certain. Brad needed some time alone. As they walked into the living room, he checked his watch. "How's your headache?" he asked Tori.

"Still there. But I'll bet with a little distraction, I might be able to get my mind off of it." Her eyes looked hopeful, like she was thinking that he was planning on some way to make it better.

But he had a headache of his own. And if he'd ever felt more inferior than at this moment, he couldn't think of when it was.

"Let's get some rest, Tulip," he said, giving her a kiss on her forehead. "It's late, and I'm really beat."

"Sleep well," she said, watching as he headed toward the guestroom.

He shut the door tight behind him and started to take off his shirt and pants. That look of rejection on her face told him he'd hurt her, but right now there wasn't anything he could do about it.

He felt beat all right. Downright defeated. His whole life had been a damned roller-coaster ride. Every time he started to soar, he'd be sure to come crashing down. His insides hurt from the motion of it all.

Worse yet, now he'd begun to drag Tori along on the ride with him. He'd been running hot and cold with all of his hang-ups and insecurities since he'd met her. He'd gotten her hopes up tonight, as if they might have a chance at some kind of future together—because he thought they might. Now again, he had doubts. He threw his clothes on the chair and climbed into bed. He wasn't sure anymore about anything. Except that he was tired. Real tired.

It was six o'clock in the morning; a disagreeable time to be phoning anyone. But it was an hour later in New York, and that's where Brad could reach Mike Sweeney. Mike was his best friend. He was the only person who really understood Brad's situation, and he would know what to do. Besides, they had business to discuss.

Luckily there was a phone in Tori's spare bedroom. A sleepy voice at the other end answered. But Mike was one of those guys who could open his eyes in the morning and actually be awake. Within minutes Brad explained what had been happening, starting with the fact that he'd been arrested.

Mike had been listening quietly, and Brad knew that meant he was thinking. "What about publicity?" Mike finally asked. "The tabloids will have a field day if they get wind of this—not to mention the papers."

"The cop who handled everything was the fatherly type," Brad explained. "Luckily I was in a small town that doesn't have its own newspaper."

"Yeah, but the major papers always call around for the police reports."

"The officer implied that he wasn't in the business of deciding what was newsworthy and what wasn't. He seemed like a really nice guy. We'll just have to keep our fingers crossed."

"You know, if that's the case," Mike said, "when you stop to consider it, nothing's really changed all that much since last week, except your feelings for Tori."

"I got arrested last night!" Brad whispered loudly. "That's a first!"

"Yeah. But not for some major criminal offense. It's not even like you screwed up the driving. You did fine. You didn't know she had a missing taillight, and she still doesn't know you don't have a license. If you want my advice, ride it out until you're ready to trust her with the rest of your story. Kiss off last night as a streak of bad luck, and kiss her good morning like nothing happened. And pray the press doesn't get wind of it."

"Are you trying to cheer me up here—or make me paranoid?"

"Well . . . uh."

"It's not your style to hem and haw, Mike. What's goin' on that I don't know about?"

"I just want you to watch your back."

"No, there's more to it than that. The whole thing smacks of Leona. What the hell is she up to now?"

"Nothing. Not that I know of anyway. But I found out yesterday that her mother took a fall. She hit her head, and they say it could be serious. She was transferred to the hospital. You know what that means."

"Josie fell? She's gonna make it, isn't she?"

"I don't know. I'm not a doctor. But I heard Leona's taking this whole thing real bad. When she gets stressed, she gets vicious and demanding. I wouldn't be surprised if you hear from her in the next day or so."

"She already called me last Sunday. Didn't take her long

to figure out I was staying here. But she didn't say anything about her mother. She just dished out some line of crap about how she was worried about me and all."

"Yeah, well if you want my opinion, I wouldn't dismiss it as bogus information. Personally I think the woman's still fantasizing about another roll in the hay with you."

Brad snickered. "Ain't it a shame. It'll be snowing in Tahiti before I rise to that occasion."

"All the same, be careful."

"Always. Say, what hospital did they take Josie to?"

"Oh, man, I hope you're not entertaining any ideas about paying her a visit. You'd only be asking for trouble."

"That was the one good thing that came out of my connection with Leona. Josie treated me as if I were her own son. It tore me up when her MS got so bad she had to move to the nursing home. You know her mind is still as sharp as a single-edge blade. It's her body that won't cooperate."

"I know. But if the psycho bitch catches you hanging out with her mom, she's only going to get more ideas. You don't need that right now, especially not with everything else that's going on with the tour and with your new lady. You've got your hands full."

"Don't worry," Brad assured him. "I've got a plane to catch today, and I'm on a pretty tight schedule." Even so, Brad made Mike tell him the name of the hospital, and they talked business for a while longer.

"Remember what I said about you and Tori," Mike urged in closing. "Don't let your mind dwell on the bad stuff. Get past this or it will get you down to a place you don't want to be—again."

"I hear you," Brad said. "And Mike?"

"Yeah?"

"Thanks, Man."

Brad hung up the phone, and then dialed information for the phone number of the Chicago hospital and the nearest florist. Later, when the flower shop opened, he would send Josie a bouquet of two dozen roses in an assortment of her favorite colors.

The next call was to his accountant. "I want you to arrange for all of Josie's hospital bills to be sent to me," Brad ordered.

That taken care of, he threw on his jeans and headed to the bathroom for a quick shower. When he finished, he walked out into the kitchen.

Kevin was already at the table, pouring milk over his cereal. "Hey," he said. "Last day here, huh?"

"For a while," Brad answered.

"Tori's planning on riding with you to the airport, you know. Her first patient won't be here till one o'clock."

"Where is she?"

"Probably in the office setting up charts for later. I asked her if I could skip school to go along, but of course, she said no."

Brad smiled. "This isn't the last time you're gonna see me, Kevin. I told Tori that I want the two of you to come out to my summer home on the Cape for a visit."

"Wow! You mean that?"

"I wouldn't have said it if I didn't."

"Wow!" he said again. "That would be great. She actually agreed to take a vacation?"

"She did," Tori confirmed, her sudden appearance a surprise. "As soon as she can figure out who's going to take care of her patients while she's away."

She was all dressed and ready to go, making Brad wonder whether she'd been awake half the night too.

"Mornin', Tulip. How long have you been standing there?" he asked.

"Long enough to realize that Kevin is going to miss his bus if he doesn't get a move on," she said.

"Sure you won't change your mind about letting me come to the airport with you?" he pleaded.

Tori's green eyes flared.

"Only if you'll let me tag along the next time you have a hot date," Brad teased, in an effort to avoid another school-related confrontation between Tori and the kid.

"Fine. I get the message," Kevin said, choking down one last spoonful of cereal and jumping up from the kitchen table. He walked up to Brad, and the two shook hands. "Brad, it's been a slice. I won't forget it."

"I won't give you the chance to. I told you, I'll be around," Brad assured him.

With that, Kevin headed toward the door. "I'll send you a copy of the interview when it's published," he called, on his way out.

Finally, Tori and Brad were alone. "Hi there," he said, with a grin.

"Are you upset with me over last night?" she asked.

He swept her into his arms and planted little butterfly kisses all down her neck. "Does that answer your question?"

"Nicely," she said with a smile. "You know I could drive you to the airport. We don't have to go in a limo."

"Not a good idea, Tulip. It's one thing to hide out in a small town for a few days in secluded restaurants and bike paths in the woods. But I can't chance going to a busy place like O'Hare without some security alongside me. People can get real crazy. You've seen it first hand."

"I understand," Tori said.

But the look on her face told him she probably didn't. Not fully anyway.

"When are they coming?"

"We still have a couple of hours," he said, glancing at the clock on the wall.

"Time enough for one last treatment."

"My hand is fine," he assured her. "Maybe we could skip the treatment and do something a little more creative—and a lot more fun."

"If we manage our time well," she said with a crinkle of her eye, "I'll bet we can fit business and pleasure into the schedule."

A while later Tori had finished giving him his last adjustment. "I think that should take care of the problem," she said, as Brad got up from the treatment table. "Of course, if you have any more trouble, you could always fly out here for an emergency visit." She was fighting to keep the yearning out of her voice.

"That's right, I can," he emphasized, tilting her chin upward with his fingers. "So don't be acting like this is the last time we're gonna see each other."

Bending down, he pressed his lips to hers in a kiss that started out gentle, like the early-morning breeze of spring. She wrapped her arms around his waist and moved against him until their mouths were locked in contact that was full of passion and need.

His fingers moved to the buttons on her silk blouse, and he began to create an opening large enough for the expanse of his hand. Her breasts were aching with arousal as he traced the satiny fabric of her bra.

"You understand that we're all alone in the house," she said coyly, "and that Kevin will be at school for several more hours."

Brad grinned. "So what does that mean?"

"It means that my bed is a lot more comfortable than this treatment table."

"Is that right?" Brad took her by the hand and began to lead her out of the office area.

But as they got to the waiting room they realized someone was knocking at the door. Brad shot her a look of half-startled wariness. "Pretend you don't hear it," he said in a pleading whisper.

"I can't do that!" she whispered back. "It might be one of my patients."

"That's what I'm afraid of," he said, tightening his grip on her hand.

"Brad, please." Reluctantly she broke from his hold and quickly began buttoning her blouse. When she was finished she opened the office door to the outside.

"Mr. Lemont!" she exclaimed, at the appearance of one of her regular patients. His fists were clenched, there was tension in his breathing, and he was leaning on his wife for support. One hip looked obviously higher than the other, and the expression on his face told Tori that he was in serious pain.

"I told him not to try to carry that air conditioner up from the basement by himself," Mrs. Lemont explained, before Tori could even ask what happened. "But the man is so darned stubborn!"

"Let's get you into a treatment room," Tori said, taking him by his other arm to offer support.

"My leg hurts real bad," he said. "Pain goes all the way from my hip down to my toes—like I got needles in me.

"You just try and relax," she soothed. "The sooner I can figure out what the problem is, the sooner we can start to alleviate your pain."

But things were not happening quickly. The poor man was barely able to move. By the time she'd maneuvered him under the X-ray machine and had done the initial exam, almost an hour had passed. She hadn't even begun treatment when she realized that she'd forgotten about Brad. "You just sit here for a little bit now," she instructed, as she propped Mr. Lemont up with an ice pack. "I'll be back in a few minutes."

She went racing out of the office and into her living room, where Brad sat on the sofa quietly strumming his guitar. "I'm so sorry," she apologized. "This isn't at all the way I'd planned to spend the morning."

"Well, you know what they say about the best laid plans," Brad quipped, his tone caustic enough to tell her he was upset. "Is your patient gone?"

"No, I'm afraid he's going to be around for a while."

Brad looked at his watch. "The limo should be here any minute."

Tori's adrenaline surged, and her stomach knotted. "You're leaving, and I'm not even going to be able to ride to the airport with you."

"No, I guess you're not," he agreed. She watched his jaw tense while that vein in his neck stood out.

No sooner had he said the words than Tori looked out the window. The limo was pulling into the driveway. She could feel a heaviness in her chest as he laid his guitar in its case and locked it. Then he stood.

"I miss you, and you're not even gone yet." She bit down on her lower lip in hope that the action would keep her from bursting into tears.

The men got out of the car, and one of them walked toward the front door. "Got a pencil and paper?" Brad asked.

Tori opened the drawer of the nearby end table to get

what he'd requested. The doorbell rang. "Let them wait a minute," he said, quickly writing. "This is my home phone number. If you need to reach me—if you ever want to reach me, just call. Leave a message if I'm not home. I check my machine every day."

He handed her the piece of paper, and she clutched it to her chest. The bell rang again, making her jump. She started for the door, but he took her by the hand and pulled her back. He wrapped his arms around her and kissed her with a lingering sweetness. Desire, sadness, hope, confusion; she was a flood of emotions. There was a loud knock at the door, and Brad let go of her.

One last look into those sapphire eyes, his penetrating gaze. And then he would be gone. She was determined not to cry. "Have a safe trip back," she said softly. She could not bring herself to say goodbye.

"See you later, Tulip. I'll call you soon."

A moment later she stood by the window, tears streaming down her face, as she watched him get into the limo and drive away. He had taken a piece of her heart right along with him.

With a start she realized she wasn't the only one who was hurting. She reached for a tissue and willed herself to gain control. This was no time to be falling apart, not when poor Mr. Lemont needed her so badly.

Much later that night, Tori closed the door after her last patient. She hadn't taken a break all day, not even to eat. There hadn't been time. She hadn't made time. It had been easier to stay busy than to give herself even two minutes to think about Brad—about the fact that he was really gone. And that maybe—just maybe—she might never see him again.

Oh, he'd said all the right things, and she was sure he'd meant them. But she knew the best intentions could go by the wayside, especially when they were complicated by matters people couldn't control. Like distance. *Face it, Tori. The man travels all around the world for a living. When is he going to make time to see you?*

Tori walked into the kitchen, only to find a note from Kevin that said he was tired and had gone to bed. That was exactly where she ought to be herself. She was exhausted from too many nights with too little sleep. But her mind refused to shut down. Unless she could find some way to quiet her thoughts, she doubted that this evening would be any more restful for her than the previous nights.

Alone in the darkened stillness of the hour, her focus was totally on Brad. He was probably at his home in Worcester, and she considered calling him—just to see if he'd made the trip all right—or to ask how his hand was doing. He had, after all, given her his personal number. But it was nearly eleven o'clock there. Not a very respectable hour for her to be phoning. Especially since he obviously hadn't thought to phone her.

Well, he was probably sound asleep. He'd probably eaten too. Something she needed to do, she thought, as she foraged through the refrigerator for some food. There were still a few eggs left. She'd cook those and make toast. Then she'd crawl into bed. But not before taking out Brad's phone number and staring at it for a full ten minutes, and then deciding—absolutely—not to dial it. Not tonight anyway.

Brad hung up the phone for about the twentieth time since the minute he'd returned home. It seemed all hell had broken loose while he'd been away, and now he was scrambling to get things back on track. The biggest problem was that Tom Mallone, the band's bass player, had cut his finger, and he was going to be out of commission. Luckily the injury wasn't too serious, but it had been tough trying to find someone skillful enough to take Tom's place for a couple of weeks. Now that they had, they were going to have to rehearse every spare chance they got. The band had to be ready by Thursday night, and it was already Tuesday. That meant Brad would be out the door by five o'clock the following morning.

On top of it, the band's manager had been called out of town on an emergency, so Brad had taken on even more responsibility. But those were the breaks, and Brad was used to the stress of the business.

What he wasn't used to was the emotional flip-flop he'd been on ever since he'd left Tori. Couldn't get the woman out of his mind, even when he was supposed to be concentrating on all the problems at hand. He'd wanted to call her the minute he'd left her side. He'd almost called her from the plane. But the voice had stopped him from calling during her office hours. *She's busy doing important work, helping sick people.*

He looked at his watch, it was late. *Should I call now? What if she's sleeping? What if she's not?* Just when he'd made up his mind to dial her number, his phone rang again.

"Bradley, Darling," the unwelcome caller purred. His heart sank, and so did he, right into a nearby chair.

"What is it, Leona? It's not your mom, is it? She's not worse, is she?" His throat tightened at the afterthought.

"Mama's better, Bradley. The doctors were concerned that she might have a concussion, but it turns out she doesn't. They're putting her on some new medication, and when they figure out the right dose, they'll be sending her back to the care facility. Maybe in a couple of days or so."

"That's good," he said, with a genuine feeling of relief. "I was worried about her."

"I know that," Leona said. "It was so terribly sweet of you to send her those beautiful roses. Mama adores roses, and she adores you."

"Please give her my best," Brad said.

"Why, Bradley, you can do that yourself, this very minute. I'm standing right next to Mama's hospital bed, and she can't wait to thank you."

Before he could respond, he heard the faint, sketchy whisper of Josie's voice. It was a voice that had been badly tampered with, due to the effects of her illness; a sound that required great patience to comprehend. But he had enough respect for this lady to want to take the time to understand what she was trying so desperately to say to him.

By the time Leona came back on the line, nearly forty-five minutes had passed. "Thank you, Darling, for being so kind to Mama," she said.

"It's easy, Leona. She's a great lady." Josie was a woman who'd accepted, with dignity and grace, the cross she'd been handed. And she'd still managed to retain her sense of motherhood and personhood, even though her husband had abandoned his family when Leona was a small child. Hard to believe Leona was her daughter. Yet he had to admit, to Leona's credit, she did seem to have genuine compassion for her mother's circumstances.

"Well, Bradley," she whispered in a tone that made him think she was cupping the phone to offer privacy from Josie's ears, "once Mama gets out of the hospital, I'd really like to come visit you."

"Leona, I'm on tour. I'm busy, and there's no reason for

you and I to be seeing each other. My accountant can handle whatever business we have in common."

"I miss you," she said, in a voice that sounded pleading enough to rankle him.

"Well the feeling's not mutual! I'm tired, and I'm not in a good mood. I've got an early day tomorrow, so if you don't mind, I'll just buzz off now."

With that he set down the phone. Hanging up on Leona was getting to be a habit. Sooner or later he figured she'd find a way to get even. Though maybe when she learned he was footing her mother's hospital bill, she'd back off for awhile. But knowing Leona, probably not.

Brad checked the time again. It was really late now, and he was pissed off. Any way you cut it, it wasn't a good time to be phoning Tori. He'd have to put that off until morning.

Tori woke the following day to a thunderous bang. The rain was coming down in torrents, and she'd already had her first patient cancellation. She suspected it wouldn't be the last. An early morning report stated that there were no signs of the storm letting up any time soon.

The weather was a perfect match for her mood. Kevin had already left for school. She poured herself a cup of hot tea and took out the piece of paper with Brad's phone number. She wanted to hear his voice—needed to hear it. She was so nervous her hands were shaking, and her heart was pounding. Still, she dialed (508) 555-1746. *Answer, she willed silently.* But the next thing she heard was the sound of a recorded message telling her that the number she'd called was not in service.

You dialed wrong, she told herself, in an attempt to override the feeling of panic that had set in. Once again she tried, this time with a slow and deliberate preciseness. And once again she heard the same message. With a deep breath she set the handset in its base and took a swallow of her tea.

So, she'd been right all along. He was gone and out of her life. He hadn't even had the nerve to tell her the truth. Instead he'd given her a fake phone number along with some false hope. Much easier than having her make a scene over his departure the day before, she supposed he'd figured. But the fact was that nothing about this was easy, and she gulped hard as hot tears ran down her cheeks.

The loud crackle of thunder and the bolt of lightning she saw from the window jarred her, making her aware that her next patient would be arriving soon. She needed to get a hold on her emotions.

Somehow she got through the rest of the work day, though it seemed like it might never end, with patients streaming in intermittently and others not bothering to show up or to call. That was unusual. People were normally more considerate. But Tori was beyond getting upset about that. She had other things on her mind.

Kevin hadn't come home from school until nearly dinnertime. The buses had been running late because of the weather. "Have you heard from Brad?" he asked, the moment he came through the doorway.

"No," was all she said.

Even Kevin looked disappointed, but he made no comment. Instead he picked up the phone to make a call. "Maybe this is why," he said, without even dialing.

"Why what? What are you talking about?"

"The phone is dead. There's no dial tone. I'll bet the office phone is dead too. The lines must be down because of the storm."

"No wonder my patients weren't calling to cancel their appointments."

"Maybe Brad tried and couldn't get through either," Kevin suggested.

For a moment Tori's heart soared. She wanted to believe that. But then she remembered about the phone number he'd given her. "Time will tell," was all she said.

Chapter Eleven

Thursday morning at seven o'clock the ring of the telephone woke Tori out of a long overdue sleep. "Tulip, is that you?" she heard a voice say.

"Brad?" Instantly she was alert and sitting up in bed.

"I know it's early," he apologized. "But I hoped you'd be up already, and I knew if I didn't call you now I might not get another chance, at least not anytime soon. I've got rehearsals all day, and a concert tonight. Tom cut his finger, so we're playing with a different bass player for a while."

Brad was talking so fast she could hardly keep up with what he was saying. "Is he going to be all right?"

"He'll be fine in a few weeks. It's just that things have been crazy since I got back."

"I'm glad you called," she said. "When I didn't hear from you . . ."

"I tried to phone you at least ten times yesterday, but your lines were down. I got kind of worried. Are you and Kevin okay? I heard about the storm."

He'd been worried about her. Suddenly her mood was buoyant. "We're fine," she said. "The rain has finally stopped. In fact, I suspect the sun is going to come up real soon."

"I miss you, Tulip."

"I miss you, Brad," she said at exactly the same time.

They both laughed, and suddenly they were conversing with the exuberance of two teenagers. "You first," Brad insisted.

"I was just going to ask how your hand is doing?"

"Couldn't be better," he said, "and I've been playing my guitar non-stop."

"I'm so glad. I tried to call you, but the number you gave me isn't in service." She reached for the piece of paper he'd given her, which was sitting on top of the nightstand.

"That can't be. What number were you dialing?"

"(508) 555-1746."

"Jeez! I'm sorry. That last part is supposed to read 1764. I have a habit of inverting my numbers, especially when I'm in a hurry."

She didn't need a mirror to know her smile was as wide as her face. "Well now that I have the right information, I'll have to test it out soon."

"You'd better," he said, in a voice that was deep and sensual. "I have to hang up now. Believe it or not we've already started to rehearse this morning. We took a short break, but the guys are waiting for me."

"Knock 'em dead tonight," she said.

"I'll give it my best shot, Tulip. Talk to you soon."

Tori jumped out of bed, singing all the way to the shower. She had energy to spare, and all was right with the world.

Much later that afternoon the office phone rang. "Doctor Glenn speaking," Tori answered. "How can I help you?"

"Tori? Is this Tori?" The female voice was hesitant, but there was a familiar-sounding quality about it.

"Yes, who is this, please?"

"This is Leona Farnsworth. We met during Brad's last concert. I played guitar with the band that night."

"Oh, right," Tori acknowledged with a slight quickening of her pulse. She had an uneasy feeling about this call. "I remember you."

"Well . . ." Leona said, her breathing audible and punctuated with effort, "I understand you're a chiropractor . . . a very good chiropractor."

"I like to think so," Tori responded. "But I'd be curious to know who told you as much."

"I'm a journalist. Word gets around."

Obviously the woman wasn't going to reveal her source of information.

"In any case, that's not the issue. The problem at hand is that I have a headache . . . a really severe headache. And it's not my first."

"I see. Do you get them frequently?"

"Actually it's something that just started in the last six months or so. But they seem to be occurring more often as time goes on, sometimes twice a month."

"Are they ever in line with your menstrual cycle?" Tori questioned.

"I thought of that too. But no, they don't seem to correlate."

"Do you feel it's a migraine?"

"I'm not sure. I was hoping you could tell me." Her voice exuded suffering and had become more pleading. "I'd like to make an appointment with you, since the pain is really bad right now. Do you take new patients, and do you see people on an emergency basis?"

Hmm. That would mean Leona Farnsworth would have to come over to Tori's office. Was that a good idea? "Yes on both counts, but tell me, Leona, where do you live?"

"Oak Park."

"That's quite a distance from here. Are you sure you want to start up with a doctor that far away? At this time of day, it might take you an hour or more to get here. Maybe it would be a better idea to set you up with one of my colleagues. There are a number of good chiropractors out your way."

"No, if it's all right with you, I'd really like you to take a look at me."

Somehow her answer came as no surprise. *Watch your back with that woman,* Sherry's warning screamed loudly. Still Tori could not refuse to help a person who was in genuine need of her services. Though at this point it was impossible to tell if that was the case. "Do you have someone to get you here, or do you feel you're well enough to drive yourself?"

"I'm used to working and driving around in pain, and I'd be grateful if you could see me," Leona said.

"Why don't you start out now. By the time you get here I should be finished with all of my scheduled patients for the day. Do you need directions?"

"No, that won't be necessary. I'll see you soon."

No directions? So Leona already knew where Tori lived and worked. Tori found that a bit unnerving. "All right then, I'll be expecting you." With that she hung up the phone.

An hour and a half later Tori walked into the waiting room. There, with Kevin, sat Leona Farnsworth. The two of them were talking like it was old home week, and Leona didn't look like a woman who was suffering great pain.

"Tori," Kevin said, his face beaming with approval.

"Look who's here. Pretty soon you'll be taking care of Brad's whole band."

"Let's hope that won't be necessary," Tori said with a forced smile.

Leona stiffened in her chair and rubbed her forehead. It was still too early to tell if the gesture was for real or an added touch for Tori's benefit.

"Leona, how are you feeling?" Tori asked.

"Actually, the pain is very bad right now. I'm hoping you can do something to alleviate it."

Tori handed her a medical questionnaire. "I'm sure I can do something to improve the situation, but I'll need you to fill this out before we begin."

"She's already been answering a bunch of my questions," Kevin piped up. "Do you realize she's a musician and a writer?" Clearly her brother was impressed with Leona's credentials. "It's too bad I've already finished the interview with Brad. She's been giving me some great tips!"

"That's nice, Kevin. I'm sure you can use the information on your next writing project. Though, for the time being, let's not lose sight of the fact that Ms. Farnsworth is here because she's in pain."

Leona looked at him and flashed him a flirtatious smile. "I really appreciate all your enthusiasm, Kevin. I'll be sure to tell Bradley we spoke. But your sister is right. I am in need of some relief for this awful headache. So if you'll excuse me, I'd like to get started."

A short time after Leona had filled out the paperwork, she sat with Tori in one of the treatment rooms. After a lengthy examination and a number of additional questions, Tori concluded that Leona's problem was, for the most part, a tension headache and not a migraine. Not that tension headaches weren't painful. Sometimes they could be every bit as distressing as a migraine, especially when neck and shoulder muscles were involved.

However, in Leona's case, Tori couldn't be sure how much of this pain was exaggerated and how much was real. The only thing she could do was treat the woman as she would any other patient—in a caring and thorough way.

"We'll start with some trigger-point therapy," Tori explained, positioning Leona on her back on the treatment table. Tori stood behind Leona, and with her index finger she began to press upward against the edge of the bony eye socket.

"Ouch!"

"I'm sorry that hurts, but it means we're in the right spot, so if you can bear with me . . ."

"I think you'll find I'm pretty stoic," Leona said. "Just do whatever you have to do."

Tori continued to circle both eyes, all the while Leona was running off at the mouth.

"You know, Kevin is truly a love," she said, much to Tori's surprise. "I understand he's quite a musician in his own right. You really do have a responsibility to encourage that talent."

Tori stiffened at the unwelcome advice. "Did Brad tell you that?" *Please let the answer be no.*

"Oh, heavens no! I could see it for myself, and in talking with him I can tell he's a very special young man."

Exactly how much had Kevin told the woman that she could be drawing such conclusions in the short time she'd been speaking to him? "I didn't realize you'd been in the waiting room that long."

"Darling, it doesn't take a rocket scientist to see potential."

Careful, Tori. Remember, you're a professional. But she

could feel herself bristling, and if she wasn't cautious, she was going to start exercising more pressure than necessary in order to help this woman. "Yes, Kevin is very special," she agreed. "He has aptitude in a number of different areas." *Let that be enough said on the subject.*

"So how long have you known my Bradley?" Leona asked, in an abrupt shift of gears.

Her Bradley? The implication could hardly be missed. "Long enough to realize that he's incredibly talented, and that I really enjoy his music," Tori answered. *Had she been evasive and nonreactive enough?* "How about you?"

"Well, of course, Bradley and I have been quite close for a very long time," she emphasized.

How close? Had they been lovers? Were they still in a relationship? Could Brad possibly have made love to Tori and still be involved with Leona? Tori's adrenaline was on the rise, and she could feel her face becoming blotchy with anxiety. She would not take this topic any further, not with Leona Farnsworth, at any rate. She doubted the woman could be trusted to tell the truth anyway.

Tori switched to the trigger points at the top edge of Leona's eyebrows, gently pushing the muscles downward on both eyes. "Tell me how this feels," she directed, in an effort to sway the conversation back to the treatment at hand.

"Actually, it feels wonderful, very soothing."

"So you like Brad's music," Leona continued. "He is incredible, isn't he? You know he has some very unique methods of composing songs. In fact, I can remember helping him on a number of occasions."

"Oh, you're a songwriter, too?" Tori asked.

"It's not exactly my forte," she explained, her voice suddenly thick with innuendo. "But Brad works on inspiration.

And I like to think that often times I've provided that for him."

I'll bet you have! "Really? Are you the one who motivated him to write Evil Diva? I love that song, don't you? It's so rich with emotion and realization."

Leona twitched into a facial expression of displeasure, much to Tori's guilt—and satisfaction. "You know, Leona," she chided coolly, "you're flexing your levator labii superioris alaeque nasi muscle. You really shouldn't do that, because the muscle houses a trigger point which could cause a terrible headache if it should cramp up. Fortunately, we can address the matter right now," she added, pressing against the sides of Leona's nose with controlled force.

By the time Leona left, she'd claimed to be feeling much better. Tori hoped so because she doubted either one of them would want to go through another treatment session like that again.

Brad called after the concert the following night. "How did the show go with the new bass player?" Tori wanted to know.

"I wouldn't exactly say we brought the house down, but things went all right. Between you and me, I'll be relieved when Tom gets back. He knows all our moves. It takes a lot of the pressure off when everything goes like clockwork. How was your day, Tulip?"

"Funny you should ask that question. I had a new patient yesterday. A friend of yours."

"Did you say a friend of mine? I can hardly hear you. We're back stage, and there's a lot of noise. In fact, hold on, I'm gonna try to find a more private spot." The sound was muffled for a minute, then Brad came back on the line.

"I'm talking on a cell phone, so the connection might not be that great. Now what were you startin' to tell me?"

"Your friend Leona Farnsworth came to my office today. She had a very bad headache and was in need of a chiropractor." The next thing Tori heard sounded like a choking noise. "Brad, are you all right?"

"Yeah," he answered, after several more seconds of trying to catch his breath. "I took a swig of beer to water my vocal cords, and I guess it went down the wrong pipe. So, you, uh . . . fixed her headache?"

"More or less. She was awfully chatty for someone who was in as much pain as she claimed to be."

Brad's muttered curse was confirmation that Tori had struck a nerve. "Just what did she have to say, if you don't mind my asking?"

Tori took a deep breath. "Well, she said that the two of you were very close. In fact, she implied that . . ."

"Listen, Tulip," he interrupted, "can you hear me?"

"Yes, Brad, I can hear you."

"Leona Farnsworth and I are not friends. Not anymore. There was a time when she and I were seeing each other, and I thought we were close. But I was wrong."

"So, the two of you are not . . . in any way . . . at this time . . . ?"

"Someday I'll explain about Leona. In the meantime, I'm asking you to trust me, Tulip. You're the only woman I have any interest in being with. Do you believe me?"

"Yes I do," she said, with a sigh of relief. And she did. Gut instinct assured her that Brad was a man of his word. But she was still going to be very much on her guard when it came to Leona Farnsworth.

Three weeks went by. Tori and Brad talked on the

phone daily. He always asked about Kevin, and occasionally the two of them would talk as well. Most of the time Brad called Tori. He was on the road so much, it was easier that way. Besides, they usually talked so long, she imagined his phone bill must have looked like the national debt. But they never ran out of things to say. They were growing closer, and she could hardly wait to see him again.

"Don't you have to come back to this area for your court date pretty soon?" she asked him one night.

"Yeah, but I'm gonna take a private flight in. I have to leave town the minute the hearing is over. We're playing in Oregon the same night."

"What day will that be?" she pressed. "Maybe I could meet you at the courthouse. Even if we only get to see each other for an hour or so . . . I miss you, Brad."

"Tulip, it wouldn't be worth your time," he insisted. "We wouldn't even have two minutes alone without a whole entourage listening in on our conversation. Security's gonna be tight. They're concerned about bad publicity and trying to keep this hushed up."

"Good heavens. It's not like you're on trial for murder. You just let your driver's license expire."

"Listen, I'd much rather talk about when you and Kevin are coming to Provincetown, which ought to be real soon. He is out of school now, isn't he?"

"Yes."

By the time she'd hung up the phone, the two of them had decided that she and Kevin would visit Brad at his home on the Cape in two weeks. He'd insisted on paying for the tickets, especially since she'd never billed him for her chiropractic services. Somehow she was going to have to shut the office down for about five days. But she was so anxious to see him that she knew she'd find a way to work things out.

Still, it nagged at her that he didn't want her to meet him in the nearby town for his upcoming court appearance. Something about the whole thing didn't gel. In fact, she realized he'd never even given her the date. She supposed that with a little digging she could find out. Maybe she would surprise him and show up anyway. Though she had the feeling that might be a bad idea—especially since he'd been so adamant about her not being there.

Like a thief in the night, Brad had snuck into Tori's neighboring town. Only it wasn't night. It was broad daylight. And he was no thief. *A liar? Maybe.* He'd certainly lied to her when he'd told her his reasons for not wanting her to show up at the courthouse. If only he could have been honest, she might have stood by his side during the ordeal. *Might have,* the voice emphasized. But he hadn't had the courage to find out.

So the attorney had haggled on Brad's behalf, a fine had been imposed, and everything appeared to be settled. Brad and his lawyer walked out of the courtroom, and there in the hallway stood Leona Farnsworth! For all the security and confidentiality money could supposedly buy, nobody seemed able to protect him from the ravages of this conniving, ever present, piranha.

Her appearance here could only mean one thing, and he broke a sweat just thinking about the newspaper headlines. As she attempted to get closer to him, his security people began to surround her, but Brad waved them off. Better to find out what her terms were privately than to have them announced to the whole freakin' entourage.

"What do you want?" he demanded, steering her off to the side.

She linked her arm in his and looked at him with adoring

eyes, flashing him a smile full of sensual implication. Sickened, he broke from her hold, but not before some photographer took a picture of the two of them. His first thought was to have someone confiscate the camera, but years of dealing with the media had taught him to keep cool. No sense in pissing off the press over something as insignificant as a picture of him and a woman who had been known to play in his band a couple of times.

"Dammit, Leona!" His tone was muffled. "What the hell do you think you're doing?"

"Thanking you," she said. "I found out that you paid my mother's hospital bills, and I'm here to express my sincere appreciation."

"Oh, so you're gonna reward me with a little courtroom publicity for that rag you write for?"

"Not at all, Darling. In fact, I'm going to see to it that your little secret remains exactly that—your little secret. No one needs to find out why you were in that courtroom today."

"Yeah, right. We both know how good you are at keeping a confidence."

"Now don't be cruel," she said. "Besides, it isn't good for you to upset yourself right before a concert performance. I hear Oregon is beautiful this time of year."

"That's right, and my plane will be leaving shortly. So if you'll excuse me, I'll send you a picture postcard."

"You won't have to. I'll be right there by your side, Bradley. My bags are packed and waiting to be loaded onto your jet."

"In your dreams!" he exploded. "There's no way you're coming with me to Oregon."

Leona clucked her tongue, making that revolting noise that told him she was about to pull out all the stops—again.

"Did I mention to you that I met your little friend, Tori? She's quite the chiropractor, though I think her bedside manner could use a little work."

"Why's that, Leona? Because she's not under your thumb?"

"You know," she continued, pretending not to have heard, "I think I might be getting another one of those dreadful headaches." She rubbed her fingers over her forehead and feigned a painful moan. "Doctor Glenn's office is only the next town over. I wonder if I should try to schedule another appointment with her—while you're on your way to Oregon. I'll bet she'd see me. Then she and I could chat. You know, compare notes about your various . . . performances."

The entendre made him snap. Conscious of the nearby security people, he gripped her tightly by the arm and pulled her off to a more secluded area around the corner. Once they were out of sight he took hold of her other arm as well, pinning her against the wall.

"You're hurting me!" she whimpered.

He knew that he was.

She struggled to get free, but he could not let go of her. For once in her life, Leona looked scared. She'd pushed his buttons too hard this time, and he was out of control. The rage he felt was blood chilling, and it scared him, too. *Don't do this! She's not worth it.*

"You stay away from Tori," he warned, his voice low and deliberate—and very much in her face, "or I'll give you a real reason to visit a chiropractor."

She grimaced with pain. *Let go of her!* the voice urged. Brad released his grip. "Do I make myself clear, Leona?"

Her skin was red with marks he'd made, and she stood rubbing her arms and staring at him in disbelief. But she would not give him the satisfaction of an answer.

"Do I make myself clear?" he repeated.

Without responding, she turned and walked away. It was anyone's guess as to what she was going to do next. About the only thing that was certain was that Leona Farnsworth was capable of bringing out the very worst in him. For the first time in his life he'd almost gotten violent with a woman, and for that he felt shame. Yet that same woman made him feel wimpy and inadequate. He hated himself for letting her best him again. When it came to Leona, no matter what he did, he could not win.

"What was that all about?" The question was posed by Brad's attorney, who'd suddenly appeared.

"Nothin'. Let's just get out of this one-horse-town," Brad said. "I've got a show to do tonight, and the plane is waiting." For as much as Brad longed to see Tori, he was grateful she hadn't shown up to witness this scene. Some reunion that would have been. Now he could only pray that Leona would heed his warning.

One more week, he consoled himself. In one more week Tori would be coming up to the Cape to be with him in the secluded privacy of his beachfront home. Maybe by that time his life would be a little less muddled and a lot more focused.

Chapter Twelve

The envelope lay on the kitchen counter, along with all the other mail that had arrived that afternoon. Kevin had already sorted through it, and the pile that was left was addressed to Tori. Most of it was junk mail, along with a bill or two. But the cream-colored, hand-stamped envelope that had been set off to the side looked like expensive parchment, and the penmanship was calligraphy. The letter had apparently caught Kevin's attention as well.

Tori picked it up and ran her fingers over the surface, carefully examining the outside for a clue as to who had sent it. There wasn't any return address. Odd, she thought. Judging by its thickness, it could have been a wedding invitation, but she couldn't think of anyone who was getting married.

"Are you going to keep playing with that thing or are you going to open it up and see what's inside?"

Tori jumped at the sound of Kevin's voice. "You startled me!" she said. "How long have you been standing there?"

"About ten seconds. Are you finished working for the day?"

"Yes. My last patient canceled. What do you say we order a pizza? I really don't feel like cooking and besides, I want to do a little shopping tonight for our trip out to the Cape."

"No argument from me there. But aren't you going to open your mail?"

"Oh, sure." She'd almost forgotten about the letter. Almost, but not quite. She had an eerie feeling about this, not unlike other eerie feelings she'd been having as of late.

Cautiously she pried open the edges, being careful not to rip anything.

Dear Tori, the note began.

I wasn't sure whether or not you had any pictures of Bradley, and since he photographed so well in this one, I thought you might like a copy. It was taken inside the courthouse just a few days ago when Bradley flew back to this area to clear up that messy little legal entanglement he was involved in.

By the way, I'm feeling much better these days. I haven't had a headache in weeks. Do take care of yourself, Dear, and say hello to that adorable brother of yours.

Fondly,
Leona

Inside the note was another piece of folded parchment, no doubt housing the picture. A wave of dread washed over Tori as she freed the photo to take a look. It was Brad all right. There beside him stood Leona, her arm linked in his, and her eyes brimming up at him with lust.

Tori's knees went weak as she was assaulted by a mélange of feelings: anger, pain, jealousy, confusion, mistrust. Though, at this point, she wasn't sure whether her doubts should be cast on Brad or Leona—or both of them.

"You're about as white as a cloud on a warm, sunny day, Sis," Kevin said, pulling out a kitchen chair for her to sit down. "I hope that letter isn't bad news."

How was she going to answer that? She longed to share

her feelings with him, but Kevin was only fifteen. How was she going to tell him what she was thinking and expect him to understand? She didn't even understand herself.

She'd all but begged Brad to let her be with him for his court appearance. But he'd been so adamant about there not being enough time for the two of them to be together and about them not having any privacy. Yet it seemed he'd found the time for Leona. The moment that had been captured on film looked very private and intimate to Tori.

She was near tears now as she wondered whether she should even bother to continue with her vacation plans to be with him.

"Tori," Kevin insisted. "Tell me what's wrong."

Without saying anything, she handed him the letter and watched as he read. As he neared the end, she noticed a bit of heightened color in his face.

"Hey, I guess I am pretty adorable," he said with an embarrassed laugh.

When Tori didn't respond, he brushed her hand with his. "Don't tell me you're worried about Leona and Brad. There's nothing going on there, Tori."

"How would you know that? How would I know?"

"Haven't you ever watched him around her? I did backstage at the concert. Body language tells a lot."

"What do you mean?"

Kevin snickered. "Sure, she's a sex goddess and everything."

"Oh, that makes me feel a whole lot better."

"Yeah, but you're much prettier in a different way. Anyway the point is, he doesn't like her. Look at this picture, Sis. Look at his face. You don't need a magnifying glass to see that he's scowling, which is the way he usually looks when he's around her. Besides, there's something else I didn't tell you."

"What's that?" she asked, her interest in Kevin's perception of the situation piqued.

"Well, I didn't mean to be eavesdropping, but one time I overheard Brad talking with Mike about her. It was that night she played guitar with the band. They were both really steamed about something. I couldn't exactly hear everything they were saying, but I got the idea that they don't trust Leona.

"So maybe you ought to ask him about this picture before you go jumping to conclusions."

"You really think so?" Tori asked, brightening.

"Figure it this way. She's a reporter. Reporters can always smell a story, and they come with built-in photographers. You know Brad didn't want this thing publicized, so he's probably mad that she even showed up, which would explain the expression on his face."

Tori took a more scrutinizing look at that photo. "You know," she said with a smile, "you do have a point."

"Yeah, well all that thinking made me hungry. Let's order that pizza now."

"You call. I'm going to get cleaned up."

Moments later Tori stood under the showerhead, letting the warm droplets of water soothe her body along with her thoughts. She hadn't given Kevin enough credit. For a fifteen-year-old kid, he made a lot of sense.

Now she had a choice to make. She could go to Brad and ask him about the picture. Or she could do what he'd asked her to do, which was to trust him. He'd already told her that he and Leona were no longer friends, and he'd promised to explain the situation—when he was ready.

Tori had already given her heart to this man. It was time she gave him her trust as well.

He was wearing dark sunglasses and a fishing cap, but Tori spotted him the minute she and Kevin stepped off the plane in Provincetown. He was waiting by the gate at the tiny airport, as he'd promised.

"Br . . ." she started to call out his name, but then stopped herself as she realized the last thing she needed to do was bring attention to his presence. Her adrenaline was pumping with anticipation and excitement.

A second later he saw her, and flashed her a grin that sent her pulse racing. "Tulip!" he said, as he reached her side. Oblivious to anyone else's presence, he took her into his arms and gave her a tender welcoming kiss—until the sound of Kevin clearing his throat broke the spell.

"Hey, Kevin, how ya doin'?" Brad asked, extending his hand to the teen.

"Great, now that we've landed. The flight from Boston was bumpier than I'd expected."

"This is the first time he's ever flown," Tori explained. "He's a little queasy, but he'll be fine once he's on solid ground for a while."

"In that case, let's get the rest of your luggage and grab a taxi," Brad said. "I don't have a car here. Most places are within walking distance, and it's easy enough to get a ride when I have to. Cuts down on pollution."

A short while later the Mercedes Cab Company dropped the three of them off in the flower-lined driveway of one of the most picturesque Victorian homes Tori had ever seen.

"You live here?" Tori gasped, spellbound.

"Wow!" was all Kevin seemed capable of saying.

"It is beautiful," Brad said, his tone almost apologetic.

"Come on, let's get both of you settled in so I can show you around." With that he picked up Tori's luggage and led the way.

"You handle those bags as if you're carrying feathers," Tori said. "I gather your hand isn't giving you any problems."

"Everything's back to normal," he assured her, setting her things down on the huge front porch to unlock the door.

The entrance foyer was larger than Tori's living room, and from what she could see of the nearby parlor and dining room, the house was spectacular. The ceilings must have been fourteen feet high. "I want to know who cleans this place?" she asked.

"Well, I'm not here as much as I'd like to be, but I have an older woman who takes care of things year round. Let's head upstairs first," Brad suggested. "That way you can unpack if you want to."

"How many bedrooms you got up here?" Kevin asked in amazement, as they started down the expansive upstairs hallway. There were gothic arches over almost every doorway and decorative woodwork surrounding the windows.

"Actually five. You get to sleep in this one," Brad said, as they reached the far end of the house.

Kevin walked in and set his things down underneath the shallow bay window. "Jeez!" he exclaimed. "Would you look at this!"

Tori walked over and gazed outside at an expansive stretch of beach that was blanketed with sand the color of parchment. And beyond that, for as far as the eyes could see, water—the bluest water anyone could possibly imagine. The view was majestic. "Oh my! I didn't realize your backyard was the Atlantic Ocean."

"It is pretty incredible when you think of it," Brad said.

"It's awesome!" Kevin chimed in. "This whole place is something. I even have my own private bathroom!"

Brad laughed. "Why don't you hang up your stuff while I get your sister situated," Brad said.

Then he flashed Tori a sly wink and motioned for her to follow him.

"You can put your things in here," he said, leading her into the bedroom at the opposite end of the hall. He dropped her suitcases to the floor, then closed and locked the door behind them. "This room just happens to be next to the bedroom where I usually sleep," he said with a cagey grin. "Coincidentally this door that looks like the entrance to a closet . . ." he explained, while opening the door to demonstrate his point, "well it's not a closet at all."

"It's an entrance to your room! How convenient," she teased, with a naughty smile.

"I was hoping you'd think so," he said, standing behind her and wrapping his arms around her waist. "I missed you, Tulip." His voice was husky and his arms possessive.

"And I missed you," she admitted, whirling around to face him. His lips settled over hers, and a surge of pleasure ran through her as their tongues entwined in sweet exploration.

"You in there, Sis?" Kevin called, from the hallway. Tori jumped at the sound of his knock.

"Yes, I'm unpacking a few things," she answered, as Brad continued to hold her.

"Well, I'm going outside to get a better look at that ocean," he said. "So I'll see you two later." With that they could hear Kevin racing down the stairs.

"Take your time," Brad said under his breath.

"You think he'll be okay all alone?" Tori asked.

"Quit your worrying," Brad assured her, drawing her closer. "He'll be fine." There was need in his voice and a hunger in his look.

Her skin began to tingle as he undid the buttons of her blouse. Though the front of her bra was designed for easy access, he fumbled with the clasp in an effort to free her breasts. She could have helped him, but she chose not to. He was usually so self-assured and competent that she found this little show of schoolboy awkwardness endearing. Besides, she was nervous too.

A moment later she was naked from the waist up. He cupped both breasts with his hands, stroking her nipples until they were taut. Then he began circling them with his tongue. His touch made her quiver, and she could feel the liquid heat of arousal warming her body.

"You are so beautiful," he whispered.

Too overcome with desire to let her nervousness get in the way, she reached for the bottom of his T-shirt and lifted it over his head. She stroked his bare, muscular chest with her fingers, her lips, her tongue . . . gradually working her way downward.

He unzipped her jeans and hooked his thumbs over the top. In one swift motion he slid them and her satiny underpants to the floor. Then he did the same with his own jeans and briefs.

Tori's eyes were powerless to do anything but stare at his smooth length of hardness. He wore his nudity like a custom-made suit. For the moment he seemed neither self-conscious nor vain. But his good looks were breathtaking.

There was an urgency about this union that was different from the first time they'd made love. She felt it. He demonstrated it by quickly slipping on a condom. Then he laid her down on the bed, carefully positioning himself on top of her. His initial thrust was gentle as she arched to meet him. But she heard his sharp intake of breath as their passion mounted, and she gave a moan of surrender. Two bodies moving as one . . . until they both cried out together . . . until their desires were fulfilled.

For a moment after, they lay quiet and motionless, still as one, with Brad's head cradled between her neck and shoulder. Then he raised his torso far enough to gaze at her face. "When I'm with you, I'm happier than I can ever remember being," he said thickly.

"Me too," she said softly. *Because I love you,* she wanted to add. But she didn't. He hadn't said it, so she couldn't risk admitting it. Not yet anyway.

A little while later Tori put on some shorts, and walked down to the beach with Brad. Any fears about Kevin going off by himself had been quickly put to rest, as she spotted him in the distance with a small group of teenagers who seemed to be about his age. In fact he was off to the side with one very curvaceous, red-haired, bikini-clad young lady.

"So," Brad said with a grin. "I see your brother has met Megan. She lives next door with her family, and I kind of asked her to show Kevin around."

"Looks like she didn't waste any time."

"Megan's a good kid, but she does know how to go after what she wants," Brad teased as the two teens approached them.

"Sis, this is Megan O'Rourke. Megan, my sister, Tori," Kevin said, by way of introduction.

"Nice to meet you, Megan."

"Kevin tells me you're a chiropractor," Megan responded, extending her hand to Tori. "I think that is so great. We need more natural health practitioners in this country. It's the wave of the future you know."

Tori smiled broadly. "It's good to know you feel that way. I wish more people did."

"Megan and I are going to take a walk into town," Kevin announced. "She's going to show me some of the hot spots."

"Oh," Tori said, looking at her watch. "What time do you think you'll be back?"

"Hard telling," Megan answered for him. "It all depends on who we run into and what's going on in town. Could be later on tonight."

"Tonight?" Tori's reaction was one of surprise. "Well, I don't know. It's Kevin's first day here and all. Are you still queasy from the plane ride, Kevin? Maybe you should take it easy for a while."

"I'm fine, Tori!" Kevin insisted, shooting her an embarrassed look that told her to stop treating him like a baby.

"I'm sure he's right," Brad said, with a little nudge to Tori's arm. "After all, we're on vacation here, and Megan knows her way around."

That's what I'm afraid of, Tori thought, but resisted the impulse to say so. "First maybe you'd better change into some clothes; something to cover that fair skin of yours," she suggested to Megan, with as much restraint as she could muster. "I wouldn't want you to get an awful sunburn."

"Oh, I will," Megan assured her. "Let's go, Kevin, you can come with me while I find something to wear." The young girl further lured him with her inviting smile, and he turned to follow her like a lovesick puppy.

"In case we're not here when you get back, you'd better take this house key with you," Brad said, going after Kevin.

He reached into his pocket, and along with the key Tori saw him subtly slip some money into Kevin's hand.

"That was nice of you," she said after the two teens had disappeared.

"Well, I figure in case they get hungry for a snack . . ."

"It may be too late. It looks like she's already sunk her teeth into my little brother."

Brad laughed. "In case you haven't noticed, your 'little' brother is a good five inches taller than you are. And you're behaving like an overprotective mother."

"Well Kevin hasn't really done much dating. And that girl is so . . . so . . ."

"Attractive?" Brad finished for her.

"And provocative," Tori added.

"I told you, Megan comes on a little strong, but she's a good kid. Trust me, you'll like her after you get to know her. So quit your worrying and back off some. Kevin's growing up. This is all part of the process. Anyway, it's our vacation too, so let's take advantage of the time we have to be alone together."

Once again she supposed Brad was right, even though it was hard to accept. Tori flashed him a resigned smile. "Let's take our shoes off and go barefoot along the beach." She bent over to undo the straps of her sandals, and when she did the necklace she was wearing slid off. "Oh, no!" she said, picking it out of the sand. "This used to belong to my mother. I treasure it, and now it looks like I've broken it."

"Maybe it needs a new clasp. Let me look at it," Brad said, taking the piece of jewelry from her and carefully examining it. "Here's the problem. It's just the loop that came open. I can even bend it shut with my fingers."

A moment later the necklace was back in her hands—good as new. The loop was so tiny she could hardly see it, let alone fix it without some sort of tool. "You're amazing," she said, with a grateful smile. "Thank you." She kissed him on the cheek to show her appreciation and then put the necklace back on.

"It's so beautiful and peaceful here," she observed, as they began to walk. The warm sand was soothing as it slid between her toes. "There aren't that many people around, but the ones who are don't seem to recognize you."

Brad chuckled. "In the first place this is a private stretch of beach, and most of these people aren't tourists. They're neighbors. We all know each other. They're really not impressed. There are lots of celebrities living in Provincetown."

"Really?"

"Yeah, in fact Megan's mother is an author. She writes those steamy romance novels," he said, with a raise of his eyebrow.

"Is that a fact? Have you ever read any of her books?"

"Uh, no," he said, his face coloring slightly.

Was that embarrassment or the beginnings of sunburn? "Not macho enough for your literary tastes?" she baited.

"Something like that. What do you say we get our feet wet?" he suggested, leading her closer to the water.

Tori looked down and picked up a seashell. "This is going to be the best vacation I've ever had," she predicted.

"And I'm just the man to make sure that it is, Tulip." His voice was thick as he took her hand. "Have you ever gone skinny dipping in the ocean on a hot summer night, where the only lights are the moon and the stars?"

"Uh, no," she confessed, shyly. "I can't say that I have. What's it like?"

"Freeing. Very freeing. The water is full of soothing

warmth, and the waves climb up and down your body like an erotic massage."

A shudder of desire ran over the length of her spine as she turned to face him. His eyes seemed to be probing her very soul. "It sounds like a little bit of heaven," she said softly.

"It will be," he promised.

And it had been a bit of heaven, Tori recalled as she woke the next morning in Brad's arms. Kevin had gotten in shortly before midnight and had gone to bed. Afterward Tori and Brad had gone down to the beach to a secluded area where the two of them had made love, in and out of the water, until both of them were practically euphoric.

Brad was still asleep as she glanced at the nearby digital clock. Ten o'clock, she realized with a start. Half the morning was gone already. Then she caught herself. This was her vacation. She was supposed to be relaxing, and that's exactly what she'd been doing. There were no patients to hurry for, no schedules to adhere to, no responsibilities for anyone other than herself and, of course, Kevin.

Quietly she slipped out of Brad's arms, and into her satiny robe. She padded toward the bathroom. Moments later she thought she heard someone knocking on the front door. It appeared she was the only one awake, so she quickly threw on a pair of shorts and a T-shirt and hurried downstairs.

She looked out the window to see Megan standing on the front porch. But the teenager wasn't alone. There on the sidewalk was another young girl who looked to be around ten, and she was sitting in a wheelchair. "Good morning," Tori said, as she opened the door.

"Hi," Megan said, with a cheerful smile. "Is Kevin up yet?"

"No, I think he's still asleep." Tori stepped onto the porch to smell the fresh morning air. "What a glorious day."

"It's like that all the time around here," Megan explained. "Tori, I'd like you to meet my friend, Annie. She lives a block over. Annie, this is Kevin's sister. Remember I told you she's a chiropractor, and she helps people to feel better."

"Nice to meet you Annie," Tori said.

"You're a doctor?" Tori could hear that the question was worded with apprehension, even through the child's slurred speech.

Megan rushed down the stairs to take the child's hand. "Not the kind of doctor who makes people hurt," Megan reassured her, before Tori could even answer. "And anyway we're just here to see if Kevin can come out to the beach to play ball with us."

"Well, he should be getting up soon," Tori said. "Would you like to come in and wait?"

Megan glanced down at the younger child. "No, that's okay. I promised Annie we'd get some sunshine this morning before she has to go see her physical therapist this afternoon. She doesn't like those sessions, so I'm going to see if I can't get her mind on something else for a while. Please tell Kevin we'll be down by the beach, if he's looking for us. Or else I'll see him later on in the day."

"Have a nice time," Tori called after them, as Megan steered Annie down the sidewalk.

She walked back into the house and collided with Brad. "Mornin', Tulip," he said, sliding his arms around her waist. "I didn't know you were down here."

"Megan was here looking for Kevin, and she was with this young child in a wheelchair."

"That would be Annie," Brad said knowingly. "She's got muscular dystrophy. Megan voluntarily spends a few hours with her at least one or two days a week to give the parents some relief. She's great with the kid."

Maybe Tori had misjudged Megan after all. "I could see that," she said. "I think it's wonderful."

"I told you she's a good person."

Tori broke from his hold and headed toward the stairs. "Where are you going?" Brad asked.

"To wake Kevin. He's already slept away half the morning, and Megan is waiting for him out on the beach."

Tori looked back in time to catch Brad's grin and his wink of approval.

Chapter Thirteen

Tori's prediction had been right on target. Her vacation with Brad had been, beyond any doubt, the best one she'd ever experienced. Never had she spent a more relaxing week. More importantly, she realized she'd been with the man she loved. Not that she knew what she was going to do about it. But she'd gotten to know Brad in a much more intimate way, spending time with him when neither of them had had to worry about the pressures of the emergency ring of the telephone, the alarm clock, or the twelve hour work days. They'd seen the sites, talked, played, cooked, and they'd made love . . . sometimes long and leisurely, depending on Kevin's whereabouts . . . and sometimes during stolen moments, making the experience all the more dangerous and fun.

Yet for as much as they'd talked, the subject of Leona Farnsworth had never surfaced. It wasn't as though Tori hadn't been tempted to ask. It would have been nice to have some verbal reassurance from Brad that her fears about the woman were unfounded. But the right opportunity had not presented itself. Besides, he'd demonstrated such a powerful bond with Tori in so many ways during the time they'd spent together, she hadn't had the heart to disturb the magic with talk of a subject that was so distressing.

All the same, she had the nagging feeling that something was being left out—that maybe Brad was keeping a secret of sorts from her, even if he and Leona were no longer friends. Maybe it was her intuition working overtime, trying to make problems where there were none.

In any case, now, as she paid the cab driver and walked into the living room of her house, she felt the effects of a big letdown, and reality was setting in. If a future with Brad meant that life would be one big vacation, the two of them might be fine. But the fact was he had a career that took him all over the world; a career that smacked of a lifestyle far different from hers. And she had her profession. Demanding and time-consuming as it was, it left her little room for vacations and relaxation.

She'd taken the flight home alone. Somehow, some way, in a possible moment of insanity—or ecstasy, Brad had talked her into leaving Kevin with him, to spend the next several weeks on tour as one of Brad's roadies. It had been a conspiracy the way both of them had managed to convince her that, not only would Kevin get a great geography lesson, but he'd earn money while finding out whether he really wanted a career in music.

It had tugged at her heartstrings to leave behind the two people she cared about most, only to return home to an empty house. She knew that if she were going to have any kind of future with Brad, long periods of separation were inevitable, and she wondered whether she would ever be able to adjust to them.

But it was a comfort to know that she would be hearing from Brad every day and that he would keep a watchful eye over Kevin. She trusted Brad, and her brother got along well with him. Maybe a little male bonding was exactly what Kevin needed.

For years now, she'd been the only real authority figure in her brother's life. But it was plain to see that Brad's influence over Kevin was profound. Though she could only admit it to herself, this relationship of Brad's and Kevin's made her feel a bit left out and maybe even insecure.

To further compound things there was Megan. Tori found herself really liking the young girl. It was obvious that Kevin was drawn to her. But Kevin and Megan were only kids, and their growing affection for each other was just one more reason for Tori's parental concern.

The paradox of this whole thing was that while she couldn't quite put her seal of approval on Brad's free-spirit lifestyle, she was intrigued by it. In fact she was envious of his spontaneity. Guilty as it made her feel, Tori realized she was resentful that it was Kevin and not she who would be accompanying Brad on this continuing tour. She'd never had much opportunity for travel, and she couldn't help imagining what an adventure it would be to see the world with Brad.

But there was no chance to fantasize about that now. She had work to do, and was reminded of that fact as soon as she stepped into her office. She'd arranged for all of her calls to be transferred to the office of a chiropractor/friend a couple of towns away. As soon as she'd contacted Dr. Carpenter for the update on her patients, Tori reprogrammed her office phone. It wasn't ten minutes before it began to ring. An hour later people were lined up in the waiting room.

It was early morning at the beginning of August, and the day was already a scorcher. Tori poured herself a cold glass of orange juice and sat down to plan her work schedule. She hadn't even seen her first patient yet, and already she was exhausted. Maybe it was the humidity of the warm weather making her feel lightheaded and overheated.

Kevin and Brad had been on the road for more than a month now, and she desperately missed them both; each for different reasons. Not that she hadn't heard from them daily. She looked forward to those phone calls no matter how late or early they came.

But the fact was, she'd been very busy since she'd come back from Provincetown. Too busy. Her patient load had become excessive, and twelve-hour workdays were getting to be the norm rather than the exception. She'd even been seeing people on Sundays in order to take up the slack.

One of the problems was that her friend, Doctor Carpenter, had gone off on a well-deserved vacation. He'd left Tori in charge of his patients, and, of course, they'd been phoning her for appointments. How could she refuse him the same favor he'd done for her? Except that he'd had a partner then, and now that partner was off on a medical leave.

So, as each person trailed in, she willed herself to have the energy to treat them—until later that afternoon when Mr. and Mrs. Lemont arrived.

"Child, you don't look too well," Mrs. Lemont insisted. The older woman put her hand to Tori's forehead. "I think you're feverish."

"I'll be fine," Tori insisted, as Mr. Lemont stood to follow her into the treatment room. But neither of them made it that far. The last thing Tori could remember was that the room had begun to spin seconds before everything had gone black. The next thing she knew, she was on the floor, and Mrs. Lemont was stooping over her.

"You fainted," Mrs. Lemont explained, once Tori was conscious enough to understand.

"I don't understand it," Tori said. "Nothing like that has ever happened to me before."

"You're sick, child!" Mrs. Lemont insisted, while she and her husband helped Tori up off the floor. "Now you're going right off to bed. You're in no condition to be working today." Tori was in no position to argue, as Mr. and Mrs. Lemont both helped her into the bedroom and on to the bed.

"Don't you worry now, Tori," Mrs. Lemont assured her. "You just lie there and keep still. I'll call the rest of your patients and cancel for today."

"That really won't be necessary," Tori started to protest. But a moment later she drifted off.

Tori opened her eyes to the feel of a cool cloth over her forehead. Was she hallucinating or was that really Brad sitting on the edge of the bed?

"You're awake," he said, with a look of relief. "The doctor's on his way."

"What?" she asked, sitting straight up. "Brad, is that really you? Is Kevin with you? What are you doing here?"

"Take it easy," he insisted. "One question at a time."

He laid his hands on her shoulders and gently forced her back to the pillow. "Yeah, it's really me, and Kevin's in the kitchen getting more ice. We flew in to surprise you, but the surprise was on us. You're burning up, Tulip. What the hell's goin' on?"

He was here—really here. If only she could get oriented enough to show him how truly happy she was to see him. But her head was pounding, and her throat was so sore she could hardly swallow. And she was shivering. How could that be? It was probably still ninety degrees outside.

"Here, Sis, take a little of this," Kevin said, holding a

glass of water in front of her. She took a sip through the straw.

"Kevin," she murmured, trying to force a smile. *She was so tired. Why couldn't she stay awake?*

Later she heard more voices. And it was dark now. Had she nodded off again? "I'll give it the rest of the night, as long as the two of you are going to be here with her. But if that fever doesn't break by morning, I may need to put her in the hospital."

Was that Doctor Haeger talking? Who else would be conscientious enough to make a night-time house call?

"You see to it that she takes one of these every four hours, and two of these for the fever," Doctor Haeger added. "And you push fluids while she's awake. I don't want her getting dehydrated. A temperature of one hundred and four is nothing to fool around with."

"I won't leave her side," Tori heard Brad promise.

"Now don't get too close to her," the doctor warned. "She's got a strep infection, and she'll be contagious for a while."

Strep throat? Was that what she had? That would mean she'd have to cancel her patients for tomorrow too. If only she could get the energy to climb out of bed and get her Appointment Book . . .

All night long she drifted in and out of sleep. When she did sleep she dreamt. *She was on a flying carpet, and Brad was holding her close. Together they soared over the rooftops of buildings and above green forests, exploring the world. She was carefree and in love. Then she heard the call of responsibility.* "Doctor Glenn, your patients are waiting for you," the voice said. "They're lined up at the door, expecting you to take away their pain. And here you lie sleeping as if you don't have a care in the world."

Suddenly Tori was awake, and she struggled to sit. Brad lay curled up on the nearby chair. She dangled her feet over the edge of the bed and started to climb out.

"Where do you think you're going?" Brad asked, suddenly alert.

"It's morning. I have to get up and get ready for work."

"Not on your life," Brad countered, touching his hand to her forehead. Before she could protest, he grabbed the thermometer and stuck it in her mouth. "One hundred and one degrees," he said, minutes later. "It's an improvement, but you're still sick."

Tori swallowed, and the memory of her painfully sore throat came back. Her head still ached. "Am I allowed to go to the bathroom?"

Brad smiled and helped her to her feet. But she swayed, and if he hadn't grabbed her she would have fallen to the bed. "Guess I am a little weak," she admitted.

He held on to her and walked her down the short hallway and then stood outside the bathroom door until she finished. "You're going right back to bed," he insisted.

Tori didn't argue, and minutes later she lay under the covers, as Brad fed her more antibiotics. "Did you get any sleep at all last night?" she asked.

"Off and on. Then again, it's rare that I get a full eight hours anyway. Think you could get breakfast down if I made something that was easy to swallow?"

"Maybe. But first, sit with me for a few minutes," she pleaded. "I want to see your face and convince myself I'm not still dreaming. I'm so glad you're here, even if I am sick."

"The feeling's mutual," Brad said, taking her hand and flashing her that pulse-pounding grin. She was suddenly conscious of how she must have looked. No makeup, messy hair, maybe even morning breath despite that she'd quickly brushed her teeth. Yet he'd been at her side the entire night. And now he was gazing at her as if she were some sort of sex goddess. The signs of love were certainly there even though he hadn't spoken the words.

She glanced at the nearby clock and was jolted. "My patients are going to start pouring in here soon," she said. "You have to at least let me call them to cancel."

"Yeah," Brad agreed. "But you can do that right from this bed."

"Could you go into my office and get my Appointment Book, please? It's sitting in the reception area on the desk. It's black with huge gold lettering on the front. You can't miss it."

Brad left the room, and she adjusted the pillows so that she could comfortably sit up in bed. Then she grabbed the phone from the nightstand. Ten minutes passed, and still Brad hadn't returned. Maybe Mrs. Lemont had put the book somewhere else, and Brad couldn't find it. Tori was getting fidgety thinking that if he didn't hurry, patients would start arriving. Where was he?

Just as she was about to get up to go look for him, he appeared. "Here you go," he said, holding out a binder which in huge lettering read, ADDRESS AND TELEPHONE NUMBERS.

"Brad," she said, "I'm sorry, but this is the wrong book."

"Oh." His face turned bright crimson. "You said, black with gold lettering. I guess I just assumed this was it."

"Well it should be right on the desk like I said. Do you want me to go find it?"

"No!" he lashed out. "You stay put. I'll be right back."

But he wasn't right back, and several more minutes

passed. Now she was getting really agitated. Finally he appeared, holding two books, one of which was the APPOINTMENT BOOK she'd been requesting. The other was her DAILY REMINDER of things to do, and said so in large print at the front of the binder. Brad was sweating, and she hoped he wasn't getting sick too.

"I thought you might need all of these," he said, nervously. "Why don't you make your phone calls while I take care of breakfast?" Without waiting for her response, he disappeared. Something wasn't right, but she didn't have time to analyze it.

Tori quickly phoned her first patient, and then the second. The moment she hung up after the third call, it came to her. It was all beginning to make sense, she realized, as she traced her memory back to when she and Brad had first met. His handwriting—so sloppy you could barely decipher his name, the day at the zoo when he'd seemed so surprised at the flying bats, his inability to read without his glasses—which always seemed to be lost. And now, this mix-up with her appointment book. He claimed he was farsighted, and yet without his glasses or a moment's hesitation, he'd been able to read the thermometer that said her fever was down to one hundred and one. The letters on the covers of her office books were large—much larger than the numbers on the thermometer. Surely he could see them too. Then she remembered that he'd fixed her necklace on the beach in Provincetown. She could barely see the broken loop herself.

The pieces to the puzzle had been there all along. And now she'd finally been able to put them all together. *Brad wasn't farsighted at all. He couldn't read!*

Brad stood at Tori's kitchen sink, splashing cold water

over his face. He'd blown it. All Tori had asked him to do was bring her the Appointment Book, and he'd turned the situation into a damned fiasco! The woman wasn't stupid. But she was feverish. And maybe the fact that people have trouble thinking straight when they're sick would work to his advantage. Possibly she still didn't know.

Or, maybe you should come clean and tell her your reading skills aren't even at first grade level. Considering how close they'd gotten, was it too much to hope that she loved him the way he'd come to love her? That she'd stick by him regardless?

He did love her. All he'd thought about since he'd gone back on tour were those precious days the two of them had spent together on the Cape. He couldn't wait to see her again. Then when he'd found her last night, so helpless and ill she could have been hospitalized, he'd been frantic with worry. Just the thought of losing her made his stomach lurch. *Coward!*

He just couldn't work up the guts to tell her, not when he knew how important education was to her. What if she told him to get lost? No, he'd deal with that risk only if she backed him into a corner and left him with no other choice.

Meanwhile, he searched the cabinets and found a box of oatmeal. Oatmeal and bananas. Easy to swallow and nutritious. He'd have her breakfast cooked up in a jiffy, and then he'd have to shower and get ready to head out. She'd be upset when he told her he had to leave. But a short visit was better than no visit, and he could see that the antibiotics had begun to do their job.

"Hey, Brad," Kevin said, appearing in the doorway. "How's Tori?"

The kid. Now that was another problem. The original plan had been for Kevin and Brad to fly back out together, for at least two more weeks. But with Tori still sick, there was no way she could be left alone. Kevin would have to stay behind. And he wasn't going to be happy about it.

"Her fever's down," Brad answered, filling a quart-sized pan with water. "But she's sure not well enough to get out of bed. Somebody is going to have to look after her for a while."

"Hmm," Kevin hedged, as if he understood the implications of what Brad was telling him. "Were you thinking of anyone in particular?"

"It would have to be someone who knows the ropes around here. Somebody who could stay night and day in case of an emergency; someone who can handle the phone and reschedule appointments, run the washing machine, mow the lawn, make meals and keep the house clean. We'd have to have a person who really cares about her. Know anybody who qualifies?" Brad asked, stirring the oatmeal into the boiling water.

Kevin folded his arms over his chest and let out a sigh of defeat. "You're leaving me behind, aren't you?"

"Do we have a choice? This is your sister we're talking about, kid. The person who's been raising you for the past four years. She'd do the same for you in a heartbeat."

"Yeah, I know it," Kevin answered with a crestfallen look.

"There will be other tours, Kevin. Besides, for the past several weeks now, I'd say you've had a good taste of life on the road."

"But I'm supposed to see Megan again before school starts. She's counting on it," he pleaded.

The fact that Kevin and Megan had been in close touch since the beginning of summer wasn't exactly a news flash to Brad, though it might have been to Tori.

"I'm sure she'll understand, and you'll see her again." *Even if he had to fly the little beauty into Wheatfield himself. Megan had been good for Kevin, and Brad wanted to see their friendship continue.* "In the meantime, a man's gotta do what a man's gotta do."

Later that morning Brad left Wheatfield to continue his tour. Once again he'd taken a piece of Tori's heart with him. Saying goodbye wasn't getting any easier. The only difference on this occasion was that she'd been too sick to busy herself with her normal responsibilities, which meant that she'd had more time to dwell on missing him.

He'd certainly doted on her while he'd been there, and for that she was grateful. But why hadn't he seen fit to tell her he couldn't read? The more she thought about it, the more it bothered her that he didn't trust her enough to confide in her—especially after she'd poured her heart out to him about everything, including Jack.

No wonder he'd been so defensive about the fact that he'd made it big without benefit of formal education. His self-esteem was at stake. It would also explain the friction between Brad and his well-educated family members, and she wondered if they were aware of the extent of his problem. Not that she was like them. Didn't he know her well enough to see that? Didn't he think she would understand and try to help? Obviously not, and that muddied her perspective of their relationship.

"You awake, Sis?" Kevin asked, appearing in the doorway of her bedroom. "I've got your pill."

His voice jarred her from her thoughts, but she was grateful for the interruption. He carried in a tray with hot soup and some juice.

"Over here," she said, motioning for him to sit on the

side of the bed while she swallowed the medication. "I haven't seen much of you today."

"I've been kind of busy," he explained, without looking directly at Tori.

"Really? I was worried that you might be angry or that maybe you didn't want to talk to me."

"Why would you think that?" he asked, still avoiding eye contact with her.

"Because I know you, Kevin. So why don't you level with me?"

"Try the chicken soup," he said, in an obvious attempt to change the subject. "It's Brad's special recipe."

She tasted a spoonful. And then another. "It's wonderful, and I really appreciate that you made it for me." But she would not be thwarted. "The fact is you had planned to go back on the road with Brad. I got in the way of that. I want you to know I'm truly sorry."

"You didn't ask to get sick, Tori. Though you do work yourself into the ground," he added. "Even Brad said so."

"There are a lot of people who count on me. I'm the only chiropractor in this town."

"Doc Haeger says you're rundown and that you ought to take it easy for a while. Besides, you can't go treating your patients while you're contagious. So you might as well enjoy the rest."

"How about you, Kevin? How are you feeling about being back home again?" she wanted to know.

He faced her head on. "Truthfully, I miss being on the road with Brad. It was the most exciting thing I've ever done, Tori. Seeing those crowds rev up every night the minute the band hit the stage—girls screaming their lungs out. Not that Brad takes that kind of attention seriously," he assured her. "Traveling to a different part of the country almost every day, riding around on tour buses and flying in airplanes—I loved being part of all that action. I know what I want to do with my life now. It's just a matter of time before it happens."

"And what's that, Kevin?" she asked, trying to keep the angst out of her voice, despite knowing what he would say.

"I want to be just like Brad—a dynamite musician with all the wealth and fame that comes with the package."

"I understand that's how you feel now," she said, in as calm a tone as she could muster. "Though you may change your mind once you've finished your education."

"Possibly," he agreed, looking away from her, "but I wouldn't count on it."

He'd said the last part under his breath, and while Tori had heard him, she ignored the comment. School would be starting soon. Hopefully then he'd be thinking about the activities and excitement of his junior year, not to mention preparation for his college entrance exams. Then maybe he'd come to his senses. "There's something else I've been meaning to talk to you about," he added, in a tone that suggested he was about to further her frustration.

"What's that, Kevin?"

"Well, you know my birthday is in the middle of September. I'll be sixteen then, and I can get my driver's license."

As if she didn't have enough to worry about. "Not without first taking formal instructions. But they offer Driver's Education at school."

"Yeah, but now that I'm going to be around for the rest of the summer, I'd like to take private lessons so that I can get my license right away."

"Won't that be kind of expensive? What's all the rush?"

"C'mon, Tori," he pleaded. "I've saved up plenty of

money from the tour, and I'd really like to get going on this. Besides," he reasoned, "that will be one less class I'll have to take in the fall."

Tori sighed. "All right, Kevin. If it's really what you want, go ahead and sign up." She'd given in without a fight, partly because she felt he deserved a consolation prize for staying home to care for her, and partly because she sensed that he was asserting his independence. Maybe it would be healthier for both of them if she allowed him to do just that.

As for Tori, she closed her eyes and tried to shut out her worries; Kevin, her illness, her patients and all of her various responsibilities. She had no choice but to put everything on hold until she could better cope. And though it still troubled her that Brad had chosen not to confide in her about his inability to read, she would deal with that later, as well. For the moment, she preferred to dwell on the memory of his loving touch and the promise of their next meeting.

Chapter Fourteen

September had come and along with it, some semblance of normalcy. Tori had recovered from her illness and was back treating patients. School had begun, and Kevin had nearly finished with his driving lessons. Despite the fact that he had homework and other commitments, he practiced his guitar for hours on end. And Brad and Tori continued to stay in touch each day.

She missed him terribly. His tour would be ending some time in November. After that he planned to start work on a new album. But at least he wouldn't be traveling all over the country, and that meant she would be seeing more of him. Meanwhile, it was Kevin's sixteenth birthday, and Brad was due to visit later that evening.

Kevin was at a football rally with friends who'd been instructed to keep him occupied until it was time for his surprise party to begin. Tori had taken that Friday off and was anxiously decorating the house in preparation for the event. Brad's flight would be too late for him to make the party on time, but there would be another surprise guest. Megan had already arrived. Tori had picked her up at the airport earlier that morning, and the pretty teenager was exuberant.

"I can't wait to see Kevin," Megan admitted, standing

on a chair to fasten crepe paper to the ceiling. "How soon do you think he'll be home?"

"Not for at least a couple of hours. Tape this balloon at that end too," Tori instructed. "Hopefully one of his friends will distract him while the rest of them get here first. We do want him to be surprised."

"Well, I know he's not expecting to see me. I've managed to keep this secret for a month now, ever since Brad promised to fly me out here. He's a great guy, isn't he? If he hadn't been our next-door-neighbor ever since I was a kid, I'd probably have a crush on him myself," she said, without waiting for Tori's response. "But now I kind of think of him as the older brother I never had."

It seemed to Tori that Megan and Kevin, for that matter, were *still* kids, and she smiled at the irony.

"Of course, it's different with the two of you," Megan continued, with a raise of her brow. With Megan it was sometimes difficult to get a word in edgewise.

"What do you mean by 'different'?"

"Like I said, he's lived next door to us for years. You get to know someone in that amount of time. I can tell he's crazy about you."

Not crazy enough to level with her about what was really going on in his life. But she wasn't going to mention that. Nor would she dwell on it right now. It was Kevin's birthday, and she was about to spend some time with the man she loved. This was a day to be happy.

"Yes, well I've grown pretty attached to him too," Tori admitted with a smile. "I'm going to run outside and get the mail. I'll be right back."

There was a hint of fall in the air as Tori reached the end of the driveway, but the sun was still warm enough to make the day perfect. Nothing was going to spoil her good mood.

She reached into the mailbox and began to sort through the pile. It didn't take long to get to the envelope with the familiar calligraphy she recognized as Leona Farnsworth's handwriting. Only this time the envelope was addressed to Kevin. Why would Leona Farnsworth be writing to her brother? she thought apprehensively. If ever she was tempted to run interference, this would have been the time. But at sixteen, Kevin deserved some measure of privacy, and she would not allow the likes of Leona Farnsworth to push her to such tactics. Instead, she brought the mail in and set the unopened letter on Kevin's bed, where he would be sure to find it.

Kevin's friends started to arrive a short time later. Megan seemed to be at ease with them, and she handled things well in Kevin's absence. Finally, Kevin walked through the front door, and Tori was on hand with her camera to capture his surprised expression. But it was the look of elation on his face when he first saw Megan that made Tori realize her younger brother was growing up. Seeing him so happy made her happy. And she, too, was grateful to Brad for flying Megan in.

Tori slipped back into the kitchen and made herself scarce once the party began. Instinct told her it would be best if she were around if needed, but not too visible.

She glanced at the clock and with a flutter of her heartbeat, she wondered how much longer it would be before Brad appeared. She couldn't wait to be in his arms again. Though with Megan and Kevin both there, she wasn't sure how much time she and Brad would have to spend alone with each other.

Then she thought about the envelope lying on Kevin's bed. Had he seen it yet? If he had, how much information would he be willing to volunteer about its contents? Surely he would realize that she had seen it too and would be curious.

For the moment, it was best not to dwell on it, she decided. There was food to be prepared, and there were lots of hungry teenagers in the house.

Much later that evening Brad arrived at the back entrance of the house. "Sorry I couldn't get here sooner," he said, setting his guitar and luggage down to pull Tori into his arms for a hello kiss.

She was happy to see him . . . so very happy. The woman inside of her came alive once again.

"I don't suppose you and I could go somewhere and hide out for a while?" he whispered, nudging the hollow of her throat with his lips.

"I want to," Tori answered. "But we're going to have to wait a bit. Kevin and Megan are in the living room. The party's over so there's no telling when they might come looking for me."

"Oh yeah," he teased. "Maybe they want to be alone too."

"Well, maybe they do," she agreed with some reluctance. "But it doesn't mean they're going to be. Anyway, they're far too young to even be thinking about doing anything like . . ."

"Like what I'm gonna being doing with you first chance I get?" he finished for her. "Don't kid yourself, Tulip. They're thinking about it plenty."

"How do you know that?" she asked, her eyes widening with alarm.

"They're normal hot-blooded kids. Their hormones are raging—just like ours," he said, grabbing her around the waist and pulling her even closer to him—so close that she could feel him hardening right through the denim of her jeans.

Her breasts grew taut while her pulse quickened. "Kevin didn't say anything to you about . . . well, you know. Did he?"

Brad raised her chin to make eye contact with her. "I haven't seen you blush this red since the first day I laid eyes on you. Don't tell me you can't say *sex* and Kevin in the same sentence."

"Brad!" she pleaded, with an embarrassed whisper, trying to look away from him.

He grinned. "You better get used to it, Tulip. The kid is sixteen. He's not a baby anymore, and one look at Megan should tell you she's already gone through puberty. And yeah, Kevin and I had a little conversation about the subject one day."

Tori groaned. "Dare I ask? Would you even tell me?"

"Let's just say I gave him all the pros and cons of sex in the new millennium. I certainly didn't push it. I told him that it was a big responsibility and that he shouldn't do it unless he was sure he could handle all the repercussions. Then I went on to explain what all those might be. It was a guy thing."

"Do you think you convinced him?"

"Let's be realistic. That's something you and I might never know. But just in case I didn't, I also gave him a little speech on the safety aspects."

"I guess I should be thanking you," she said, nuzzling his chest and pressing her cheek to his. "I know my dad had a talk with Kevin before the accident, and, of course, kids learn about these things in school. But now that he's older I'm sure he could use some advice from a man whose opinions I respect. I know I don't qualify."

"So you respect my opinions?" he teased, running his fingers over the tips of her breasts.

"Oh, yes," she answered smiling. "You're a man with a lot of knowledge—and skill."

"I could demonstrate some of that skill right now," he offered.

"Later, after Megan and Kevin are asleep—in their own separate beds," she promised.

"Shucks," he said, with a look of persuasion. "I was all geared up for something sweet."

Tori laughed. "I saved you some cake and ice cream."

"That's not exactly the kind of treat I had in mind."

She planted a butterfly kiss on his earlobe. "Then I guess you're just going to have to be patient," she said coyly. Though she was feeling awfully impatient herself.

"All right, I know when I'm defeated. But you just wait till later."

Tori smiled. "Believe me, I am," she emphasized. "You know, Kevin's been in his glory all night, especially since he locked eyes with Megan."

"I figured he'd be happy to see her," Brad said with a grin.

"He's going to be glad to see you too. I didn't tell him you were coming, so he'll be very surprised."

"He'll be even happier when he opens this," Brad said, picking up the guitar case.

"What do you mean?" Tori questioned.

"You'll see." Brad sounded as excited as a child at Christmas. "C'mon." He grabbed her hand and pulled her toward the living room, where they discovered Megan and Kevin locked in a kiss.

Brad looked at Tori and then cleared his throat—loudly.

The two teenagers jumped apart. "Brad!" Kevin exclaimed, the moment he looked up from the sofa. "Wow! I didn't know you were going to be here too!"

"Happy birthday, kid," Brad said. He let go of Tori's hand to shake Kevin's. "How's it goin', Megs?" he added with a sly wink.

Megan blushed and then gave a wide smile, indicating that things were, in fact, going very well.

"Brought you a present," Brad said, handing the guitar case over to Kevin.

Kevin's eyes grew wide as saucers, and he stood motionless for a few seconds. "For me?"

"Sit down and open it," Brad instructed.

Kevin unlocked the case and pulled out a brand-new acoustic guitar. He ran his hand over the highly polished Canadian maple, and then he saw the mother of pearl inlay that formed his initials. He was totally speechless.

"Is this really mine?" he finally said.

"You earned it. It's not a VanLear," Brad explained, "but it is hand-made."

"I don't know what to say, Brad. I don't even know how to begin to thank you."

Kevin wasn't the only one. Tori could never have afforded to give him such an expensive gift, and she knew he would treasure it always.

"Why don't you start with a little concert? You've been practicing enough. You ought to be pretty good by now."

Kevin took a few moments to tune the strings, and then he started to play. The tones were rich and clear, the notes exacting. It was plain to see that none of the classes he had taken at school could command his attention or garner his passion the way this instrument, and what it stood for, could. Tori ran her hands over the gooseflesh that appeared on her arms. Kevin was good—really good. And with time, he would only get better.

★ ★ ★ ★ ★

The weekend had passed far too quickly, and at the end of it Brad and Megan had both gone their separate ways. Brad and Tori had managed to find some time alone together. But from the moment he'd left she longed for the feel of his arms around her, his lips and hands upon her, and the cherished intimacy that they could only share when they were with each other.

While Kevin wasn't saying so, Tori could see that he missed Megan as much as she missed Brad. At least Tori had the comfort of knowing she would see Brad again soon. He had promised. In the meantime, she had her patients to attend to, and Kevin had school.

He had made a slight reference to the envelope Leona had sent, explaining that it was just a birthday card. Tori wondered how the woman would even know the date of Kevin's birthday. It made her nervous to think that Leona had access to personal information about Kevin or, for that matter, Tori. She thought back to the day when Leona and Kevin had conversed in the patient waiting area and wondered exactly what Kevin had told the woman. But she decided not to press the issue. As she was fast learning, sometimes the less said the better.

By the middle of the week Kevin had finished his driving lessons, and the following day he passed his test and got his license. Tori let him drive the car as they went out to dinner to celebrate.

"You know, Sis," he said, while they sat in a corner booth at the restaurant waiting for their food, "I want to tell you how much I appreciate everything you've done for me." He grabbed her hand over the table and squeezed it hard. "I love you, and some day I'm going to pay you back for all the sacrifices you've made."

Tori smiled in surprise. Such an emotional display from Kevin was uncharacteristic, but she assumed it had been brought on by all the events of the past week. "The payback is to see you grown up and happy and able to make your way. That's all the thanks I need. I love you too, Kevin. We're family, and families stick together. I'll always be here for you."

"And I'll be there for you, Sis. Even if we're separated by distance."

Why had he said that? He wasn't going anywhere. At least not any time soon. Not that she was aware of.

"After all, look at you and Brad," he added, as if he'd been reading her mind. "When you need him, he's only a phone call or a plane ride away. And look how close Megan and I have gotten."

Tori wondered just how close that was. But unless Kevin offered that information, she would refrain from asking. As his guardian she wanted to know that he wasn't doing anything that would endanger his future. But to ask such a personal question now might only invite hostility into this otherwise loving conversation, and she didn't want to risk spoiling the mood. In any case, his little addendum had not eased the nagging worry that something about this exchange was being left out.

The following morning Tori was up early, and she had a full patient load. The fall season had brought many leaves to the ground, and along with it, the sore muscles of enthusiastic rakers who'd gotten carried away. She'd been busy; too busy to hear the ring of her personal phone or to check the blink on the answering machine until early afternoon, when she stopped for a brief lunch.

The voice on the taped message was that of Kevin's principal. Within ten minutes Tori had posted a *"Closed for Emergency"* sign on the office door and had driven to his school.

"I called you as soon as I read this. But by the time I received it, Kevin had already left the building," Mr. Hawkins explained, handing Tori the note her brother had written, forging her signature. "There really wasn't anything I could do."

Tori sat there in stunned silence. Kevin had dropped out of school.

"I'm afraid that with a parent's permission, it is legal to quit school in this state at age sixteen," he added. "Of course, we don't encourage it."

And neither had she. She had exceeded the speed limit in her race to get back home to check Kevin's room, in hopes of finding some further explanation. When she arrived she discovered the note he'd left revealing that he'd gone on the road to be with Brad.

Her adrenaline surged. *Think, Tori, think!* Brad had given her his itinerary for the week, and she'd written it down herself. She'd find it, find Brad, and he would send Kevin packing.

"Golden, Colorado," she said aloud, after rifling through her purse to locate the sheet of paper with the information. That was where Brad was supposed to be playing that evening. At the Red Rocks Amphitheatre. But he hadn't given her a phone number. *Calm down, Tori. That's why we have information operators.* Quickly she dialed 4-1-1.

"I'm sorry, there is no listing available," the operator explained.

"Dammit!" Tori swore, after hanging up the phone. Her hands were shaking as she dialed the number of the hotel where Brad was spending the night. Chances were he wouldn't be there, but she could at least try.

"Could you leave a message for Mr. Daniels?" Tori asked the hotel operator, after an unsuccessful attempt to get through.

"I'm sorry, but Brad Daniels is not registered here, nor are any members of the band you're referring to," the operator said.

"Look, I'm not one of his groupies!" Tori said angrily, "and this is a family emergency!"

But the operator would not change her story and kept insisting that Tori's information was incorrect.

She hung up the phone. Her stomach churned at the string of ugly thoughts that had suddenly surfaced. If she had gotten her facts wrong, maybe it was because Brad hadn't seen fit to tell her where he was really going to be that night. After all, it wasn't the first time he'd withheld important information from her.

She sat at the edge of Kevin's bed while a montage of the events that had led up to this situation played before her—starting with Brad's proud declaration that he'd dropped out of school at age sixteen to become a rock star. No wonder Kevin had been so nostalgic the night before. And no wonder he'd been in such a rush to get his driver's license. That would also explain why Brad had given Kevin such an impressive guitar. He'd been grooming him to be a member of his band. Why not? Kevin was following in Brad's footsteps. Exactly.

Brad must have known about this all along! Even on the chance that he didn't, it was still his fault. He'd encouraged it with his negative attitude toward education. Besides, how else would Kevin know where to find him? She couldn't even reach Brad other than to leave a message on his home phone. Anger, resentment, tears flooded her being. She'd trusted this man! Trusted him with her heart, her soul and her own brother! He'd stolen Kevin right out from under her; lured him with hopes of success and doomed Kevin's future, while she'd stood by and practically given her blessing. Brad Daniels had trashed her entire value system, along with their relationship—if they'd ever had one to begin with. What had she done to merit such a betrayal? More to the point, what was she going to do now?

She thought about phoning the police. Kevin was a minor, and legally she was still responsible for him. But she knew that for the time being he would be safe with Brad. Surely one of them would call her soon. Then she would decide what to do.

Meanwhile she paced and waited for the phone to ring. The office remained closed. Although she was guilt-ridden, she was incapable of treating patients in her frame of mind.

Nightfall came. Her stomach growled angrily, a reminder that she hadn't eaten since breakfast. So she forced down some tea and a bagel. Again she called the hotel on the chance that Brad may have checked in. But she was given the same story. At three o'clock in the morning she gave the hotel one final try. This time she asked for Kevin and was told he wasn't there.

Tori went through the motions of getting in bed, but she couldn't sleep. She could barely function.

Saturday morning came. And passed. Then Saturday afternoon. And still no word.

Chapter Fifteen

Brad had just stepped out of a hot shower when the phone in the hotel suite rang. The last twenty-four hours had been right from hell, and he could only hope this signaled that the phone lines in Denver were finally operational.

"Yeah," he answered, wrapping a towel around himself.

"Bradley, Darling!"

Damnation! Did that woman have radar when it came to finding him? "What do you want, Leona?" he asked, with as much calm as he could muster after a couple of deep breaths. It didn't make sense to get any more riled than he already was, not when he had a concert to do in just a few more hours.

"I need to talk to you," she said softly.

"So talk."

"No, I mean that I need to see you in person. Right away."

"Impossible," he answered. "Since I'm here, and you're . . . where?"

"Actually, Darling, I'm here too. Right in the hotel lobby. And I'm not alone."

He could already feel himself breaking into a sweat, and he wasn't even dry from his shower yet. "What do you mean you're here, and who the hell is with you?"

"I'll tell you that when I see you. I'm coming up there now. Will you clear it with your people?"

What freakin' choice did he have? If he didn't find out what the witch was doing there, she'd be riding his trail all night like the caboose on a freight train. Besides, he'd never be able to concentrate on his music if he didn't get this out of the way first. "Give me ten minutes, Leona, and make damn sure you don't bring anybody else up here with you till I know what this is all about."

He hung up before she had a chance to argue. After making a quick phone call to alert security, he threw on some jeans and a T-shirt. Exactly ten minutes later she stood before him, all decked out in her flamboyant finest; snug black, leather miniskirt and gold spandex-knit top that clung to her chest like a second skin. Her fiery red hair was tucked behind her ears to reveal the longest, gaudiest earrings he'd seen lately. Yep, her stage was definitely set for something, but it was anybody's guess as to what it might be.

"I came a long way to see you, Darling," she purred, "and in this storm it wasn't easy tracking you down."

"Yeah, well you shouldn't have troubled yourself. Now what's all this about having company? Who's your travel companion?"

"I didn't say we were travel companions. However, your assumption happens to be correct. Do you have any mineral water? My throat is a bit dry."

Brad walked over to the pitcher of water on the end table and began to pour a glass. "Pigs will have wings before you run out of enough spit to flap that jaw of yours. So why don't you quit hedging and tell me what you're doing here? Cause I'm just about at the end of my patience."

"Bradley, there's no need to be crude," she said, taking the glass from him. "I was kind of wondering if you'd like a roommate. The weather being what it is and travel plans so turned around for people, there seems to be no room at the inn . . . so to speak."

He couldn't stop his mouth from dropping open, but for the moment he was completely unable to get any words out.

"Think about it," she said, moving far closer to him than the safe distance she ought to be keeping. "I'm warm, I'm cuddly. And I know all of your hot spots—even the one underneath . . ."

"You know, your audacity is mind staggering!" he interrupted. "Is that why you're here? For a roll in the sheets!"

"It wouldn't have to be merely a roll, Bradley. Though that wouldn't be a bad start."

"You're delusional! Now get the hell out of my face before I really lose my temper."

"Don't you want to know who else is in this hotel?"

"Not unless you spill it within the next five seconds!" he bellowed.

"Kevin. Kevin Glenn."

He gave her a sidelong glance of disbelief. "What are you talkin' about, Leona?"

"The boy hopped on a plane and flew out here with me. He seemed determined to quit school and join up with your band."

"Kevin dropped out of school? And coincidentally he gets on a plane with you? Go figure!" Brad said, as she wisely backed away from him. "What are you up to, woman? I want some answers, and I want them now!"

"I can't help it if the boy idolizes you. As it happens, he likes me too. We've become rather friendly as of late. Anyway, he confided to me that he was considering dropping out of school after his sixteenth birthday. Apparently he thinks there's a place for him in your band."

"And you encouraged this?"

"Well, he has become rather skilled as a musician. Anyway, I did let it slip that I was coming out here to do another concert with you, and he decided to tag along." She folded her arms in front of her chest. "That's about it in a nutshell," she finished.

"In a nutshell!" he repeated, with the robotics of a trained parrot. "The hell you're doing another concert with me! You mean to tell me Kevin's downstairs in the hotel lobby?"

"That's right."

"Does his sister know he's out here?"

"I don't think so, Bradley. Evidently he hasn't chosen to reveal his whereabouts to her as yet."

"That's great! She's gotta be worried sick!" Brad picked up the phone to dial Tori's number, but the hotel operator intervened.

"I'm sorry, Sir," she explained. "The outside lines are still not operational."

"Dammit!" he said, slamming down the handset.

"Bradley, I think now is the time to lay all my cards out on the table," Leona said.

He fought an odd, volatile feeling as his rate of respiration increased. "There's more?"

"I miss you," she said, sweetly. "I mean I really miss you. I made a mistake in letting you go, Darling, and I want you back. I truly do." She swung her hips and sidled up to him, tracing the front of his T-shirt with her long fingernails. "We were good together once. We could be good together again. Give us a chance, Bradley."

He looked at her, and for a moment his contempt was

overshadowed with feelings of downright pity. "It's over, Leona," he said, gripping her hands firmly, and removing them from his chest. "Accept it. Get some therapy for yourself if you have to. But accept it, and let it go."

"It doesn't have to be over," she pleaded. "Not if you would listen to reason."

"Tell me where Kevin is," Brad said, as if he hadn't heard her. "I want him up here. I have to talk to the kid."

"Not until we straighten this thing out between us."

"It's straight, Leona! Believe it, we're through. End of story. Now where is Kevin?"

Her nostrils flared angrily as she tossed her hair over her shoulders. "You want Kevin up here. Oh, I can arrange that. And while we're chatting, perhaps I should tell him about the sorry mess that took you out of school at age sixteen. He might be very impressed by the entire truth of your success. While I'm at it, maybe I ought to give Ms. Tori Glenn a call too. Doctor Tori Glenn!" she emphasized with fury. "I bet she'll be fascinated with your story. Unless, of course, you've already told her."

Rage hung in the air as Brad locked eyes with her in open warfare.

"No, of course you haven't told her. I can see that now," Leona said smugly.

If ever he wanted to wrap his hands around her self-righteous little neck and choke the life out of her, it was now. Though wanting to do it and actually doing it were two different things. He was going to stop this woman once and for all. But it would not be with violence. He was better than that, and for the first time in his life, he felt like he was actually in control of the situation. It had taken far too long, but finally he knew exactly what he was going to do.

Catherine Andorka

★ ★ ★ ★ ★

Saturday night at seven o'clock the telephone rang.

"Tulip," Brad said.

"Where are you?" she demanded, frantic with anxiety.

"Denver, and before I say anything else I want you to know that Kevin is with me, and he's fine."

"Well that takes the worry right out of my day," she said sarcastically.

"There was a bad storm, and the concert got moved to the McNichols Sports Arena in Denver. The phone lines have been down. This is the first time I've been able to get through. You and I have a lot to talk about."

"Too bad you didn't think so before my brother dropped out of school to join your band. But you have what you wanted."

"Look, this isn't a conversation I want to have over the phone, and I'm due on stage pretty soon. I'll see you on Monday. Till then you're gonna have to trust me."

And with that, he hung up. Tori was both furious and relieved at the same time. At least she knew Kevin was safe. But as far as trusting Brad, she doubted she would ever be able to do that again.

Monday morning Tori received another call from Mr. Hawkins. Without going into any details he'd asked her if she could come down to the high school. When she arrived, she was ushered into the auditorium and given a front-row seat at an assembly that was about to take place. She had no idea what was going on, but the students were filing in, and a moment later Kevin sat down in the empty seat next to hers.

"Kevin!" she said, with startled elation.

He looked around, seemingly conscious that others

might be watching. Still he grabbed Tori's hand and gave it a squeeze. "I'm sorry I had you so worried and upset, Sis. But Brad and I had a long talk, and I think we can work this thing out."

Before she could ask how, Mr. Hawkins came on stage to say a few words, and the next thing she knew, he was introducing Brad. The students began screaming and cheering the moment he appeared. But Brad took the microphone and silenced them.

Fumbling with the mike, he acted nervous; not at all like the self-assured performer she was used to seeing. "I'm here today for a number of reasons," he began. "One of them is to clear up some misconceptions many of you may have about me because of an interview that appeared in your school newspaper a while back. So far I've been lucky in my music career. Most of my records have hit the top of the charts. The problem is that when you're that high up, it's a long fall down. In a sense, that's why I'm here now."

Brad cleared his throat and then locked eyes with Tori for a few seconds. "One of the things I said in that interview was that I'd made it in this business without much formal education. That I'd been to the school of 'on-site experience'. While that's true, I suppose the implication was that I really didn't value the educational system. But the fact is that I don't reject it. I'm intimidated by it. I'm in awe of someone who can make the honor roll. I never could. A couple of days ago a good friend of mine dropped out of this school because of some of the things I'd said and because of an example I'd set. That's when I knew I had to be straight with him—and with all of you." He stopped talking to take a drink of water, and once again glanced at Tori.

"I got into the record industry because I love composing songs and playing my guitar, and because I knew I could do those two things without having to know how to read."

The students' gasps were audible, and they began talking in low tones. Brad gave them a moment to react before silencing them so he could continue. Tori was close enough to see beads of perspiration on his forehead, and she felt sorry for him.

"That's right," he admitted. "I can't read. I'm not even sure why. Someone once suggested that I might have something called dyslexia, but I never had it checked out. What I did do was spend a lot of time and energy trying to fool friends, family, and especially my teachers into thinking that I could read. I'd guess on the multiple choice tests, disrupt the class if I had to, pretend to be asleep, pay some other kid to do my homework—the tricks were endless. I cheated and got away with it because I was an athlete. We attach a lot of importance to sports in this country. I knew the system well, and that's how I got through school . . . till I dropped out," he added.

"And the cheating continued right on into adulthood. I'd tell people I forgot my reading glasses, when the fact is I have twenty/twenty vision. I order the same foods in restaurants because I can't read the menus. It's a good thing I can afford a chauffeur because I don't even have a driver's license. I can't read well enough to pass the test."

Brad paused to look at Kevin. "So what I'm telling you people is, stay in school. Learn all that you can because knowledge is power. Once you have that power, a lot of other doors can open up. My friend Kevin is back in school as of today. It's not too late for him. And you know what? I'm convinced that it's not too late for me either. I'm going to get that evaluation to find out what my problem is. Then I'm gonna learn how to read, no matter how long it takes. That's a promise."

The students stood and clapped and cheered, and Tori hoped that no one would notice that she was crying. She was happy that Kevin was going to finish school. And she was happy for Brad that he had finally unburdened himself—even proud of him that he'd decided to do something about his problem. She had to admit that Kevin could have done a whole lot worse than to have chosen Brad for his mentor.

But she felt devastated that Brad had chosen to reveal his secret to her at the same time he'd told the rest of the world. It was clear she was no one special to him; that after all these months he still couldn't trust her. Whatever they'd had together; whatever she'd thought they'd had never existed. And it never would.

She gazed up at him one final time, memorizing his face, his smile, and his eyes. "I'll see you later," she said to Kevin, before slipping out of the auditorium to drive home. Somehow she'd have to find a way to work through the hurt and get on with her life, a life that was no longer going to include Brad.

The house seemed empty and inert as she walked through the doorway. But it was Monday, and she had responsibilities. People were counting on her, and it was time to get back to her patients. She made her way to the bedroom to change into some working clothes, and when she came out she heard pounding on the door.

"Open up, Tulip!" Brad insisted.

Her heart began to hammer, and she thought of pretending she wasn't home.

"I know you're in there!" he yelled. "I'm not leaving until you talk to me."

She went to the front door and opened it a crack. "I don't think we have anything more to say to each other."

"Is that right?" He looked wounded. "Is that because I don't measure up intellectually?"

Tori threw the door open all the way. "That's what you think? That I'm just like your family? Oh, excuse me, but you never gave me the chance to show you how I felt. You couldn't trust me enough to let me in!"

"Trust!" he exploded, walking into her living room. "You want to talk about trust? You practically accused me of kidnapping your brother. I didn't even know he was in Colorado until an hour before I called you."

That was a jolt. "Where was he?"

"Stranded at the airport because of the storm. He was with Leona Farnsworth, of all people, until they got to my hotel."

"Leona Farnsworth?"

"Yeah. Apparently she knew about his plan to leave school. In fact, I think she encouraged it, but that's something Kevin ought to explain to you himself. Anyway, I had quite a talk with him once we did hook up."

"Would you mind telling me what he said?" Her concern was mounting.

"Could we sit down and discuss this?" His tone had softened, and the two of them sat on the sofa facing each other. "Kevin is very troubled. He hasn't resolved this thing with your folks at all. He feels that because of the way they died, all education ever did for them was to give them a death sentence. I tried to explain the illogical reasoning behind that, but he wasn't convinced. I think that a part of him relives that accident every day of his life. Maybe he needs some professional help to sort this whole thing out. Of course, I'm no expert on psychology, but . . ."

"I agree with you," she interrupted, as a knot formed in

her stomach. "But I feel ashamed that I wasn't the one to see this first."

"Don't go blaming yourself, Tulip. There's such a thing as being too close to a situation. Anyway, I did tell him that he couldn't be in the band until he at least finished high school. I also told him that I think he has a brain for college. But he loves the guitar. You can see that. The kid has potential. I suggested that maybe he should major in music."

Tori smiled. "For an amateur psychologist, you're pretty good."

Brad smiled back, inching a little closer to her on the sofa.

"It hurt me that I had to learn about your reading problem along with five hundred kids. Why couldn't you tell me, Brad?"

"I was afraid of losing you. Trust doesn't come easy for me."

"Tell me why," she pleaded.

His blue eyes darkened, clinging to hers, analyzing. "Yeah, it's time," he agreed. "Several years ago I was crazy in love with Leona Farnsworth. At least I thought it was love," he amended. "Back then she was a reporter for one of those 'tell all' magazines. In fact, she still freelances for them when the occasion suits her. Maybe you've read some of her trash."

Tori listened intently, trying not to squirm at the idea that he'd been in love with someone else.

"I thought we had something really special," he admitted, with a look of hurt. "But like I said, she's a reporter, and reporters dig."

"She found out you couldn't read?" Tori guessed.

"Worse." His voice broke with emotion as he looked

away. "She found out I couldn't read, and she threatened to go public with the story. Unless I could come up with some money."

"She blackmailed you?" Tori was dumbfounded.

"Well, to her credit, she didn't want the money for herself. She used it to pay her mother's medical expenses. The woman is very sick, and right now she lives in a nursing home. Anyway, I paid her off. I've been paying her off every stinking month, not only with my checkbook, but with my integrity. That's how she wound up on stage with the band.

"Once that stuff starts, you know, it's insidious. She made me feel like a worthless, stupid piece of garbage that she'd thrown away for the almighty dollar."

"Oh, Brad," she said, taking his hand. "I can barely imagine anyone being so vicious."

"Yeah, well the one thing I always had going for me was my common sense. If I hadn't let my pride get in the way of that, she never would have gotten away with it." Once again, Brad made direct eye contact with Tori. "The hell of it was that I would have paid her mother's medical bills if Leona had just asked me. I actually care a great deal for the woman. I knew Josie when she was still well, and she was good to me, Tulip. Better than my own family."

"No wonder you have a hard time trusting people, Brad." *But he had trusted her just now, with a humiliating account that had been very difficult for him to share.*

"Like I said, I didn't want to risk losing you. Then I realized I was losing myself. I was starting to believe my own lies. When Kevin showed up with Leona, it was the last straw. I knew if I didn't square the situation in my own head, I could never face up to things with you and him. Truthfully, I wasn't sure I could tell the story once, let alone twice. That's why I decided to go public. Now it's out in the open, and I can finally quit pretending. Leona Farnsworth has blackmailed me for the last time."

"That's right," Tori said, softly.

His hand closed over hers tighter, and his eyes were penetrating. "I didn't realize I'd be hurting you. I really didn't. For that I'm sorry. But now that you know, how do you feel about the fact that I can't read?"

"Oh Brad, it wouldn't occur to me to stop loving you simply because you don't know how to read. Not now, not ever. But not knowing how is different from *'can't.'* You just haven't found the right way to learn yet. I think that with the proper technique, someone can teach you. Though it's your decision whether or not you want to do it."

Suddenly he had that familiar twinkle in his eyes, and that devilish grin swept across his face.

"What?" she pressed, feeling somewhat shy.

"You said you loved me."

"So I did." She could feel a warm splash of color invading her face.

"Well, that's real good. Because I love you too. And when you love somebody, you want to do things for them—and with them. I've got some money, Tulip. You've got a lot of property here. There's enough land to build a clinic. Let me do that for you so that you can take on a couple of partners. That way you won't have to work yourself into the ground, and you'll have time to do some traveling with me."

"A clinic?" she repeated, trying to take in the magnitude of the whole idea.

"Yeah. Then we can convert your office into a recording studio for me, so that I can spend more time with you and Kevin."

"A recording studio?"

"We can soundproof it," he added, giving her a few seconds to digest the idea. "But if we're gonna be married I think we should spend as much time together as possible. Don't you?"

"Married?" She took in a quick breath as her pulse began to race.

"You're the best thing that's ever happened to me, Tulip. You and Kevin. I want you to be my wife. Will you marry me?"

"Oh yes!" she said, without any further hesitation.

He took her into his arms and gave her a kiss that was full of passion and need, filling her senses with his essence. It was then that Tori realized she hadn't lost Kevin to Brad at all. Rather, they'd found a way for all of them to share each other's love.

"I have the feeling this family is going to be making a lot of beautiful music together in the years to come," she said, as she buried her face in his chest.

Thanks to the International Dyslexia Association (800-222-3123) for the information they provided and for the valuable work they do.

About the Author

Catherine Andorka is multi-published, both in short story fiction and non-fiction. Her career as a writer began one morning at 3 o'clock, after receiving a speeding ticket. (In her opinion, undeserved.) The poem she authored lamenting the injustice of the justice system served her well, both in the courtroom and later, when it was published in a local newspaper. That was in 1979, and the rest, as they say, is history.

Catherine is a member of Romance Writers of America and belongs to the Chicago North RWA Chapter. She is a romantic at heart and has always been intrigued by the genre. She is also a born matchmaker, so now that she is writing romance novels she can make sure all of her couples live happily ever after.

Catherine and her husband reside in a Chicagoland suburb. They have one "particularly wonderful" daughter who is married to one "particularly wonderful" son-in-law.

Once Upon a Secret is Catherine's first full-length novel, though she is hard at work on a second. When she is not writing fiction, she is busy serving as Editor-In-Chief of the Weddingpages Bride and Home Magazine (Chicago edition).

The employees of Five Star hope you have enjoyed this book. All our books are made to last. Other Five Star books are available at your library, through selected bookstores, or directly from us.

For information about titles, please call:

(800) 223-1244

or visit our Web site at:

www.gale.com/fivestar

To share your comments, please write:

Publisher
Five Star
295 Kennedy Memorial Drive
Waterville, ME 04901